SWIFT HAT-TRICK TRILOGY

Vital Blindside

BOOK THREE

HANNAH COWAN

Portions of this book are works of fiction. Any references to historical events, real people, or real places are used fictitiously. Other names, characters, places and events are products of the author's imagination, and any resemblances to actual events or places or persons, living or dead, is entirely coincidental.

Special Edition

Edited and Proofed by: Sandra @oneloveediting

Cover Design by: Booksandmoods @booksnmoods

ISBN: 978-1-990804-02-1

Dedicated to my beautiful mother –
You are a superhero. Thank you for everything.

And to my littlest sister –
Embrace your red hair. Bad bitches have red hair.

Authors Note

This story contains some sensitive topics and portrayals.

These topics include:

Mention of bipolar disorder and brief mention of past self-harm.
Alzheimer's disease

Reading Order

Even though all of my books can be read on their own, they all exist in the same world—regardless of series—so for reader clarity, I have included a recommended reading order to give you the ultimate experience possible.
This is also a timeline accurate list.

Lucky Hit (Oakley and Ava) Swift Hat-Trick trilogy #1

Between Periods (5 POV Novella) Swift Hat-Trick trilogy #1.5

Blissful Hook (Tyler and Gracie) Swift Hat-Trick trilogy #2

Craving the Player (Braden and Sierra) Amateurs in Love series #1

Taming the Player (Braden and Sierra) Amateurs in Love series #2

Vital Blindside (Adam and Scarlett) Swift Hat-Trick trilogy #3

Disclaimer

The real Canadian Women's Hockey League ceased to exist in 2019, but for the purpose of my story, I have written it to still exist. Like the NHL team names in my other novels, the CWHL team names have been altered.

Playlist

Like A Man — Dallas Smith	♥ 3:08
Kiss Me — Ed Sheeran	♥ 4:39
I Blame The World — Sasha Alex Sloan	♥ 3:16
Spin You Around — Morgan Wallen	♥ 3:32
I Don't Wanna Be Your Friend — ayokay, Katie Pearlman	♥ 2:33
LOVE ME HARD — Elley Duhe	♥ 3:38
In Case You Didn't Know — Brett Young	♥ 3:44
All Nighter — OVERSTREET, Dark Heart	♥ 4:18
Don't Blame Me — Taylor Swift	♥ 3:56
As You Are — The Weeknd	♥ 5:39
Till Forever Falls Apart— Ashe, FINNEAS	♥ 3:42
Wildest Dreams — Taylor Swift	♥ 3:38
Die For You — The Weeknd	♥ 4:20
Your Soul — RHODES	♥ 3:51
Addicted To You — Picture This	♥ 3:13
Why — Sabrina Carpenter	♥ 2:51
I GUESS I'M IN LOVE — Clinton Kane	♥ 3:24
Dandelions — Ruth B.	♥ 3:53
King Of My Heart — Taylor Swift	♥ 3:33

Family Trees

SWIFT HAT-TRICK TRILOGY

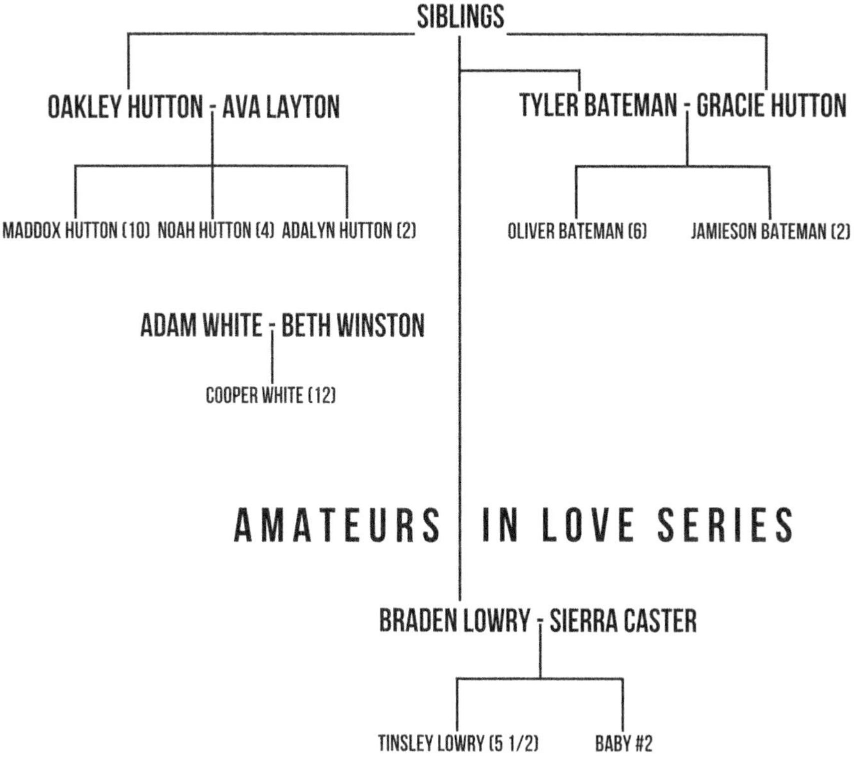

1

Adam

The lumpy clouds above Vancouver, British Columbia, groan into the sky before opening up to drown us beneath a heavy pour of rain. It wets my hair, making it stick to my forehead as I continue my morning run.

I'm on my seventh mile, and even though the weather just gave me the middle finger, my house is only a couple of blocks away. I can't exactly stop now, even if that means I'll have to listen to my twelve-year-old son scold me for bringing wet clothes into the house as soon as I walk through the front door.

Cooper loves to poke at the bear, as long as that bear is me. I can't help but take complete responsibility for that. He learned at a young age that the majority of the time, I'm all bark and no bite, which only makes him enjoy picking on me like a little shit even more.

Our two-story craftsman-style house pokes its head around the eyesore of a spruce tree planted dead smack in front of Mrs. Yollard's house. It's almost the size of her entire front yard and looks like it hasn't been trimmed once in its lifetime. I've tried convincing the widow to have it cut down, even going as far as to offer her my assistance, but she's shut me down each time.

My persistence has no limit, however. I'll get her to agree one of these days.

I jog past the neighbouring yard and toward my house, noticing the open garage door. Cooper's bike is leaning up against my workbench inside, his Marvel-sticker-decorated helmet dangling from the handlebars.

Neither my son nor dog are anywhere to be seen, but I can only assume they're close by. My kid wouldn't dare leave his precious bike out in the open without protection, and Easton doesn't move from his best friend's side for a second longer than necessary.

Slowing to a walk, I move up the driveway, patting the hood of my Mercedes when I pass it. I maneuver around the array of hockey gear and dog toys scattered on the concrete pad in the garage before shaking my hair free of rain and opening the door that leads to the mud room, stepping inside.

The mud room is as big of a mess as the garage, with large piles of laundry stacked in front of the washing machine and a collection of shoes everywhere but the designated rack. I've been telling myself I'll get this room cleaned up eventually, but I may have put it off a bit too long.

"Coop?" I yell, slipping off my wet sneakers.

Taking a step out of the mud room, I wince when my socks make a squelching noise and water seeps to the floor. With rushed movements, I pull off my socks and add them to a pile of dirty clothes before collecting all of it in my arms and tossing everything in the washing machine. I'm throwing in a pod of detergent when I hear the familiar click-clack of nails on the floor.

"You're lucky Dad wasn't home to see that, East. You would have had to sleep outside—" Cooper's words cut off when he enters the mud room.

Chuckling, I start the washing machine and turn around. Easton, the ninety-pound German shepherd we adopted when

Cooper was five, flops onto his back immediately, his tongue lolling out of his mouth and paws folded beneath his chin.

"Yeah, that's not suspicious." I snort and look at Cooper as he rocks back and forth on his heels. "What did he do?"

Cooper is the spitting image of me. Staring at him is like going back in time and looking in the mirror.

His milk-chocolate-coloured eyes have the same green flecks around the irises as mine do, and his puffed bottom lip twists to the right just enough to rest in a half-smirk that's gotten me in trouble once or twice over the years. He's tall for his age, coming in at just under five foot four—just like his dad was.

"Uh . . ."

"Cooper," I groan. "Let's do this the easy way, please. What did he do?"

His eyes roam around the room, focusing on everything but me. "He might have eaten one of the jerseys you had lying in that pile." He points to the laundry on the ground.

"He might have? Or he did?"

Cooper gulps. "Okay, he did. But in his defense, he probably thought it was going in the trash anyway. It had been sitting there for at least a couple weeks."

He's not completely off base there. It's been over a week since I brought WIT's spare jerseys home to wash, and they have yet to see even a dollop of detergent. I'm sure they smelled ripe for the picking.

"Did he eat the entire thing?" I ask with a weighted sigh.

Cooper shakes his head. "No. Just the sleeve. And he puked it up in the backyard already."

Flicking my gaze to the dog wrapped around Cooper's foot, I give my head a shake. The troublemaker is smiling at me.

"Fine," I say. "But make sure he doesn't do it again, Coop. This room is off limits, yeah?"

"Got it, Dad."

I nod before checking my watch for the time and muttering a curse. Cooper raises a curious brow.

"No bike today, bud. I'm gonna drive you before you're late for school. Get your stuff, and I'll meet you in the car as soon as I change."

My boy doesn't put up a fight, despite how excited he was to ride his bike to school. Instead, he raises his hand in a salute before grabbing his backpack from its hook and slinging it over his shoulder. Once he heads into the garage, I take off toward my bedroom.

Despite the chaos that is our laundry room, the rest of the house is clean and organized. I've never been a messy person, but being a single father is no easy feat. Between chauffeuring Cooper to band practice four out of seven days a week, art lessons another two, and owning and managing a booming business, I've allowed myself just one room to not give a crap about. One room where I can shove everything I don't want or don't have time to deal with away where I can't see it.

Out of sight, out of mind, right?

My bare feet thump against the cold wood planks lining the hallway before meeting the plush carpet in my bedroom. The walk-in closet is too extravagant for my taste, with the built-in maple shelves and drawers and collection of mirrors that make it impossible to avoid staring at yourself, but it came with the house, and I haven't had the time to change anything yet.

I quickly change into a pair of black track pants and a hoodie, both featuring the White Ice Training logo, before slipping on a pair of socks. Stepping in front of the mirror beside the rack housing my suit jackets, I shake my hair out again and run my fingers through the brown curls.

Every day that passes where I don't find a grey hair on my head is a day to celebrate. Knowing that my father went grey in his early thirties has been hanging over me like a piano on a thin wire since the day I turned thirty. It's been three years since, and every day, I count my blessings.

The beeping of my smartwatch has me quickly flicking off all lights and jogging through the house to the garage. Easton watches me run down the hallway from his place on the couch, and I flip him off before heading outside.

Cooper is already waiting for me in the car, and when I slide into the driver's seat, he levels me with a disapproving stare that makes him look far older than he is.

"Are you finally ready, beauty queen?"

With a quick burst of laughter, I reach over the console and ruffle his hair. "Careful, tough guy. I might drop you off on the side of the road and leave you there."

"I dare you," he sniffs, slapping my arms.

I pull back and start the engine. "Triple doggy dare me and you have a deal, bucko."

WHITE ICE TRAINING is a hockey arena located a few minutes from East Vancouver, housing a half rink, a full-size gym, and several rooms specialized for position-specific training.

We coach over a hundred athletes, with ages ranging from five-year-olds learning to skate, players in their late teens preparing for their chance at the big leagues, and anywhere in between.

Besides Cooper, WIT is my pride and joy. My blood, sweat, and bucketloads of tears. I've put everything I am and have ever had into building my company, and it still feels like a dream come true to stand here—a handful of feet away from the entrance—and stare up at what I've built in utter awe.

I pull open the heavy glass door and step inside, welcoming the slight chill that settles on my cheeks from the busy rink. I'm very late this morning, and after having to call Banks, my second-in-command, and deal with his chiding when I asked him to come in early and open the building, I've already determined it'll be a hellish day.

"Good morning, Adam," Brielle, one of our front desk workers, greets me with a smile.

"Hello, Brie. How was your morning?" I ask, closing the gap between us and leaning my forearms on the half wall separating me from her desk.

Brielle is a young single mother of triplets. Her ex-boyfriend left before the three girls were even born, and although she has a lot of help from her parents, I've offered to help her out whenever necessary.

Usually, a couple of days a week, I pick her girls up for school since I'm already taking Coop in that direction, but she's been adamant recently that she can handle it on her own. It's not my place to push her on it. Lord knows I didn't love taking handouts when Cooper was young, even if that's not what I'm offering.

Brielle smiles warmly. "It was pretty good. I think we've finally worked out a good morning schedule for the four of us. One that doesn't have me rushing out of the house with my hair still up in a towel and three six-year-olds wearing Halloween costumes."

I toss my head back and laugh. "That's great. But I'm sure they're the life of the classroom in those costumes."

"Oh yes. I've heard all about how much their teachers love chasing child-size hot dogs and pickles around during morning announcements."

"I remember when Cooper was in the third grade, he went to school on Halloween with one of those Scream masks that was filled with fake blood. The tubing attached to the pump ended up ripping open, and whatever they used to create the blood squirted all over his math teacher. I received quite the scolding from the principal that day."

Brielle covers her mouth with her hand and giggles.

"I know, I know. I'm a cool dad." I wink.

She shakes her head, her lips tugging at the corners. "That's exactly what I was thinking."

I push myself back and plant my hands on my hips. "I better get to work before Banks sees me slacking off. There are three interviews on the schedule today. Just page me to my office when the applicants get here, yeah?" It's been a long search for the perfect addition to our team, and at this point, I'm losing hope that we'll find anybody worth hiring.

She nods. "Sounds good, boss. Good luck with Banks today. He's already nearly thrown down with Brooklyn Danvers."

Great. One of our best clients and an Olympic gold medalist. Mornings and Banks don't mix, so as much as it might annoy me, I'm not surprised.

"Thanks, Brie. I'll see ya later." I throw her a grateful smile before spinning around and heading for my office.

As I walk through the busy halls of WIT, I can only hope to make it out of this day in one piece.

2

Scarlett

"Mom?" I yell, stepping inside our house and out of the scalding sun.

Silence is the only reply I receive.

I close and lock the door before shuffling into my childhood home, soaking in the smell of burnt orange and an array of fresh flowers as I go. When I enter the kitchen and pass the thick stack of envelopes full of unpaid bills on the table, my muscles grow taut, bunching beneath the cover of my running gear.

Grabbing the stack, I flip through them for the fourth time this week and make a mental note to pay them for my mother before we end up without electricity. I would—should—have done that for her already had my head not been in the dirt all week.

Heaving a sigh, I grab a cup from one of the mint-coloured cabinets and fill it with cold water from the tap. The greenish-blue paint on the cabinets is chipped in several places, but my mother wouldn't dare touch them up.

"It gives the kitchen a rustic feel, my darling," she says whenever I mention sprucing the space up a bit, as if in her terms, rustic means unique, not outdated and falling apart.

I all but inhale my water before placing the cup in the dishwasher and heading back through the house, past the small den and half bathroom. My room is at the back of our home, with a window that looks out to our small backyard that's more like the inside of a greenhouse now than anything else.

Since I moved back home and discovered the state my mother had fallen into while I was gone, she's spent more time pruning the hedges and caring for her vines of tomatoes than she has doing anything else. I'll admit that she has quite the green thumb—something she most definitely didn't pass down to me.

I can't even keep a succulent alive.

Gardening helps her feel sane. Like the disease plaguing her mind hasn't poisoned her yet.

Stepping into my room, I keep my focus on the window. On the flowers swaying in the light Vancouver breeze like a bride and groom on the dance floor and the sun's glittering reflection off the small pond that rests below our giant oak tree, warming the home of the koi fish that live there.

And when my mother's small figure wanders out from behind the garden shed, I smile—a big genuine smile—at the happiness that stretches her features.

Mom's sunflower-yellow watering can is in her hand. She's wearing a floppy hat on her head and a pair of oversized overalls. Her feet are bare, showing off the pedicure I gave her last night.

Neon green.

That's the colour she wanted me to paint her toenails, and I sure as hell wasn't about to say no. Even if I were the only one who remembered how much she hated when I painted my nails that colour growing up. How she had always said it reminded her of snot.

I shake my head to clear away those thoughts and step up to the window, tapping it with my knuckles, hoping to draw her attention.

Amelia Carter spins in my direction and lifts her watering can into the air, waving it around.

A rough laugh escapes me as I wave my fingers in reply. Mom's cheeks and shoulders are pink from the sun, and I can't help but wonder if she remembered to put sunscreen on before going outside.

After a few seconds of smiling and waving, she turns back around and heads toward a clump of daisies. I release a breath and let my smile slip as I grab a change of clothes from my dresser and go to the bathroom in desperate need of a shower.

I've just put the freshly poured glasses of lemonade on a tray to take outside when Mom comes tearing through the porch door.

"My darling Scarlett!" she sings. There's dirt smudged between her brows and on her chin. "When did you get home? I would have come inside had I known you were back."

My grip on the tray wavers before I steel myself and force a smile. "Just long enough to pour some drinks, Mom." The damp hair on my shoulders from the shower I took nearly forty minutes ago suddenly weighs a ton. "How is the garden looking?"

"Oh, it's lovely. We'll have so many tomatoes we won't know what to do with them all!"

"That's great," I say genuinely and tip my chin to the patio door swinging open in the warm breeze. "Sit with me outside and tell me all about it."

She nods giddily. "I would love to. We'll have to sit in the shade, however. I'm feeling a bit crispy from the sun."

"Of course, Mom."

Stepping ahead of her, I lead us through the door and onto the back deck. I place the tray of drinks on the glass table and pull out one of the four patio chairs surrounding it. Mom flashes me a grateful smile and sits. When she looks comfortable, I set her glass in front of her.

The patio umbrella in the centre of the table is closed, so I make quick work of opening it. When my left shoulder groans with the effort, I chomp down on my tongue to stifle my whimper as I finish and then sit on the chair beside her.

The open umbrella provides more than enough shade to keep Mom safe from the sun, and she sighs happily before taking a long sip of her drink.

"So, my sweet, sweet girl." She sets her glass down and pins me with a knowing look. "How is your shoulder?"

I stiffen, subconsciously rolling said shoulder. "What do you mean?"

"Don't play coy. I saw your pain just now."

Like she had just reached over and shoved at it, a shallow pain trickles up my back, contracting around my left shoulder again.

"It's fine. I hardly notice it."

"Unless you're doing something as simple as cranking open a patio umbrella?"

"Mom, please don't start."

She guffaws, "Oh heavens, Scarlett. You can't expect me not to show concern for you. Especially when it's my fault that you had to quit your physiotherapy."

Tears fill her eyes, and I want to beg the earth to crack open and swallow me.

I reach across the table and cover her calloused fingers with mine. "I chose to come home, Mom. You didn't make me do anything."

What was the alternative? Fly back to Alberta and continue rehab with therapists who worked for a team we all knew I would never play for again while my ill mother was home alone, struggling with a new Alzheimer's diagnosis?

Not likely.

"They were taking good care of you over there," she states.

"It was time for me to come home."

She shakes her head furiously, sending tears flying through

the air. I flinch when she smacks the table hard enough to shake the pitcher of lemonade. "You're stuck here because of me. I will never forgive myself for that."

"Mom, look at me," I beg, squeezing her hand tight. She does so reluctantly, her piercing green eyes the shade of freshly watered grass meeting my sky-blue-coloured ones. "There is no place I would rather be than right here. Look around us. This is the most beautiful place I have ever seen. And I've travelled the world."

She blinks at me, squeezing my hand back before slipping her stare to the background. At the sight of her garden, she relaxes.

"I'm here because I want to be. Don't even for a second think otherwise."

"I'm sorry, darling. You know how I get."

I nod and brush the bulging blue veins on the back of her hand with my thumb. "Tell me about what you did while I was on my run."

Her eyes light up. "Oh! How could I forget? I have such exciting news."

"Let's hear it, then," I encourage.

She leans forward and pulls her hand away from mine to clasp it with her other one before tucking them under her chin. I brace myself for the gossip that usually follows that move.

"So, when I was at Charlotte's Flower Shop Saturday, I ran into this man and his son. And I mean really ran into them. My arms were full with my new fiddle-leaf fig—you know, the one in the corner of the den, by my reading chair."

I nod, and she continues. "Anyhow, I hit that poor man right in the chest with it. I obviously started apologizing profusely, but he started laughing and took it from me. Oh, Scarlett. He and his son brought it to my car like true gentlemen."

"That's nice, Mom. But you should have asked an employee to help you in the first place."

A call from the hospital informing me that my mother had

gotten hurt while trying to carry a heavy plant out of a garden shop would have been a nightmare.

She slices a hand through the air. "Save the scolding for another time. I have more to say."

"Go on."

"As I was saying, he brought my plant to the car, and before I could ask his name, I recognized the name on his jacket. You remember White Ice Training, right? It was you that mentioned it to me, wasn't it? Oh dear, that must have been years ago."

Of all the things she has forgotten over the past six months, I'm not surprised one bit that she hasn't forgotten WIT or anything to do with my hockey career. It will be a devastating day when she does. If there's anybody who loves hockey as much as I did, it's my mom.

"I remember WIT, yes. That's where Leo trained before getting drafted."

I'm sure there isn't a single person in the North American hockey world that doesn't know of White Ice Training and Adam White himself. Leonard Orlo is just one of many who spent most of his career there before making it big time. As one of my closest friends, I've heard a good amount about the place.

"Oh great! Because I got you an interview there with Adam on Wednesday."

My jaw slacks. Annoyance licks my spine. "You did what? That's tomorrow, Mom."

"Oh, you're right." She blinks a few times before shrugging. "He has a position open for a new trainer, and as soon as he heard your name, he insisted you come in. I barely even had time to talk you up, and you know how much I love doing that." She has the nerve to look disappointed.

"An interview is pointless. I don't want the job." I push away from the table to put our glasses back on the tray. Mine is still full, but the idea of drinking from it now makes my stomach sour.

Mom's mouth drops open. "What do you mean you don't want the job? It's perfect for you."

"I appreciate the thought, but I'm done with hockey. I don't want to work there."

"That's the most ridiculous thing I've ever heard."

"You need to call him and cancel the interview. I'm not going."

"Scarlett Jasmina Carter. You are going even if I have to drag you there myself. I refuse to let you stay here and act as my shadow. Until I need that from you, you will continue to live your life as a regular, twenty-three-year-old woman. That's final."

She jerks to a stand and stalks off into the house before I can tell her how *not* final it really is. The door slams shut, and I hold the edge of the table in a white-knuckled grip.

Hockey has already broken me once. I'm terrified I won't survive if it happens a second time.

3

Adam

THE WORDS ON THE RESUME IN FRONT OF ME BLUR INTO INKY SWIRLS. I'm only half listening to the woman seated on the opposite side of my desk as she tells me about her brief year-long career with the Calgary Blaze for the third time in the past forty-five minutes.

We're already well over her interview time, and I can't keep myself from looking at the door, curious if my next applicant has shown up and whether she's debating to stay a few more minutes or take off.

I'm praying she's not the impatient type.

"I was so close to getting promoted to second-line centre when I broke my wrist and spent the rest of the season healing," Lilliana says.

I nod subconsciously and push the flimsy paper away. Looking up, I catch her chewing on her thumbnail before she drops her hand to her lap.

"What have you been doing since? When did you leave the team?"

"Oh, I didn't leave," she replies with a forced laugh.

My brow quirks. "So you still play for them?"

"No. They released me from my contract."

"Why?" I can't help myself from asking. There are usually only two reasons a team will release a player from a contract early, and neither of them is promising.

Her nostrils flare as she sits up straighter in her chair. "I was too physical of a player on the ice."

"Physical? In a mild-contact sport?"

Her laugh has an edge sharp enough to cut steel. "There lies the problem, don't you think? The question you should really be asking is why do women with the same skill set as men have to play a milder version of the same sport we encourage them to hit and fight in?"

I tuck my knuckles beneath my chin and lean forward in my chair, chewing on what she's said. It's not a new topic, but still one that carries heavily opinionated views. Views that I don't particularly want to get into today.

"You have valid points, Lilliana. I won't argue otherwise. However—"

I'm interrupted by three harsh knocks on the door. The wheels on my chair screech against the floor when I abruptly stand and head toward the noise.

Grateful for the distraction, I throw a quick "Excuse me" at Lilliana before flinging open my office door. An immediate grin tugs at my mouth.

"My interview was twenty minutes ago, Mr. White," says a clearly livid red-headed woman. She stands in front of me with her arms crossed, chin high, and robin-egg-coloured eyes blazing. My smile drops at her harsh tone.

Flaming red hair falls in loose curls over her shoulders, skimming the tips of her heavily muscled biceps. And freckles—so many dark brown freckles—are splattered across her porcelain cheeks and over her nose, like someone has flicked melted chocolate on her face and let it dry. I'm bombarded with the urge to take a pen to her skin and connect them all. I drag a hand over my jaw to collect myself before flashing a warm smile.

"You're right. Um . . . if you just give me—" I risk a quick glance in Lilliana's direction just in time to see her stand and grab her bag from the floor before I'm looking at my next interviewee again. "—a couple of minutes. I was just ending my last interview."

"That's unnecessary, Adam. I'm leaving now," Lilliana says, sidling up beside me. I take a small step away, creating some distance. "Oh. Hi, Scarlett. You're a rare sight nowadays. What are you doing here?"

Scarlett Carter eyes her old teammate with subtle annoyance and says in a monotone voice, "Trying to talk to Mr. White."

"I meant in Vancouver," Lilliana clarifies. "Last I heard, you were still in Alberta doing rehab on that shoulder of yours."

Scarlett bristles. "It's personal."

"Right. Of course. Well, good luck. I hope the shoulder isn't giving you too much trouble. If you cut your therapy short, I can't imagine it's feeling the greatest," Lilliana says smugly. I clench my jaw.

Gripping the doorknob, I pull it open as far as possible and say, "It was nice to meet you, Lilliana. I'll be making my decision soon."

"Looking forward to hearing from you," she says before giving Scarlett a condescending smile and walking away.

Good riddance. I will most definitely not be calling her.

As soon as she's gone, I gesture to my office and release a tight breath when one of Canada's best and most well-known female hockey players walks inside. Scarlett maneuvers around me swiftly and stops behind the chair Lilliana was just sitting on.

"I'm sorry about that," I say.

She cocks a brow. "For what exactly? Making me wait outside your office for twenty minutes or for Lilliana?"

"Both?"

"Thanks."

Swallowing, I nudge my chin toward the chair in front of her.

"Please, sit. It's nice to formally meet you. I know we've briefly spoken in passing."

She hesitates but after a few silent moments nods her head and rounds the chair, sitting stiffly. I follow suit in my own chair but don't hesitate to flash her another warm smile. There is no way I'm letting Lilliana Adino's catty behaviour ruin this interview before it's even begun. If you can even consider it an interview at this point. It's more a formality than anything.

I clear my throat. "How long have you been back in Vancouver? When I ran into your mother, she mentioned it was a recent move."

"A little over a month," she replies.

Her blue eyes skate curiously over the shelves on the walls and the countless framed pictures and sports memorabilia that line them while I rub at my stubbled jaw, trying to form an estimated timeline in my head.

Scarlett Carter's career is one that I've followed over the years, having watched her win an Olympic gold medal in 2018 with our Canadian women's hockey team, and I trained a few of her friends before and after that. However, my knowledge only goes so far, and I can't help but let my curiosity get the better of me.

We have only met once previous to this interview, at a charity game put on by the national league a year ago, and it was more of a passing greeting than a Q&A opportunity. She was playing her second season with the Calgary Blaze and was set to hit a record number of goals that year. To no one's surprise, she hit that record and then some.

"You only injured yourself at the beginning of last season, correct? A grade III AC joint separation on your left side?" I ask, hopping right in and poking at the elephant in the room.

Her stare snares mine, guarded but not afraid. "So that *is* a kinesiology degree on the wall."

I huff a laugh. "Yeah. It pays to have that knowledge around here."

"Do you work a lot with sports medicine?"

"Not as much as I used to."

She hums, considering me before saying, "Yes. It was a grade III AC separation. My third one."

I hiss through my teeth and sit back in my chair. That's shit luck. The recovery time for an AC separation isn't the "end of the world" type, but a reoccurring separation would require surgery and a hell of a lot of rehab afterward. Not to mention being labelled *injury prone* in the eyes of the suits signing your paychecks. Her sudden disappearance from the Blaze and missing attendance at the Olympics this year starts to make more sense.

"If I'm right, you should still have another month or two of physiotherapy to go with that shoulder if you intend on ever playing again. You had surgery, right?"

Scarlett ever so slightly rolls said shoulder, and my eyes latch onto the movement, refusing to look away. My eyebrows pinch with concern.

"I had surgery six months ago. I feel fine now," she says tightly, and when I finally look away from her shoulder, I'm met with an icy glare.

"Fine?" I release a tight breath. "So if I asked you to stand and do a shoulder extension right now, you're telling me you wouldn't feel any pain? Not even a slight twinge?"

If looks could kill, Scarlett would be my executioner.

"Is this a job interview or a clinic visit?" she snaps, digging her nails into the leather arms of her chair. I should stop pushing, but I won't.

"Right now, it's both." I try to keep my tone level, easy. "If you ever want to play again—"

"I can't play again. I'm done."

Just like that, the frustration building inside of me depletes, leaving my tank empty of anything but a slight brush of surprise. I should have seen that coming.

"The odds of another injury are too high. It's too risky," I confirm. She jerks a nod.

"I'm here for my mom now. My shoulder is good enough the way it is to live with every day."

"I'm going to take a stab in the dark and guess that you being here today is your mother's doing?" I ask, smiling sadly. There's a pang of disappointment in my stomach that I ignore.

"She was pretty adamant about me getting this job and out of her house."

I lean forward, bracing myself on my desk by my elbows. I'm staring at the slight dimple in her chin when I say, "She wasn't the only one. You're my top choice. Injury or not."

She blinks slowly. "I'm not sure I would be the best choice."

"Why not? You have loads of experience, not to mention success."

"I do, but I'm not exactly in the best shape."

I barely manage to hold back my laugh. A brief flick of my eyes from her head to toes is all it takes to prove that statement incorrect.

Scarlett is in incredible shape. You don't get to the athletic level she is without spending countless hours working your body to the bone, sculpting it into its highest form.

The way her thigh muscles bulge beneath the thin material of her yoga pants when she quickly crosses one leg over the other has me averting my gaze before I get caught drooling.

"If it wasn't for your shoulder, I don't doubt for a minute you would have just finished another winning season with the Blaze. You're still in your prime, and it's your choice whether you're going to spend your best years wallowing with regret at home or helping train a very talented girl here at WIT. I know which option I would choose."

Faint interest sparks in her eyes. "How old?" she asks reluctantly. "And what exactly did you have in mind? Because I'm extremely busy at home right now, and I have no interest in hurting myself further."

"Sixteen. Willow Barton. She's good. Really good. Might even be the best female skater I have. And as far as training goes, your shoulder would be safe. I can have somebody else handle the aggressive aspects of her training, but I need you to teach her everything else you know. I want you to help her perfect it all. Can you handle that?"

"She's that good?"

I nod once. "She's that good."

I've had bundles of talented athletes come to WIT before making it to the professional level, but Willow is something special. For such a young girl, her future is brighter than most people double her age. She deserves the best. That's why she came here in the first place.

Scarlett sighs, still looking torn on what to do. Before I have a chance to stop myself, I'm saying, "Take the job and I'll help you with your shoulder. I might not be as good as whoever you were working with in Calgary, but I'll try." Her lips part as she prepares to no doubt turn me down, but I stop her with my next words. "You can try to fool everybody else by pretending you're fine, but I've been taking care of athletes—injured and not—for too long not to notice that you're in pain. I won't judge you. Let me help."

I haven't worked on rehabilitation clients in six years—back when WIT was so new, I didn't have any rehab therapists employed and had to upgrade my college degree—but there's no chance I'm going to tell her that. The break hasn't deteriorated my knowledge or experience, let alone my will to accomplish everything I try.

Scarlett runs a hand through her curls and exhales heavily. A scowl pulls at her rosy lips, and I almost laugh at how perfectly it fits her harsh demeanour.

"Fine," she says. My jaw nearly drops. "I'll take the job. But I need weekends and every day after five off. I won't budge on that."

"Done," I agree easily.

She nods once before standing and placing her hands on her slightly flared hips.

Our eyes meet, and I offer her my hand. She hesitates for a brief second before our palms meet in a quick shake.

I grin. "Welcome to the WIT family, Scarlett Carter."

4

Scarlett

As soon as I pull out of the WIT parking lot, I call Leo. The professional hockey player is my closest friend and someone who has spent days upon days up close and personal with my new boss. If there's anyone who can tell me if I made the right decision by taking this job, it's him.

The dial tone rings three times before he picks up, panting into the speaker. "Letty?"

"Tell me about Adam White."

"Woah, girl. First, hello. Second, why? Are you planning something I should know about?"

I roll my eyes and turn off the gravel road that leads to WIT, heading onto the highway. The GPS in my mom's car updates to show I only have six minutes until I'll arrive home.

"Hey, Leo," I sigh. "And no, not really. He offered me a job today, and I took it. I need you to tell me if that was a stupid idea."

There's clanging and a muffled curse. "Say that again?"

I groan. "I knew it was ridiculous."

"I didn't say that. I'm just surprised," he says over the sound of shouted voices. "How did that happen, anyway? I doubt you wandered into his arena begging for a job."

That makes me laugh. "Maybe I did."

He snorts, and I relax for the first time since leaving Adam's office. Leo and I have known each other since we played co-ed hockey together when we were twelve and have somehow stayed in contact since then. It's impressive, considering we still call and text daily eleven years later, even with him playing pro hockey for the Minnesota Woodmen now.

After so many years, I can't imagine not talking to him as often as I do. It's become a habit that I don't intend to break anytime soon, if ever.

"Try again, Letty. This is the first time in years I've heard you mention the guy. There's no way you went there of your own free will."

I pass the East Vancouver sign and slow to a stop at a red light.

"Fine. It was my mom. She hit him with her new plant in the parking lot of Charlotte's Flower Shop and told him all about how her hockey star daughter was back in town, newly retired and bored out of her skull."

Leo's laugh is a deep rasp in my car's speakers. "Yep, sounds like her."

"It's not funny," I scold. "She's dead set on not letting me stay home to take care of her. That's the reasoning behind her sudden chattiness." The light turns green, and I hit the gas.

"Are you telling me you haven't been bored?"

"Sometimes, yeah. But I enjoy taking care of her. I've missed out on so many years already. I'm here now, and I don't want to miss any more. You know better than anyone how it is for us."

The confession is like dropping a stone in water. There's the initial plop when it hits the surface before it sinks deep, surrounded by silence. My lungs constrict, and I tighten my grip on the steering wheel as if to steady myself.

Leo mutters something too quietly for me to make out the words—like he's muffled the speaker—and then the shouting around him stops.

His voice is clearer, steadier, when he says, "I do know how it is. And I know you mean well. Just try to look at it from your mom's perspective, babes. She already feels guilty because you came home for her, right? Now add that you won't even leave the house out of worry for her safety to the equation, and I would do the same thing she is. Good intentions or not."

"You're not supposed to be on her side," I grumble.

"I'm not. I'll always be on your side. But just try to consider how she's feeling before going all Scarlet Witch on our asses."

A laugh bursts out of me at the same time I turn into my neighbourhood. The childhood nickname has a wave of nostalgia crashing into me. Leo and his comic references go together like two peas in a pod.

"How many times have I asked you not to call me that?" I ask.

"Too many. But you know I won't stop. Might as well just accept it."

I drive up the steep hill that serves as an unofficial entry to our community and spot the pointed roof of my childhood home —all nine hundred square feet of it.

The muted, yellow-painted bricks stand out like a sore thumb amongst the newly renovated dark stone and siding of the neighbouring houses, but I don't hate it as much now as I did when I was a kid referred to as the ginger with the yellow brick house at the top of the hill.

Tall hedges trimmed just a smidge crooked line the small front yard, and a matching yellow birdhouse that's seen much better days is perched dead smack in the centre. Add in a mailbox that no longer opens and shuts because of its broken lid, and I'm sure we're the subject of discussion in the HOA meetings at the end of every month.

Each morning I run past said mailbox and peek inside, I'm surprised not to see a letter from Mrs. Evansburg, the head of the committee, ordering us to spruce the place up a bit.

"Leo," I say, preparing to shift the subject back to something way too heavy for a Monday afternoon. "I need you to be honest with me. Do you think I can do this job? Training someone to help them reach the dream I had and lost? I haven't even touched the ice since that game." Pulling into the short driveway, I shift the car into park and rest my forehead on the steering wheel.

"I really hate when you word it like that, Scarlett. You lost nothing. Your injury wasn't your fault. Your career was taken from you because life can be an entitled asshole to the best people. But yes, I think you can do it. If anybody can, it's you. Adam's a really good guy. I owe him for how much he helped with my knee."

I release a tight breath and lean back in my seat. That's exactly what I was dreading he would say. Leo has never lied to me, and hearing his support only makes my decision more real. There's no going back now. I can't hide from this anymore.

My eyes catch the flapping wings of a small brown bird as it swoops into the bird bath by the porch steps. The damn thing doesn't have a care in the world as it lifts its wing and uses its beak to bring water to the exposed skin. I never cared much for birds growing up. There was always so much to do, so many places to be, that I never even paid any attention when one would sing on my windowsill or chirp at me from a tree branch in the backyard.

Stopping to smell the roses, so to speak, was never my thing.

Now, though, I've noticed several things and actually paid attention to them in a way I hadn't before my injury. The slower pace I've adapted in my daily life has been the second-best thing to come out of my destroyed career. The first one being my ability to be here, taking care of my sick mother so that she doesn't have to struggle alone.

"If you were into girls, Leonard Arlo, I would have snatched you up a long time ago. You never fail to stroke my ego when it's in the dumps."

He laughs. "Oh, baby. I would have made you mine the first

time we met and you told me your great-grandma Betsy could outskate me blindfolded and going backward."

"It's safe to say you've gotten better since then."

He has, and he knows it too. I haven't watched him play in a while, but he's quicker than me on my best days. I've lost far too many bets over the length of our friendship to dare say otherwise.

"Damn right I have. But hey, maybe this job is a blessing. I would love for you to join me on the ice again sometime. Preferably before I retire."

"Cool it on the dramatics."

"Hey! Can't blame me, Letty. You've been avoiding the rink. Don't pretend otherwise. If you keep going on this way, I'll be a wrinkly old man before I get to see you skate again."

He's right. I've avoided so much as looking at a pair of skates since my last game. They do nothing but remind me of a failed career and the blatant fact that I don't know what to do next. I put everything I had and wanted to be into hockey, and when that stopped becoming an option, I realized pretty damn quickly there was no plan B.

"I'll work on it," I mutter. My mom's figure appears behind the living room window, and she waves enthusiastically. "Thanks for talking me off the ledge, Leo. I should head inside before Mom comes and drags me from my car. I'm sure she's bursting to hear about my interview."

"Anytime. You know that," he says. "If the Woodmen make it past the second round, we'll be playing against either Vancouver or Vegas in a couple of weeks. If we play Van and I get you a ticket to one of the games, would you be there? For me?"

A sliver of panic creeps up my spine before I shove it away. There's a slim chance Minnesota will lose to their current second-round playoff opponent, the Colorado Knights. Not when they've been outplaying them in all three of the previous games and are up two to one in the series. Minnesota will be here in Vancouver in no time since the Warriors also look like they'll come out above their opponent, Vegas.

Anything can happen in the playoffs, but I'm loyal to my hometown team until the end of time.

"Yeah. As long as you don't mind me wearing a Hutton jersey."

"A Warriors girl through and through," he groans, like me cheering for the Vancouver player pains him. It actually might, now that I think about it. "Fine. But don't you dare bring a sign."

"We'll see. Gotta go, talk soon." I hang up the phone when he starts to protest.

I've only just made it out of the car when Mom comes barrelling through the front door. Her smile is bright enough to light the darkest tunnel.

"Took you long enough. I've been just buzzing with anticipation," she says when I step up beside her on the porch.

The hot rollers in her thin hair bounce as she grabs my hand and pulls me to one of the two wicker chairs decorating the corner of the porch we call her coffee nook. A metallic, glossy purple-and-blue wind chime swings above her chair, playing a high-pitched song in the breeze.

I give my head a slight shake and smile softly. "Well, sit down, busy bee. Let's talk."

5

Adam

"We're late, Dad," Cooper states from the passenger seat. He hasn't stopped tapping his fingers on the window since we left our house.

It's only a fifteen-minute drive from our house to Ava's, but I was stuck in the office longer than usual today despite clocking in way too early, leaving us running around trying to get ready for our weekly family dinner at my best friend's house.

We've been having these dinners since Cooper was a toddler. They started as Ava and her husband, Oakley, offering to help me once a week by cooking and feeding us while watching Coop, but over the years has turned into a giant get-together with all of our friends and their kids. We now alternate who hosts each week, and I won't lie and pretend I'm not relieved that it's at Oakley and Ava's tonight.

Oakley has a man cave worthy of a magazine article, and Ava is a far better cook than I am. Not to mention their place isn't nearly as cramped as mine after everyone arrives.

"We never eat on time, anyway," I reply and point to the metal gate up the road. "Look, the gate is right there. Take a breath, buddy."

He makes a point of looking at the time displayed on the fancy touch screen at the centre of the dash. "It's 6:13. We should have been here thirteen minutes ago."

As we close in on the massive acreage and the locked gate that guards it, I toss my phone to my co-pilot. "Yeah, yeah. Call Oakley and tell him to open the gate."

He does, and by the time we get there, it's already open. I turn off the service road and onto the paved driveway leading to the house.

The six-car garage at the end of the driveway is blocked by Oakley's lifted F-350, a Jeep Wrangler that belongs to Ava, and a blacked-out Escalade belonging to Oakley's brother-in-law, Tyler.

I've barely shifted the car into park before Cooper jumps out and runs toward the circle of kids watching us from the yard. Oakley and Ava's oldest son, Maddox, is only two years younger than Coop, so I'm not surprised when he's my son's first stop.

I watch the two greet each other with clapped hands and laugh at the maturity of it. Ava is waiting for me on the huge wraparound porch by the time I get out of the car and start up the cobblestone sidewalk. The smell of the fresh flowers hanging in planters around the porch should be overwhelming, but I've grown to love it over the years. I never would have thought Ava —the girl who baked countless pots of flowers in the sun in university—would grow to have a green thumb, but here we are.

"You're late," she scolds me before smiling warmly. Her long, coffee-brown-coloured hair is swept out of her face and tied in a loose bun at the back of her head, and she's wearing a Minnie Mouse apron that rests over a pair of jean cut-off shorts and a muscle tank. She's the epitome of casual, like always.

"And you're looking beautiful this evening."

"Always with the flattery."

In an instant, I'm up the stairs and wrapping my arms around her in a tight hug. "Don't pretend you don't love it," I say.

She returns the hug just as tight. "You're right."

A symphony of voices coming from inside the house has me pulling back and slinging my arm over Ava's shoulders as we head inside. Ava bumps her hip against mine.

"I hope you're hungry. I may or may not have gone a little overboard at the store today."

I snort. "What does a little overboard mean?"

"It means you'll be taking food home with you," Oakley says as he heads toward us. His grin pulls at the wrinkles by his eyes.

Ava gives my side a squeeze before slipping from beneath my arm and moving to place a kiss on Oakley's jaw. Her husband scowls like the quick kiss offended him and wraps a hand around the back of her neck, bringing her lips to his. I laugh, shaking my head, and a second later, Ava swats at his chest and pushes back.

"You just saw me five minutes ago."

Oakley shrugs. "Okay. And?"

"And this argument is pointless. I'm going to check on dinner," she says, shooting the two of us an exasperated look. "At least get out of the entryway and come sit down."

"Yes, ma'am," I reply and move further into the house as she disappears to the kitchen.

The front entry opens into the sitting room, decorated with a grey couch opposite a white-painted brick fireplace with two family photos placed on either side. One photo is from last summer, at their vacation home on the island. The photographer posed their three kids in front, with Oakley and Ava behind them. Their two-year-old daughter, Adalyn, was only a year old then and looks like she's poised and ready to take off.

The second photo is of everyone this past Christmas. I'm on the far left, followed by Ava, Oakley, his sister Gracie, Tyler, Tyler's brother Braden, and his wife, Sierra. The kids—all six of them—are placed in front of us. To a random person, we look like a crazy bunch, and we are to an extent, but we're just one massive family. We may not share DNA, but this is the best family I could have asked for.

I tear my eyes from the photos and flop down on the couch. Oakley joins me.

"How are you doing?" I ask once he gets comfortable.

Oakley rolls his neck. "Almost as good as new."

"I wasn't just referring to your injury."

"Right." He clears his throat. "I love being home more, obviously. Being on the road so often was something I hated more than anything. But I fucking miss playing, man."

It's hard to keep the sympathy I feel tucked away and out of sight. The last thing Oakley wants is for us to feel sorry for him, but I can't help it. I was sitting right here on this couch with Ava and the kids, watching Oakley play his last professional hockey game before anyone even knew that's what it was. Including the man himself.

One bad hit and his mind was made up. He wasn't going to go back after he healed.

"I would be concerned if you didn't miss it. You've been playing hockey for almost two decades. But if you're doubting whether you made the right decision, I would say that you did. Those kids out there love having you home, and I think Ava does even more."

He nods once, twice, and then grabs my shoulder, squeezing it hard. "You're right. Thank you."

I pat his hand. "Don't gotta thank me, Lee."

There's a loud cough from the kitchen entry, and I look over to find Tyler smirking at us. He folds his arms across his chest, and a dainty hand slithers up over his shoulder. His wife, Gracie, slips around him and snuggles into his side.

"Don't mind us," Tyler says. "We just got tired of waiting for you to stop gossiping and join the rest of us."

Gracie scowls at him before looking back at me with warm eyes. "What he meant to say is that we're happy to see you,

Adam. I, for one, was not surprised to find you fashionably late."

"Long day at the office," I say. Gracie parts from Tyler and moves toward me, arms held open. When she reaches me, she gives me a half hug from my spot on the couch and hums her understanding.

She runs a non-profit dance studio for children whose parents can't afford to spend thousands of dollars a year on lessons. If there's anyone who understands the struggles of working in an office well after closing hours, it's Gracie.

"Sounds about right," Tyler says sympathetically. "Anything going on?"

"No. Just busy with the preparations for next season. I hired a new trainer yesterday, though, so hopefully it'll be smoother sailing from here."

"Oh! Is it anyone we would know?" Gracie asks, pulling out of the hug and walking back over to her husband. He collects her beneath his arm and brings her to rest against his front.

"You could say that."

Curiosity lights up her eyes. "I'm going to need a bit more than that."

"I'm not sure how I managed it, but I wrangled Scarlett Carter into working for me."

Oakley coughs into his fist while Gracie gives me a confused look.

"Should I know who that is?" she asks.

Tyler rubs his hands up and down her arms, murmuring, "She won an Olympic medal with Team Canada's women's hockey team in 2018, princess."

Gracie's jaw drops.

"She was injured, though, pretty badly from what I remember hearing. Wasn't she?" Oakley asks me. He's recovered from his coughing fit and looks more curious than anything now.

I wince and nod. "Tore her shoulder. She recently moved back home."

"How does her recovery look?" Tyler asks.

There have only been a handful of times when I have refused to share something with my best friends, but this is one of them. If I learned anything about Scarlett after talking with her yesterday, it's that she isn't one to share things with people she doesn't know. I have to respect that.

"She's doing alright" is what I choose to say. It's not technically a lie.

"Well, I want to meet her. She's got to be a total badass," Gracie chimes in. "Oh! Invite her to my birthday party!"

I blink slowly. My automatic response is to say no, but I know that won't slide with Gray. Luckily, Oakley must notice my silent panic because he steps in to help.

"Who knows if she'll even stay around that long. Adam is a hard-ass at work." *Or not*. I scowl.

"Well, either way. *I* wouldn't miss it. It's already on my calendar," I say. My answer satisfies her, and she relaxes in Tyler's arms.

"Adam would never turn down a boat ride on a private yacht, Gray," Oakley chips in with a laugh.

"He's got a point," I hum, a teasing smile pulling at my mouth. "I've never been invited to such a prestigious event before. I'm honoured."

"It was Ty's idea," she argues. "I would have been okay with a small dinner at our house."

Tyler scoffs. "You're turning thirty. We're not celebrating that by doing something we already do together every weekend."

"Another good point," I say. "It's your dirty thirties, Gracie. Let your rich husband throw you a party that will make his wallet weep."

"I'm not sure that even renting a yacht would make a dent in Tyler's wallet," Ava teases, joining us again.

"Says the one married to the previously highest-paid hockey player in the world," Tyler pokes.

"Oh, hush." She waves him off. "Dinner is done, and I was about to call the kids in. I figured I would give you a chance to prepare yourselves for the chaos."

A collective groan fills the room, and I can't help but smile to myself.

Now the fun really begins.

6

Scarlett

I'M PRETTY SURE I COULD SKATE BEFORE I COULD RUN. I DON'T remember the first time my little feet hit the ice, but I know deep in my bones that I'm right.

From the very first time the icy chill of the arena pushed a shiver through my toddler-size body, it was game over. I might not remember much from those first few trips to the rink, but I do know that they became an addiction as I grew older—something I needed to do to *feel*.

Hockey isn't just a sport to me—it never has been. It's a way of life. My everything.

I was raised by a single mother, so money was always tight. She worked two jobs—both of which still barely paid the bills. Our house was small, but it was ours. The fridge had *just* enough to keep my belly full. But I didn't miss a single season of hockey. Not since my very first practice. My mom made sure of that. And to this day, I'm still not sure how she pulled it off.

But now? Now there's a void inside of me that I can't fill. An empty feeling that threatens to spread like a disease, eating away at me more and more each day.

Working for Adam White, training athletes who will go on to do things I will never have a chance to, will only be rubbing salt in the wound. But I've never been a quitter. Going back on my word isn't an option.

So here I am, standing in front of WIT with my freshly sharpened skates thrown over my shoulder and my stomach hanging between my knees.

I wipe my palms off on my leggings and scold myself for getting so nervous. It seems ridiculous to be scared right now—I've played in the Olympic games and been under more pressure than some people will ever experience. Yet I haven't been able to calm my racing pulse since the moment I slipped my arms into my new White Ice Training embroidered track jacket this morning.

If my old teammates could see how I'm acting, I would never live it down.

The sound of sneakers scuffing the pavement behind me makes every muscle in my body tense up. *Great.* I've been caught staring at the front doors like a terrified child waiting for their mom to check the closet for monsters.

Squeezing my eyes shut, I breathe in a massive lungful of air through my nose before letting it out of my mouth. Once I've relaxed as much as possible, I open my eyes and look over my shoulder.

Adam's lips part on a grin when I meet his gaze. He's shaved since the last time I saw him, making him look a few years younger than I know he really is. Not like he looks his age in the first place. He has a naturally youthful appearance, but I think he owes most of that to the genuine happiness he wears like a second skin.

There may actually be some truth behind the whole *scowling takes decades off your life* saying I was always told as a teenager. Adam certainly won't have to worry about that.

"Good morning, Scarlett," he says, and I notice the tray of coffee cups in his hand when he extends it toward me. "I didn't know how you liked yours, so there's an assortment."

I double blink at the Starbucks cups.

"If you don't like coffee, I can have Brielle bring you something else when she comes in," he offers a second later, sounding far too genuine to be considered normal.

With a quick shake of my head, I grab a cup labelled as a plain black coffee and hold it to my chest. "Thank you."

He eyes the cup in my hand before dangling a pair of keys between us. "Let's get to work, then."

Adam makes quick work of opening the doors and leading us inside before setting the extra coffees down on the reception desk and showing me around.

The tour is quick, but he doesn't seem to miss anything. We move around the arena with precision, and by the time he's leaving me to put my stuff away in the staff-only locker room, I'm feeling more comfortable.

It surprised me how quickly I relaxed during the tour, but I guess it shouldn't have. I've spent more time in locker rooms and training facilities than I have at my own home. It should be second nature to find comfort in this setting by now.

Adam left me with instructions to meet him on the ice after I'm finished here but didn't elaborate on why. I can only guess that it has something to do with why he asked me to come in today before the rink even opened.

I shut my locker door and sit down on the wooden bench lined along the opposite wall. My skates rest on the floor in front of me, but I make no move to slip them on. Instead, I fidget with the elastic band holding my unruly curls up and out of my face and spend far too long picking at the edges of the sports tape I placed around my shoulder after my shower this morning. I do everything and anything I can to avoid doing what I'm supposed to be doing and hating myself for it.

With a groan, I drop my head back against the wall and fight the urge to stomp my feet like an insolent child.

"You can put them on by the ice if you want."

I jump at the deep voice, my hand flying to my chest. "Shit. You scared me."

Adam chuckles, the sound smooth yet raspy in a way that makes the hairs on my arms rise. He's leaning a hip against the doorjamb, one hand in the pocket of his track pants, and watches me with an open expression that does little to hide his curiosity.

"I'm sorry. I just wanted to check on you and make sure everything was okay. You've been in here for a while."

I inwardly wince. "It didn't feel like that long."

"If you're not feeling comfortable, we can skip the ice for today," he offers. "I can have you go sit in on a few sessions instead. Willow isn't in until Wednesday."

I'm quick to protest. "No. You brought me in here today for a reason. You wanted to test me, right? See what I can and can't do?"

"Yes, that was my intention. But I'm not the guy that's going to push you into something you're not ready for. Help guide you, maybe. But not force."

My hackles rise even as I try to brush off the hidden challenge in his words, and I snap, "What makes you think I'm not ready?"

He lifts a brow, looking from me to the skates at my feet and then back at me again. "Did you forget how to put skates on?"

"No. I didn't *forget* how to put skates on."

"A bit rusty when it comes to lacing them, then?"

I'm not an idiot—I know when someone is trying to anger me enough into doing something, but I'm also not above falling right into the trap. With a scowl, I adjust my socks and slide my left foot into my skate. Just like I remember, it's a perfect fit.

Filled with the urge to prove him wrong, I stare at him from beneath my eyelashes and quickly tie the laces. It's muscle memory at this point, like riding a bike or driving a car. A ripple of satisfaction moves through me.

Adam's mouth pulls at the corners as he watches, but he doesn't say another word. I appreciate that he doesn't interrupt me, but I keep that tidbit of information to myself.

In what seems like no time at all, I have both skates on and tied perfectly. "Happy?" I ask.

He grins. "Very. Are you?"

Standing, I shift my weight on my feet in an effort to get comfortable with the sudden change and then nod.

"Let's get to it, then. We have half an hour before everyone else starts showing up," he says, nodding to the door.

I'm suddenly flooded with determination, having hopped that first small hurdle. One that I hadn't been able to on my own. It's a small thing, but a win is a win.

I don't think twice before following him.

MY HEART THUMPS in my chest as I stand on the edge of the ice. A nervous sweat breaks out on the back of my neck. I've never felt like this before. Not with this. Not with hockey.

My stomach tightens with fear, pure terror at the thought of diving back into this world. Of letting it consume me again.

Memories come crashing in, bringing me back to that game. To the pain—both physical and emotional—and how broken it left me.

There are three minutes left in the third period. I'm dripping sweat. It's in my eyes, hanging off my nose. I shake my head and let it fling away.

My grip on my stick is near-painful as I rest the blade on the ice and hold the stare of the Mississauga Bears first line centre. She settles her stick across from mine and grins wickedly. I ignore it.

The puck drops between our blades, and our shoulders touch when we move forward, but it's me that scoops the puck and passes it back between my legs. It's my seventh consecutive faceoff win this period.

Cassidy Lion spits my name as I skate around her and lead my team toward the Mississauga zone. My teammate passes me the puck, and it hits my blade before two Bears players cover me, pushing us toward the boards. I battle them for the puck, pushing at them and kicking the puck, trying to dislodge it.

Another player moves behind me, and I recognize the red and gold on their jersey as one of my teammates. There's no time to feel relieved. We're still outnumbered, but by some miracle, I manage to kick out the puck and push it out and away with my stick, hoping a Blaze player is ready to collect it.

The pressure on my shoulders alleviates as everyone skates off toward the puck, and I spin around, ready to do the same.

I don't see her. Not until it's too late. A blindsided hit.

The pain is instant. By the time I realize what's happening, my helmet is already smacking the boards, and my body follows. I gasp, winded.

Crumpling to the ice, I fight back a wretch at the pain in my upper body. I can't tell what's wrong. It hurts everywhere. Am I bleeding? Did I hit my head?

A cry escapes me when I try to lift my arm and pull my helmet off. Searing pain slices through my shoulder. No. *Fuck.*

I shut my eyes and let the first of many tears escape.

"Are you okay?" Adam asks gently. I wince at the memory and ignore the phantom pain in my shoulder.

He's standing a few feet away, his face tight with concern. I swallow and force a nod.

I can do this. *I can do this.* This isn't the same as before. One step in front of the other, Scarlett. Slowly, I move my skate forward and push myself into a slow glide.

Adam's eyes watch me as I push off my other skate and move further down the ice. It's like breathing after years of suffocating. Each swipe of my skates across the ice has the debris clearing from my lungs.

Pride quickens my pulse. It's such a small win, but the importance of it doesn't escape me. *I did it.*

"Can you do a couple laps?" Adam shouts when I start creating a distance between us.

Can I do a couple laps? I scowl. "Yeah."

He doesn't reply, and I tune him out, focusing on not letting my knees shake like a newborn deer. I'm not even going fast, but I'm already panting.

And as we continue with our first session, it only gets worse. Half an hour later, I'm huffing, "I quit."

Adam's laughter echoes around the rink from his place by the boards, and I halt my wheezing just to flip him the middle finger. With my fingers digging into my waist, I lean back and try to catch my breath.

Sweat pools at the back of my neck, my forehead, and between my boobs. The idea of falling to my belly and placing my cheek to the ice is an attractive one. I haven't worked this hard in months, and it shows.

We didn't touch on anything beyond simple stick handling and skating tests, yet I feel like I've just run a marathon with weights tied to my ankles. There's a bright feeling of success there too, but I don't pay it too much attention. There's still so much to do.

"No you don't. Catch," he says before throwing a bottle of water at me. I catch it and unscrew the cap before drinking the entire thing in one go.

"I wasn't under the impression that I was the one in need of training," I state.

Keeping my eyes on him, I skate to the boards and set the empty bottle by the exit, the muscles in my side straining and crying as I do. There's a twinkle in Adam's brown eyes that makes me narrow mine.

"You're not. But what kind of boss would I be if I didn't know your strengths and weaknesses before throwing you into a position to teach someone else?"

"A shit one."

Adam tips his head back and laughs freely. I've noticed that he does that a lot—laughs without a care in the world. More than anyone else I know. "You're honest. I like that."

"Do you drink liquid sunshine from a bottle every morning?"

My brash words only make him laugh harder. "That was a serious question."

"Oh, I know," he says before placing his hands on the boards behind him and pushing himself up to sit on the small surface. His cheeks are stained a light pink from the cold as he pats the spot beside him.

"There are perfectly good seats behind you." I point to the stands on the other side of the ice.

He shrugs, and I frown, refusing to move. My fingers twitch at my sides, wanting to grab at my shoulder as a soreness awakens. Wrinkles grow between his eyebrows as he watches me begin to panic. Suddenly, realization floods his features.

"Tomorrow," he begins. I stare at him blankly. "Meet me here at the same time. We're going to work on that shoulder. I need to know how bad it is."

I'm about to protest when he pins me with a look more serious than I've seen him wear so far. Realizing that this isn't a battle I want a part in, I roll my lips and nod.

My agreement is incredibly reluctant, but agreement nonetheless.

"Okay. Tomorrow it is."

7

Adam

I've never had a favourite colour, but if I had to choose one, it would be whichever ones combine to create the vibrant red of Scarlett's hair.

Multiple shades of brown, red, and even a little blond blend together to create a rusty copper colour that I wouldn't doubt forces heads to turn whenever she walks into a room. On more than one occasion over the past two days, I've wanted to slip my fingers into the mass of curls and search through them to try and locate a strand of each individual colour.

Of course, I haven't done that. Not only is that a ridiculous idea, but it's an outrageously creepy one for a man ten years her senior to think up in the first place. Unfortunately, that reminder has done little to stall those intrusive thoughts.

I blink twice, lift my coffee cup to my lips, and take a generous gulp of the hot liquid in hopes of bringing myself back to reality. Scarlett does the same with her black coffee, and I fight back a wince. I've never liked the taste of black coffee. It's too bitter, harsh. I much prefer something a bit sweeter. Quite the opposite of the woman in front of me.

Scarlett was at the arena before me again this morning, and it wasn't hard to tell by her rigid, guarded posture that she would have rather been anywhere else. Not like I could blame her. I was clear when I told her what we would be focused on today. It was no surprise to see that she wasn't excited to have her biggest insecurity poked and prodded at by someone she barely knows.

Still, she accepted the coffee I brought her with a small thank you and followed me inside. We skipped the ice altogether and instead headed straight for the therapy room.

That's where we are now, and after she sits on the raised bench, I place my coffee down on the small counter behind me. With a soft smile, I hold my hand out in front of me, and she shoves her coffee into it like she can't get rid of it fast enough. It hits me then that she's nervous.

Quite nervous.

"I'm not going to judge you, Scarlett. You have my word. I only want to see where you're at so we know where to go next."

She nods stiffly, watching as I place her cup beside mine. "I know."

"If it gets too much, let me know and we'll stop," I reassure her. The last thing I want is to push too hard.

Having not worked with a physical therapy client in a while, I'm pretty nervous myself. I'm confident in what I'm doing—I wouldn't have volunteered to help Scarlett if I wasn't—but I can't help but feel a bit rusty. Maybe I should have Quinn, our actual physical therapist, take over for me from now on.

"It's not like it's going to get much worse. Not unless you suck at your job."

I stumble over my words. "Was that a joke?"

She avoids eye contact. "A bad one, apparently."

"No it wasn't." I smile wide enough that my cheeks burn. "You just surprised me."

Scarlett makes a face like she doesn't believe me but drops it. Instead, she starts examining the room. Her eyes stray to the framed photo of me and Leonard Orlo the day after he completed his physical therapy and hit the ice at full capacity again. It was a long, hard road, as it usually is with professional athletes. The need to get back out there is one that's extremely difficult to ignore.

"Leo told me that you were the one that helped with his knee."

The wall is full of photos of me and my staff with rehabilitated clients, but she focused on that one in specific. Curiosity gnaws at my stomach at the prospect of learning more about her and her life, and I speak before I can stop myself.

"You and Leo are close?"

She rips her stare from the photo before placing it on me. "Yeah. He was the one that convinced me to give this place a chance."

"I should thank him, then."

The slight catch of her breath is the only reaction I get. She ignores my comment, and I swallow to avoid asking why.

"Was Leo the last injured athlete you helped?" she asks.

"No. Oakley Hutton was." Tension builds in my muscles. "After he healed from his collarbone injury."

"The one that ended his career?"

I suck in a breath at her blunt question. "It wasn't a career-ending injury, but it was close. He made the decision to retire based on other things at the time."

Scarlett hums deeply, like she's thinking about something too complex to share. It feels like forever before she answers me. And when she does, I have to fight to hold back the extent of my surprise.

"Well, if Oakley Hutton trusts you to help him, I guess I should too."

"Just like that?" I ask in disbelief, expecting more resistance.

She looks at me again—this time with defiance in her eyes—and lifts one dark brow. "Were you expecting me to throw a tantrum and stomp my feet like a child? I might be young, but I'm nowhere close to immature."

"I didn't mean it like that." Did I? *No.* But she's right about one thing. She is young. "Don't get me wrong, I'm thrilled to have your complete acceptance—it will make my job easier. But you seemed incredibly reluctant earlier. You just took me by surprise."

"I seem to be doing that a lot."

"You have," I agree, trying—and failing—to hold back my smile. What can I say? It's refreshing to be kept on your toes.

My phone dings from the pocket of my track pants, and I quickly pull it out, scowling at the time. WIT opens in fifteen minutes, and we haven't even started doing what I had planned. I check the text to make sure it isn't from Cooper or his school before tucking my phone away.

"Okay, enough distractions. Let's get an idea of where you are with this shoulder."

Her throat bobs with a swallow, and I try my best to reassure her with a gentle smile before taking a step toward her. She's wearing a tank top today, and I have an unrestricted view of her carved biceps even after months without use.

"Tell me where you were with your old therapist."

"We were working a lot with resistance bands and strengthening. My range of motion was getting really good," she says.

"Okay. We'll start with a couple of stretches and then try a resistance band. Place your left forearm on the doorframe and—"

"Turn my body away from it?" she cuts me off.

"Yeah, exactly."

She seems okay with that idea because she doesn't hesitate to do as I said. After about a minute of watching her stretch, I tell her she can stop and do a few more basic stretches.

After she's done, I turn around and move to a basket of multicoloured resistance bands before picking up a slim band with more stretch than the others. Holding it out to her, I say, "Step on one end and grab the other."

She does as I say, bending down and placing one end of the red band beneath her running shoe while holding the other end in a tight fist. Before I can tell her what to do next, she's fixing her posture, straightening her arm at her side, and stretching the band toward the ceiling, up and away from her body.

Crossing my arms, I lean back on my heels. "Ten reps. Get your fist as level with your shoulder as possible."

With a crease between her brows, she nods subtly, keeping her concentration on the task at hand. I'm instantly impressed at the range of motion she has with this exercise. It's not full range, but it's better than I anticipated.

Scarlett huffs a breath of frustration by her fifth repetition, when she can't lift her arm any further, hitting her limit at about an inch from her fist being level with her shoulder.

"That's really good, Scarlett," I encourage. "Better than I expected."

She scowls. "Not good enough. I was doing better months ago."

Before she stopped.

"Fallbacks happen. You'll get there again."

In under a minute, she finishes the ten reps and drops her arm like it weighs a thousand pounds.

"I want to do another exercise before the rink opens. We'll leave everything else for tomorrow morning," I tell her.

"Tomorrow morning?"

My smile starts small, slowly growing into a full-fledged grin. "Yes, tomorrow morning. And the morning after that. I want you here working on that shoulder every morning before work. Unless that's a problem with you?"

She wears an uneasy expression but reluctantly agrees. "No, it's not a problem."

"You'll meet Willow tomorrow as well. She's coming in at 10:00 a.m."

"I'm assuming you have an outline for me to follow?"

"I do. We'll go over it this afternoon."

Usually, it would be the trainer's responsibility to draw out a training program for their client, fit specifically to what they need or have requested, but the circumstances here are a bit different. So for now, she'll use my plan. Besides, I have a strong inkling that Scarlett will want to create one herself after her first session with Willow.

I take a step back and click my tongue. "Let's move on before we get distracted again. You can drop the band on the bench. We won't be using it again today."

She does but not without cutting me a curious glance that I try to ignore. I'm confident that she'll have done all of the stretches and exercises I had planned for today, but that doesn't mean they'll be easy. Nothing about restrengthening a muscle that's been sitting near-dormant for months is easy.

Tapping my fingers on my thighs, I move toward the far corner of the room. There are three yoga mats spread along the wall beside a collection of dumbbells, yoga balls, and balance boards. I point to the mats while grabbing a balance board and gently moving a yoga ball over with my foot.

"Do you care which mat you use?" I ask.

She shakes her head and moves to the one closest one to her, the one on the end. I place the balance board on the front end of the mat, watching it wobble on its small circular base before setting the yoga ball off to the side for the time being.

"Okay, you're going to get down on the floor, place your hands shoulder width apart on the base, and try to keep the board stable. If you need to support yourself on your knees for now, then do that. There's no rush here. I want you to feel comfortable," I assure her.

She releases a slow breath, and some of the previous tension in her shoulders disappears. I find myself doing the same. I'm tenser than usual, and I can't deny that's because I feel a heavy pressure not to mess anything up when it comes to this woman.

The only noise in the room is the shuffle of her sneakers on the cold tile floor before she's lowering to her knees on the mat and inching toward the board. Her vibrant red curls fall in her face, regardless of it being tied back, and my fingers itch to pull one to see if they're as springy and soft as they look. I give my head a rough shake, dispelling that thought before it has a chance to sink in.

Scarlett places her hands on the board exactly how I instructed, but after about a minute she swiftly pushes off her knees, holding her body up in a shaky, full plank position instead. I chuckle, completely unsurprised by the confidence she has in her body.

A bolt of excitement shoots through me when she glances up and holds my gaze with a silent dare. One I don't turn down.

"Move the board in circular motions," I order, and I swear her lips twitch.

Muscles rippling with the effort, she shifts her weight around, forcing the board to tilt in a clockwise motion before dropping back to her knees and starting again. The neck of her tank top hangs open, exposing the navy blue sports bra beneath it, and I dart my eyes to her natural, unpainted fingernails.

"Anything else, boss? Or have I passed inspection?" she asks, tone dripping with attitude. Attitude that entertains me far more than annoys me at this point.

"Are you in any pain?"

She looks at me like I've just asked the most ridiculous question. "I've been holding a plank on a balance board for at least a minute now."

I roll my eyes. "It was longer than a minute. And I meant your shoulder."

"A bit. It feels more wobbly than painful, though."

Nodding, I say, "Let's call it for today. We can pick back up tomorrow morning."

Scarlett drops her knees to the mat before leaning back on her heels. Her forehead is slightly damp, and her cheeks are a pale pink, but other than that, she looks cool, calm, and collected.

"That's it?" She looks confused, which in turn confuses me.

"Were you hoping for more?"

"Not really. You're just more relaxed than I expected," she admits, standing back up. With her hands on her hips, she tilts her head to the side and rolls her shoulder. I watch for the first sign of pain but only see relief as she stretches.

"That's a compliment, right?"

She blinks. "Yeah. I guess it was."

"It's nice to know that you're capable of those. You had me worried for a minute there."

"Don't get used to it."

My smile is wicked. "I'll try, Scary Spice."

Her eyes narrow into slits as soon as the words hit the air. I bite back a laugh. "No" is all she says.

I quirk a brow. "No? No what?"

If the death glare she's giving me is anything to go by, I think it's safe to say she's not a fan of the name.

"Don't call me that."

"Not a Spice Girls fan?"

She huffs, frustrated, and it only eggs me on. I've always loved a good challenge, and getting Scarlett to loosen up might be my new favourite one.

"Do you not like it because you don't know who the Spice Girls are?" I stifle a laugh when she glares at me—hard.

"I'm not a child. I know who the Spice Girls are."

"Then you'll learn to love the nickname," I tease.

"I'm positive I won't."

I run my fingers through the long pieces of hair at the top of my head and smirk. She has no idea how wrong she is.

8

Adam

The relationship I have with my mother and father—if you could even call what we have a genuine relationship—has always been strained.

With two highly successful criminal defense lawyers as parents, I spent more time alone than I did in their company. Whether it was long hours at the office or a late-night hookup with the people they were cheating on each other with, I was always set on the back burner, left to simmer and wait for even a sliver of their attention.

It's been years since they've retired, yet I can't say that's made much of a difference when it comes to spending time together. In all honesty, it doesn't bother me as much as it used to. By the time their jobs no longer held top priority in their lives, we were strangers. They had already missed too many years to make up for, left too much space between us. I'm content with the once-a-year meeting my mother plans every Thanksgiving.

Cooper barely knows his grandparents, but I know that's for the best. It's better not to give them the power to hurt him down the road when they inevitably find something wrong with him or his actions in the future.

They were very outspoken about how disappointed there were when I brought a two-year-old boy to their door, terrified out of my mind and shaking in the rain. I wouldn't have gone to them at all had I not been in such a terrified place after Beth, Cooper's mother and an old college fling, found me at a bar and confessed that I was a father to a son I had no idea existed. But my mom was still my mom, and all I wanted was a hug from the woman who carried me for nine months.

Instead, I got to listen to an hour-long rant on how negatively my actions could affect our family and, more importantly, their careers, while cradling a sleeping child in my arms that I had no idea was mine just hours prior.

It's safe to say they were no help to me. They didn't know the first thing about being parents, and I beat myself up for days afterward for thinking that these circumstances would have made my mother's maternal instincts come to light. But it's hard to find something that doesn't exist.

As I look down at Cooper now, watching as he misses the dribbles of melted ice cream as they flow down his waffle cone and drip onto his swim trunks, I can't imagine being anywhere else, missing out on these moments.

I grab a napkin from the stack between us and hand it to him. He flashes me an innocent, toothy grin before patting his shorts dry and making quick work of licking up all the melted ice cream from his cone.

We both smell like sunscreen and are wearing matching Warriors hats, but his is on backward in that typical cool-guy fashion. I've been fighting the urge to flip it around since we got to the beach.

"How is your hat supposed to protect your face from the sun if it's on backwards?"

Cooper rolls his eyes while crunching on the last of his ice cream cone. The umbrella I stuck in the sand the moment we picked a spot on the beach is doing a good enough job of keeping the majority of the sun away, but I would rather be safe than sorry. Not to mention, Cooper is a massive baby when it comes to his sunburn pain tolerance.

"Don't pretend like you don't wear your hat backwards too, Dad."

I tap the brim of my hat, the one facing forward. "Not in the sun I don't."

"I'll flip mine around when we actually go in the sun, okay?" he offers, sounding mighty annoyed with this conversation.

"Deal." My phone beeps from my pocket, and I pull it out, sighing in relief when I see the message lighting up the screen.

Beth: I'm here!

Me: Look for the blue starfish umbrella

"Your mom is here," I tell Cooper and put my phone away again. He nods once, wiping his hands on his Iron Man swim trunks. There's a slight hesitation in his eyes, and it makes my stomach twist.

Cooper and Beth's relationship is . . . fragile. How could it not be when they went years without any contact, only to meet again and be limited to seeing each other once a week?

Beth has struggled with bipolar disorder since she became pregnant with Cooper, but it wasn't until he was two and she faced a life-changing manic episode that she was properly diagnosed. Once she was, she brought him to me, asking for help, and not a day goes by where I'm not grateful for that.

Shortly after, she admitted herself into a psychiatric hospital, where she spent two years recovering and coming to terms with her past and what she could expect from her future.

By the time she left the hospital, Cooper was four. It took her another year after her release to feel confident enough in herself to reach out to me and ask to see him again. But it had been years, and Coop had grown into a whole person, one who felt betrayed and angry and refused to believe anything other than his mother abandoned him. That she didn't want him.

It didn't help Cooper's viewpoint on the situation when Beth granted me sole custody of him, with the exception of her weekly visits. I easily agreed to the visitation, knowing she was doing something she felt necessary for herself and Cooper.

She never needed to do what she did, but she did it with the strength of a mother who wanted what was best for her little boy, and at the time, without stable ground beneath her feet or a family to fall back on, she saw that as me.

She's grown in leaps and bounds since then, and we're figuring out life as it comes. As a real family.

"Hi, guys!"

Cooper and I both turn at the same time to see Beth come bouncing over to our spot on the beach. She's bright-eyed and bushy-tailed today, and I'm glad. Those are her best days.

Sharp blue eyes catch mine and hold for a moment as she silently lets me know she's okay. I nod and grab Cooper's shoulder, giving it a reassuring squeeze. His nerves are heavy in the early summer air.

"Aren't you two just the cutest guys on the beach with your matching hats. I feel like I missed the superhero memo, though. Next time, I'll come prepared in my best Marvel outfit to match those awesome Iron Man shorts," Beth chirps when she reaches us. She's wearing a pale yellow sundress today and slip-on sandals. There's even a bit of colour to her usual pale skin, like she's spent a few hours out in the sun.

"Would you be Wanda or Black Widow?" Cooper asks her.

Beth hums for a moment, scratching her chin. "Wanda."

He nods, accepting that answer, and then turns to me as his mom drops her bag beside our small cooler and sits on his opposite side.

Cooper's mouth twists to the side before he asks, "The Winter Soldier or the Falcon?"

"Crap, buddy. That's a tough one."

He shrugs. "I know who I would pick."

I tip my chin at him. "Well, don't leave me in suspense. Who's your pick?"

"Nuh-uh. You first so I know you aren't just copying me."

"Fine. The Winter Soldier."

Cooper's lips part in surprise, and he scrunches his face like he's genuinely appalled at my answer. "The Falcon has Cap's shield, Dad."

"Spoilers!" Beth shrieks, covering her ears. "I haven't finished *Endgame* yet."

"What?" Cooper and I cry at the same time. I peer at her over Cooper's head and say, "Looks like you have homework."

"I'd say," she agrees.

A strong gust of wind blows past us, and Beth is quick to swipe her long blackish-brown hair out of her face and secure it with a hair tie. I'm about to look away and double-check that none of our stuff has blown away when I spot a swirl of black ink on her wrist, protected with a clear wrapping. Curiosity nips at me, and I tilt my head at her.

"Cooper, why don't you go test out the water? You know I'm a big wuss when it comes to cold water," she says.

He laughs and starts to stand before brushing off the sand from his legs and hands. "Sure. Be right back!"

After watching him jog down the beach and cautiously dip his toes in the soft waves at the shoreline, I twist myself around until I'm facing her and my toes are only a hair length away from her legs. She grins at me, extending her arm and offering me a full view of the inside of her wrist.

"When did you get this?" I ask, gently grabbing her wrist and bringing it closer.

A beautifully drawn daffodil covers years' worth of self-harm scars. My throat grows swollen when I see Cooper's full name and birth date written in the petals.

"Daffodils symbolize rebirth. A fresh start. And, well, Cooper was mine," she whispers.

My eyes burn, but I blink away the wet before it escapes. I brush my thumb over the slightly shaded flower. "That's amazing, Beth. Truly."

"It breaks my heart that Cooper doesn't know how much I love him," she admits.

"He will. He needs you in his life, so as long as you continue to do what you're doing, keep trying the way you are, he'll feel that."

She laughs, the sound jagged, almost pained. "Cooper doesn't need me any more than you do."

"What are you talking about?" I ask, dropping her wrist, my eyes wide. "He definitely can't handle you disappearing again, and I've done this on my own for so long, Beth. It's been nice having someone to talk to that cares about him the same way I do. You've already made so much progress in your relationship. It might not feel like it now, but it *will* happen."

She sniffles then, and my muscles lock up as my brain loses communication with my body. "I didn't mean to make you cry. I'm sorry," I apologize. "Shit, I feel like an asshole."

Shaking her head, she huffs angrily. "Don't apologize. They aren't bad tears. They're happy ones. Thank you, Adam. Sometimes it just gets . . . too much. I know this is all my fault, but that doesn't make it hurt any less."

I reach over and squeeze her knee instead of hugging her like I want to do on instinct. Seeing someone upset has to be one of the toughest things, especially when you know nothing you do or say can help take away their pain.

If it were anybody else, I wouldn't have stopped myself from wrapping my arms around them and holding them tight, but Beth isn't everyone else. She never has and never will be. Our boundaries are clear-cut, and although I've never thought of her in the same light I did during that brief stint in university, I refuse to risk blurring them and destroying the current relationship we've all been building together.

Beth and I aren't meant to be, and I've known that for over a decade now.

"You didn't ask to be born with a mental illness, Beth. You made the right decision when you came to me and decided to put yourself first. He'll understand that when he gets older."

I can't even think about what would have happened if she hadn't found me outside that bar and brought Cooper to me without feeling sick to my stomach. We both know she made the right decision, even if it hurts.

"You don't think he's going to hate me for giving you full custody? He won't look at that and view it as a betrayal? Because some days, that's exactly what it feels like," she confesses. Her voice is sad, and it hits me right in the chest. "I stand with my choice. I believe it was the right decision—it still is. I couldn't provide for him the way you could, or at all, even, and the chance of me losing myself again will always be there. But having him so close yet so far feels worse than being bipolar in the first place."

I try not to show how shocked her words leave me. Beth has openly talked about being bipolar only a handful of times with me over the past few years since she was diagnosed, and even then, it's never been in such a public place or in such a casual tone.

She's been doing so well, though, that maybe I shouldn't be this surprised. Her acceptance of her disease speaks volumes to her growth.

"He could never hate you. You're his mom," I say.

A small smile pulls at her mouth as she nods. She blinks a few times before sucking in a deep breath and standing up. I look up at her questioningly.

"If we don't go join him in the water, he might forget about us altogether." She laughs.

Very true. In full agreement, I stand and wait for her as she pulls her sundress over her head, leaving her in a very modest yellow one-piece suit, before walking beside her toward the water and the boy floating on his back a few feet past the rocky shore.

I drag my toes in the sand and smile. Our family might be a bit unconventional, but I'm damn happy anyway.

9

Scarlett

Willow Barton is phenomenally talented—that much was made abundantly clear to me the moment I saw her on the ice this morning.

Not only does she skate with such a sense of agility and poise that would make any skater in their right mind jealous, but for someone so young, she carries herself with an experienced suave that immediately drew me to her.

I expected our first lesson to be a bit awkward, like most first meetings are, but it's been the opposite. She's more mature than most girls her age and shows that with her calm reactions to criticism and suggestions and excitement to step out of her box to try something new. And if she was at all nervous to meet me, she hid it exceptionally well.

Her bright, excited attitude also did wonders to help with my discomfort with being here. Standing on this ice, training—albeit someone other than myself—is unsettling.

It's different than it was on the ice with Adam. It feels much more daunting, like I could fail at any given moment. This isn't testing or a simple demonstration of what I can and can't do. It isn't even about me at all.

This is about Willow—her career and future. There's no

window for mistakes, and I feel that pressure like a weight on my back.

"Good!" I shout, clicking the stop button on the stopwatch in my palm. Willow immediately drops her stick to the ice and bends over to rest her hands on her knees. "That was better."

"My mouth tastes like a welder's hand," she grumbles as I make my way over to her.

I chew on my bottom lip to stifle my laugh and pick the heavy black stick up off the ice, placing it at my side. Slipping the stopwatch back into my sweater pocket, I make a mental note of her time.

"It should. You worked your ass off today."

She leans back, her hands gripping her hips. "Yeah, I did."

"I've made a couple of changes to the original training plan," I begin. Hopefully she won't have an issue with what I have in mind. Nerves buzz below my skin as I reach up and toy with one of the strings on my sweater.

Adam's lesson plans were a great place to start, but after spending this session studying Willow and slotting her strengths and weaknesses into their little boxes in my mind, I don't think it's best for her growth.

"You're fast, Willow. Like *really* fast. I think we would be doing you a disservice here if we didn't focus on making you even faster. You're excelling in every other aspect, with no obvious weaknesses. So until I can spot something that needs to be improved, I think we need to be focusing on speed and conditioning."

Her eyes widen, but she doesn't look put off by the suggestion. That's a good sign.

"Ultimately, it's your decision. We work for you—*I* work for you. But I really do think this would be the best route for right now," I finish on a breath.

I flinch, startled when another pair of skates cuts across the ice behind me. Did he really not think I could handle this on my own? The thought has me grinding my teeth.

Spinning around, I scowl at Adam. "Mr. White."

Amusement flickers in his eyes. "Hello, Ms. Carter." He turns to the skater beside me. "Willow."

My grip on Willow's stick turns punishing as I try my best to pretend I don't want to swat my boss on the back of the head. But if his smug grin is anything to go by, he already knows that's exactly what I'm thinking. Maybe that means I can do it—

"Hi, Adam. I didn't know you were watching," Willow says.

Me either.

Adam shakes his head. His twinkling eyes catch mine and hold as he says, "Just the past couple minutes. I was heading out for lunch and wanted to stop by and see how everything was going." Oh. "It looked like Scarlett was doing a great job."

"She was," Willow confirms proudly.

A warm feeling fills my chest. "Thank you, Willow."

"We were actually talking about changing my training plan," she adds, and the warmth drops a few degrees, leaving a cold ache behind. Little traitor.

Adam lifts a brow. "Yeah? And what are we changing?"

I clear my throat. "She's too fast and skilled to be spending her days on accuracy shooting and stick-handling drills. Those are things she can work on with her current team."

"You're right," he replies without preamble. I don't pick up anything but pure agreement in his tone.

I double blink. "I'm right?"

His lips tug into a smile before growing into a full-blown grin. "Yes. It's a good call, Scarlett. My lesson plans didn't fit her specific skill set."

Willow starts cracking up, and I look at her, confused. My scowl will be permanently etched on my face at this rate.

"He was testing you, Scarlett. Come on." She laughs.

I consider that and feel like an idiot when I realize she's right. My eyes narrow on Adam.

"I take it I passed, then?" I ask, fighting back the snark that's desperate to taint my words.

He smirks. "With flying colours."

Willow's eyes bulge when she looks at the time on the scoreboard. She pales. "Is that the time? Crap."

Adam's smile falls. "Everything okay?"

"We're done now if you need to go, Willow," I add cautiously.

"Yeah, I do. I'll see you guys Friday. Thank you, Scarlett." She sucks in a long breath before tightening the tie in her hair and rushing away from us, off the ice.

"That was weird, right?" I lift the stick in my hand toward Adam. I'm sure I look just as confused as he does.

"Definitely." He takes the stick from me, tucking it under his arm. "I'll keep this in my office tonight. Just get her to grab it Friday morning."

I hum my agreement and start skating to the exit. When I sense Adam following after me, I say, "She never did tell me if she was okay with changing her training plan."

"Write it up tonight. She didn't seem opposed to it at all, so I would say that's an approval."

He settles beside me, and his arm brushes mine. Even through the thick fabric of my sweater and his jacket, my skin tingles at the contact. I tense my jaw.

"Do you have to be so close to me?" I snap when his knuckles brush the top of my hand.

A burst of laughter escapes him, but he lets himself hang back a hair. "My apologies, Scarlett."

With a roll of my eyes, I shuffle in front of him, push the swinging door in the boards open, and step off the ice. There's a clang as the door shuts, and Adam sidles up beside me, our skates digging into the squishy rubber flooring.

My steps don't falter as I leave him standing by the boards and make my way to the stands to collect my clipboard and water bottle. It's been a very long morning between physiotherapy and training, and I'm not sure I can make it much longer without scarfing down some sort of sustenance.

"You're being a creeper right now," I mutter when I turn back around and find him already staring at me.

He makes a sound that sounds like a mix between a laugh and a cough before sputtering, "A creeper?"

"Yes. Don't you know that it isn't polite to stare?" My stomach grumbles, making me wince.

Adam tilts his head, amused with me. "I wasn't staring."

"Sure. Okay." Another unnecessary noise comes from my stomach that makes me want to shrivel up and die.

"Do you want to keep arguing with me or go get some food?" he asks, nodding to the exit.

"Like, with you?" I inwardly cringe at the stupid question. It's unlikely he would want to get lunch together. I don't know if we're even technically friends.

"Sure. Why not? We're both hungry, and Brielle is already back from her lunch break. My favourite sub shop is right on the edge of town."

I chew on my bottom lip. Is it appropriate to go for lunch with your boss? I guess we're not really going *for* lunch; we're just going to *get* lunch. Ugh. Is there even a difference? I should say no.

"Fine. But I'm paying." I give in after a few seconds and shoot him a look that says *don't test me*, releasing a breath when he doesn't.

"Awesome. Let me just go put Willow's stick away in my office, and I'll meet you by the front doors in a few?" he asks. I nod, and he heads for the exit, sending me an easygoing grin over his shoulder before disappearing through the door.

There's a knot in my stomach, and I hate that I can't tell if it's from nerves or excitement.

I'm being ridiculous. It doesn't matter. The only thing that does is filling my stomach before these hunger pains send me falling to my ass on the ice.

Adam would love seeing that, I bet. It would give him something else to tease me about.

10

Scarlett

ADAM'S CAR SMELLS LIKE LEATHER, EXPENSIVE COLOGNE, AND THE evergreen air freshener dangling from the rearview mirror. It's very similar to how he smells on a daily basis, minus the air freshener. His scent screams, "I'm a well-put-together man," and despite that I know I shouldn't, I keep taking it in in lungfuls.

He smells like a man because that's exactly what he is. *A grown man.* It's impossible not to notice the differences between him and the majority of guys I know. Not only does Adam carry himself with a maturity that comes only from age and life experience, but there's a kindness to him that shouldn't be such a rarity but is. I'm finding that it's beginning to grow harder to deny the surprising effect he has on me as the days go on.

It will be a cold day in hell before I do anything about it, though. For now, I'll continue to keep him stuffed behind the Do Not Think About door and pretend he isn't one of the best-looking and genuinely kind people I have ever met. Getting caught up in a mess of sexual fascination for my boss is not something I need or want in my life right now.

"Are you a big comic book fan?" I ask as a way of forcing myself to think about something else. "Or do you just like collecting them and keeping them in your back seat?"

He glances over his shoulder and laughs at the box of superhero comic books on the seat behind me. "Right. Those are my son's."

I nod. "Does he have a favourite?"

His eyes beat into the side of my head. His next words are sure, confident. "Leo told you about Cooper."

"He did," I confirm and chew on the inside of my lip. We turn onto a paved road and pass the new housing district starting to be built on the outskirts of town. "But if he hadn't told me, I would have heard it from someone else long before starting at WIT. Hockey players are worse than teenage girls when it comes to gossip."

He taps his fingers on the steering wheel, and his jaw twitches. "Good point. Cooper isn't a secret by any means; he just hasn't come up before now."

"I didn't think he was. You don't have to explain anything to me."

His lips part on a small, appreciative smile. "Thank you. And he does have a favourite. It's Thor."

I smile at that before replying with a nod, unable to think of anything to say. Instead, I prop my elbow on the base of the window and press my palm to my cheek. The mood has shifted to something a bit awkward, but neither of us seems to be eager to bring it back to what it was.

Instead, we sit quietly for the next couple of minutes. The steady purr of the engine and low murmurs flowing from the speaker break the silence. We're in a part of Vancouver that I'm very familiar with, having gone to school only a few blocks away from the cathedral and newly renovated playground we just passed.

I clear my throat, and Adam pulls his sickeningly expensive car—if the elaborate seat stitching and the letters AMG on the steering wheel mean anything—into a busy parking lot, stopping a car length in front of what looks like the only free space. He throws the car into reverse and grabs the corner of my seat in a tight grip, the tips of his fingers brushing my shoulder, making me shiver. He doesn't pretend to miss my body's not-so-subtle reaction to his touch because a second later, he's glancing at me, and whether it was his plan to look away quickly or not, our eyes lock and hold of their own accord.

It's impossible to ignore the tightening of the air around us as I focus in on the deep green flecks around his irises and the slight downward shift and dilation of his pupils when I lick my suddenly dry lips.

Drawing in a shaky breath, I slowly, and almost greedily, slide my eyes over his face. I make note of the old, pale scar on the jut of his bottom lip and the perfect line of his nose that shows he's one of the few hockey players who never wound up breaking theirs. Smile lines are sunk deep beside his eyes, beneath the ends of two thick, fluffy eyebrows.

We're torn out of the moment when a car horn blares from behind us. We break apart, my heart thumping in both surprise and embarrassment.

"Shit," Adam mumbles, sounding a bit breathless.

Yeah, *shit*. I don't say anything as I scoot as close to the door as I can, and he drops his hand to the centre console, quickly reversing into the parking stall. The tension from moments earlier has been replaced with an awkwardness that has me pushing open my door and rushing out of the car to get away from it.

I place a hand on my chest and suck in a few deep breaths. My heart thumps frantically against my palm, and I scowl at the traitorous bitch. Adam is not someone I should be reacting to this way. There might as well be *do not touch* written on his forehead in bright red ink. A warning my body seems to not give a flying shit about.

My nipples are stones inside my sports bra, and I grit my teeth at the buzz of pleasure that comes to life each time my chest rises. It's too easy for him to turn me on. That much I know for sure. For God's sake, he only brushed my shoulder. Something he's done multiple times during therapy. Yet now is the first time it's had this effect on me.

Fuck.

"Ready to go in?" Adam asks, his voice hinting that he's closer than I was expecting. I didn't even hear him get out of the car.

"Yep." I steel my expression and turn around.

He's waiting at the front of his car, his arms crossed as he looks ahead of him. If he was even half as affected by what just happened between us as I am, he doesn't show it. I meet him by the hood of his gleaming two-door Mercedes, and we make our way to the shop.

"I hope you're not a vegan. This place has the best cheesesteak subs in the city," he says while pulling open the door and holding it for me. A bell rings from above it, announcing our entrance as we both walk inside.

"I'm not. But I didn't know there was a competition over who had the best cheesesteak."

He places a hand on my lower back and steers me through the small gap between tables leading to the front counter. I risk a glance up at him to find his eyes already on me. He winks. "There can be competition in anything, Scary Spice."

I scoff at the ridiculous nickname that he refuses to let die as we come to a stop in front of a waist-high counter. Adam doesn't remove his hand from my back even as we wait to be served, but I pretend that doesn't matter.

"Yes, but this one seems a bit unwarranted. Are there even that many places that sell cheesesteak subs?"

A gasp comes from in front of us. An older man who looks to be maybe in his early fifties has frozen in front of one of the back doors and stares at me with pure horror in his eyes. Adam coughs to cover his laugh while my cheeks burn a bright pink.

"Are there not stars in the sky?" the man guffaws, his voice thick with an accent I can't pinpoint. "Or fish in the sea?"

Okay, I think we've gotten a little off base here. I open my mouth to say something in my defense—like maybe not all of us are sandwich connoisseurs—but end up smashing my lips together when Adam moves his hand from its previous place on my lower back to my side, or more specifically, my waist. I go rigid when his arm wraps around me, and our bodies drift closer, as if pulled together by something completely out of our control.

An awful squawking noise rushes out of me, and my body jolts in surprise when Adam quickly pinches my side. I slap my hand over his and squeeze hard, the sheer size difference between them making my mind wander to a very inappropriate place. *What the hell is he doing?*

With a soft chuckle, he bends down close enough I can feel his breath on my cheek and smell the bubble gum he was chewing in the car and whispers, "It's better not to argue with Bernard. Who knows if he'll tell the cook to put anchovies in your sub."

And then, as if unaffected by touching me, he removes his hand from my side, setting it on the counter instead, before grinning at this *Bernard*. "Don't mind the pretty lady, Bernie. Scarlett here is very uncultured in the world of sub sandwiches, but she's a quick learner." He glances at me for a second, and I nearly swoon at the smile lighting up his face.

I look at the older man and nod while pretending I didn't catch Adam's sly attempt at a compliment or the flapping sensation in my belly that followed it. "He's right. I didn't mean to offend you."

Bernard assesses me for a hard second before tipping his chin and clicking away on the order screen in front of him. "Fine. Now, go sit and wait. I will make you two cheesesteak subs."

I narrow my eyes when Adam pulls his wallet out of his pocket and slips out his bank card, prepared to pay for them both. Snapping my hand out, I snatch the card from his fingers and shove it down my shirt, into my bra. I look down my shirt, and my eyes go wide.

"I . . . uh . . . I said I was paying for my own," I stammer. *Hello, God, if you're listening, now would be a great time to snatch me up*. Without looking at Adam, I slip my own bank card from the pouch on the back of my phone and, without looking at the price, pay for both our subs.

Adam chuckles softly. He leans in close, the short hairs on his jaw scratching my cheek. "Can I have my card back now? Or do you intend to keep it?"

I inhale a shuttered breath. "I'll give it to you when you back up."

That laugh again. "Right." He leans back, and I watch as he takes a step away. "I guess I should be thanking you for lunch."

"Yes, you should," I say while dipping my hand inside my shirt and pulling his card out from the top of my bra. "I told you I would pay."

He holds my stare and, with two fingers, slowly pulls the card from my hand. He shoves it into his pocket while saying, "Consider this the first and only time, Scarlett. I'm a gentleman, after all, and a gentleman *never* lets a lady pay."

I subtly press my thighs together as the dirty undertone of his words settle like a heavy weight between my legs. It's clearly been too long since I've had any sort of release that wasn't stoked by my vibrator, and having a man that looks like Adam does speak to me with such confidence and suave is turning out to be a bigger problem than I initially thought.

I find myself wondering if he's always a gentleman or if he drops that act at the bedroom door.

"Here you go," Bernard drawls. I clear my throat and turn to see him walking around the counter, a bulging plastic bag in his hand. He squints at me while handing over the bag. "You come back and tell me how good it was. Yes?"

"Sure," I agree.

He shifts his attention to Adam. "I know *you* will come back. You can't get enough of my subs."

Adam sighs. "Too true, Bernie. You're the reason I've had to put in more time at the gym." He pats his stomach. The stomach that I have no doubt is rock fucking hard. "I'm getting a bit saggy."

I snort before I can stop myself, and Adam swings his head to stare at me. "What?" he asks, a sly smile pulling at his mouth.

As if I would tell him I don't believe there's any part of him that's saggy. I lift the bag of food in the air between us. "Our food is going to get cold."

He quirks a brow, his eyes so focused on me I can't help but fidget beneath the weight of them. "And we can't have that," he teases. Turning to Bernard, he tips his chin. "Thank you. Have a good rest of your day, okay?"

"You as well. See you both," he replies and waves at both of us before drifting behind the counter and getting back to work.

I'm not nearly as surprised this time when Adam places a hand on my back and uses it to lead me around the cluttered sub shop again. Still, it's my first instinct to tell him I'm perfectly capable of getting myself out of here in one piece. I can't get myself to snap at him, though, and that frustrates me more than looking as if I can't take care of myself.

The bell above the door rings again when we step outside, and I take a step away from Adam, forcing his hand to leave my back. Only then can I breathe easy again.

The beating summer sun has only gotten hotter in the time it took to get lunch, and I suddenly hate our work uniform and the way it produces excess heat. Sweat breaks out on the back of my neck as my sneakers slap the sidewalk.

"It's a lot hotter than I was expecting," Adam says a second later, looking toward the sky. He places his hand over his squinted eyes and groans. The sleeve of his shirt stretches around his biceps, and I nearly let out a sound of my own.

I swallow instead. "We're dressed for the rink. I don't think that helps."

"No, it probably doesn't," he agrees, dropping his arm and pulling his car keys from his pocket. "Speaking of rinks. There's a Vancouver Warriors playoff game tomorrow night, and because WIT has a box at Rogers, myself and a few of the staff are going. There's a spot for you if you want to join us."

The toe of my sneaker catches on a crack in the sidewalk, and I stumble. I spin to gape at him. "You go to enough games you can justify the cost of a box?"

I've been lucky enough to sit in a box for a couple of games while I played for my previous team in Alberta, and it's an entire luxury experience in and of itself.

He looks at me incredulously.

"Right. Stupid question," I mutter. Why wouldn't the biggest hockey training facility in the country have a permanent seat in the place most professional players will stumble into sometime during the hockey season? It's the perfect marketing strategy.

"I'm best friends with two of their best players," Adam says a moment later.

My brows furrow at the unexpected information. "Two?"

We enter the parking lot, and Adam unlocks his car. The headlights flash as he says, "I played college hockey with both Oakley Hutton and Tyler Bateman. We're like family."

I stop in front of Adam's car. "Holy shit. Are you kidding? Tyler Bateman won the Norris Trophy last season." He's one of the best defensemen in the league right now, and he wasn't even drafted.

Adam walks past me on his way to the passenger side, our arms brushing. His eyes crinkle in the corner when he smiles and pulls my door open for me.

"Damn right he did. And I'm offering you the chance to see him play game five of the second round of the playoffs from one of the most comfortable seats in the arena." His eyes shine with mischief.

I know he's trying to manipulate me into agreeing, but I'll be damned if it isn't working. It's been a long time since I've watched a game, let alone one in person, but it's long overdue.

Leo has reminded me of that hundreds of times since I moved back home.

Maybe this will be the push I need to get over my remaining hurdles. Or maybe it will only make them worse. Either way, I won't know unless I try.

I catch his hopeful eyes and nod. "What time should I be ready?"

11

Adam

"You sure Scarlett actually wanted to come and didn't just say yes because you're her boss?" Banks asks from the passenger seat of my SUV.

He's smacking a piece of nicotine gum in his mouth even though he knows that's one of my pet peeves. I've wanted to reach over and take it away more than once since I picked him up, and if it weren't for how hard I know he's been working to quit smoking, I would have already.

The guy is only four years younger than me, but some days, I swear he behaves worse than Cooper.

"She seemed like she wanted to come when I talked to her this morning," Brielle chimes in from behind me. She grabs the corner of both front seats and pulls herself between us. "I'm excited to spend some time with her outside of work. She's not really much of a talker during work hours."

I chuckle and, per the GPS instructions on my phone, turn down what appears to be Scarlett's street. "I don't think it has much to do with work, Brie."

"We'll see about that," Brie retorts. She thrusts her arm forward, pointing at something up ahead. "There! It's definitely the one with the bird bath by the porch."

I look at the GPS and nod when she turns out to be right. My pulse quickens with excitement the closer we get to the small yellow house. Scarlett's mom must be a bird lover if the several birdhouses on the lawn are anything to go by.

"Never understood why birds need baths," Banks grunts. I glance over to find him reclined in the seat and toying with the rip on the knee of his jeans.

Brielle makes a noise in her throat. "Because unlike you, they take hygiene seriously."

"Wow, good one," he replies gruffly. Rolling down the passenger window, he leans over and spits his gum out. "How long have you been holding on to that sizzling burn?"

She pushes back into her seat, and I catch her glaring at the back of Banks' head from the rear-view window. "Almost as long as it's been since you've gotten laid. That would be what? Months?"

Banks' laugh is rough, abrupt. "No, sweetheart. Not quite."

I pull up in front of the yellow brick house at the same time Brielle rolls down her window and all but sticks her head out the window. Ignoring that, I turn to Banks. "I need you to knock it off. Please behave like an adult tonight. I want this to go well."

"Yeah. You got it," he replies without hesitation, and I smile gratefully.

Nodding to myself, I smack my hands on my thighs and announce, "I'm going to get her."

When I get out of the SUV, I shut the door and wipe my sweaty palms off on my shirt. I'm not exactly sure why I'm so nervous. This isn't a date; it's not anything like that.

This is me being a friend. And fucking hell. I'll be damned if this doesn't turn out to be a fun night for her. It'll be the first time she's been to a hockey game since before her injury, and she'll be away from the crowds in a comfortable environment. Plus, she *agreed* to come. I didn't force her. If she didn't want to, I have no doubt she wouldn't have told me to fuck right off with my offer. All I did was point out the advantage of coming with us.

With a head-clearing breath, I straighten my shoulders and start up the sidewalk. The strong scent of flowers is instant when I reach the front porch. And once I climb the three steps, I realize why.

Flower pot after flower pot line the front of the porch, the petals vibrant, with not a single dead leaf to be seen, even in the dim light of the setting sun. A small table and two wicker chairs sit in the corner, and several wind chimes hang from the wooden slats above.

It's clear a lot of care went into this area of the house.

I raise my fist to knock on the front door, but it swings open before I get the chance, revealing a petite woman I recognize as Scarlett's mother. She's grinning at me, her green eyes just as piercing as they were the day we met in the flower shop parking lot.

"Oh, Adam. It's lovely to see you again," she exclaims while lifting her arms and quickly closing the space between us. I laugh softly when she attempts to wrap me up in her arms.

"Likewise, Amelia. You look lovely."

She steps back but grabs my hand in hers, squeezing it tight. I frown when her eyes become glassy. Her voice shakes when she says, "Thank you for doing this. You have no idea how much she needed to do this." Her voice breaks. "Oh, I knew her working for you would be just what she needed."

I ignore the lump in my throat and squeeze her hand. "Don't thank me, Amelia. I want to help her any way I can."

"Before you, she . . . she . . . oh dear." She trails off, her lips pursed in concentration. "I seem to have forgotten what I was going to say."

Before I have a chance to let the weight of that fully sink in, Scarlett comes rushing toward us, her red hair flailing around her. I catch her worried eyes from over her mom's shoulder and try to paint a reassuring smile on my face before she looks away.

"Mom," she breathes. With a tentative hand on her mom's shoulder, she slowly, almost nervously, meets my stare and takes in the worry I know is prominent in my expression. She cringes. "You were supposed to come get me if Adam got here while I was taking out the trash."

Amelia gasps. "I was. I'm so sorry, my darling."

"I haven't been here long, Scary Spice. Your mom is good company, anyway," I rush out, immediately hating the pain in her eyes.

There's obviously a story here, something she hasn't opened up to me about yet. Something bad enough to be causing her grief. I want to know what it is so I can fix it, ease her pain.

"Scary Spice?" Amelia echoes with a bright laugh. Scarlett rolls her eyes.

"Don't start, Mom," she says.

Her mom shrugs her off. "That is perfect, Adam."

I wink at Scarlett. "I thought so too."

Scarlett, clearly not in the mood to be picked on, turns Amelia around to face her. "It's time for you to say goodbye."

"Fine, fine, darling," she sighs, facing me again. "Take care of my girl tonight. I will be watching the game for a glimpse of you two."

Scarlett groans. I grin.

"Good night, Amelia," I say and step backward down the first porch step.

Scarlett's mother waves enthusiastically before she's pushed inside and led down a hall, disappearing from view. A moment later, Scarlett comes back out, looking only slightly more relaxed.

I watch her lock the front door before turning around and fiddling with the strap of the bag thrown over her shoulder, avoiding looking at me, opting to stare at the wooden slats above us instead. Her mind is clearly somewhere else, and I can't help but wonder where it's wound up.

"Are you okay?" I ask quietly.

"Yeah."

I furrow my brows and shove my hands in my pockets to keep from reaching out to soothe her like I want to. "Then look at me. Tell me what's going on."

She shakes her head. "Brielle told me we were carpooling tonight. They're waiting for us, right?"

"They are, but—"

"Please. Let's just go," she pleads.

I lean back on my heels and exhale. It goes against every instinct in my body to let this be, to go ahead with our plans when I know she's hurting. But I told her before I wasn't the guy that was going to push her, and I have to stay true to that. Even if doing so frustrates me beyond belief.

Softening my features, I nod in acceptance. "Okay, Scarlett. Let's go."

A brief flicker of appreciation before she's a picture of calm and collected. The pain behind her eyes is gone, leaving them guarded. I grit my jaw at how deeply that upsets me when I know it shouldn't.

I step down the porch stairs and wait for her to join me before we head for my car in silence. We're so close my shoulder brushes her arm with each step, and the scent of cherry blossoms permeates the air between us. My head is full of white noise, and when I cautiously touch the back of my hand to hers and hold it there, her sharp inhale barely registers.

We don't look at each other, but our hands stay pressed together until we reach the car.

FOR THE SECOND time in under a minute of play, a whistle blows, and the game pauses. Boos erupt in the arena as the referee calls a tripping penalty against a Warriors player, sending him to join his teammate in the penalty box.

With our team down two players and lacking a decent

penalty kill these playoffs, the Vegas Crowns have a good chance at scoring a goal to tie the game. And with only ten minutes left in the third, frustration and anger vibrates in the air.

"That ref is a fucking idiot," Scarlett hisses from her seat to my left. She has her elbows on her knees, scowling deeply. "Tremblay is a fucking diver if I've ever seen one."

Banks grunts his agreement while I take a greedy gulp of my beer.

"Both refs have been playing with Vegas blinders on all game," Brielle says. I peer over my shoulder to see her sitting in a similar fashion to Scarlett. Banks is more relaxed in the chair beside her, his legs spread wide enough for one to knock against Brielle's.

"Tyler's been insane tonight," he states, and we all make noises of agreement.

Tyler *has* been insane tonight. But that's not out of the ordinary. It's why he gets paid the kind of money he does and wears an A on his jersey. A strong feeling of pride swells in my chest.

"Let's see if he can keep the puck out of their zone. He'll get my praise then," Scarlett mutters.

My brows jump to my hairline. "This coming from the queen of the Bateman fan club?"

She turns to glare at me. "Don't be dramatic."

"You're just full of surprises, aren't you?" I tease.

She doesn't answer me because the ref blows the whistle again, signalling the puck drop. Suddenly, her attention is on the players facing off at the hash marks, her body tense and foot tapping. She slips her plump bottom lip into her mouth and chews on it nervously while watching the action on the rink. I swallow hard when my eyes get stuck there, and blood rushes to my cock.

Fuck.

My eyes are hot on her face, and when she turns to glare at me, visibly annoyed, I still can't look away. Something on my face must surprise her because before she has the chance to snap at me for staring, she's closing her mouth and turning a subtle shade of pink.

A tightness builds in my chest as the distance between us becomes a problem. I want to grab her and put her in my lap just so I can feel her body against mine. The thought hits hard enough to visibly rattle me.

With a sharp inhale, I get up on shaky legs and head for the bar behind our box. I need something way stronger than beer right now if I'm going to make it through the rest of this game.

I yank back the heavy red curtain separating our box from the private dining room we had dinner in a couple of hours ago and step out. There's no line at the bar, which isn't unusual. Not during the last period of a close game.

A young guy with slicked-back blond hair is behind the bar, his back to me, eyes on the TV on the wall that's showing the game. I catch the arm of the ref shooting into the air before an offside call against the Warriors is made. The corner of the bartender's mouth tips up.

"Crowns fan?" I ask him as I lean my forearms on the marble bar top and tap my knuckles against it. He spins around, raising two thin blond brows at me. "Whiskey neat, please."

He nods and collects a bottle of Jack Daniel's from a glass shelf behind the bar. "That obvious?"

"It was either that, or you just have no idea what an offside call is. If you did, you wouldn't be smiling."

"Busted." He laughs and pinches the neckline of his Warrior's T-shirt. "Wearing this shirt makes my skin itch." Setting a glass on the bar, he fills it with two fingers of whiskey and pushes it to me.

"Thank you." The glass is smooth in my palm as I grab it and bring it to my lips, collecting a heavy mouthful before swallowing. My stomach warms as it settles.

"I always took you as a vodka kind of guy," a smoky voice says behind me. Maybe it's the alcohol, but I could swear there's a teasing tone to the words.

I set the glass back down but don't face Scarlett when she settles beside me. Her closeness startles me, and I swallow hard.

"I'll have the same as him, please," she tells the bartender. I can sense the second her attention falls back on me by the sudden rise in temperature around us. "You missed Tyler's blocked shot. Hit him on the side of his foot."

"Is he okay?"

The bartender slides a glass toward her, and she hums. "Yeah. He was still out there when I came to find you."

"I didn't go far," I say.

A pause and a slow exhale. "Why did you go in the first place?"

I tap my fingernail against my glass. Telling her that it was her that spooked me isn't really an option right now. Even if I wasn't her boss, it wouldn't be appropriate. Right?

My beard is rough against my skin as I scratch my jaw. I'm so clueless when it comes to women now it's embarrassing. The last date I went on was when Cooper was six, and it was a complete disaster.

Not that I shouldn't have known better than to use a dating app to try and find a genuine date, because really, I should have. But at the time, it seemed like the easiest way to dip my toe back into the dating pool.

I haven't dated since that app nightmare, and not because I'm not interested in it, but because I have Cooper to think about now. Introducing him to anyone, knowing there's a chance that we—or specifically Cooper—could lose that person later on after a strong relationship is formed terrifies me.

Not to mention that even finding someone who is not only open to the idea of my son but also being with a man as career focused as I am has been an impossible feat.

Annoyance pinches my stomach. I used to be on the receiving end of a lot of female attention, to the point I wouldn't spend more than a night with an empty bed if I didn't want to. And I know I haven't completely lost my knowledge of sexual chemistry and attraction because I feel it with Scarlett. I know I do. It's strong, hard to ignore. But that's not where this—*whatever* this is—between Scarlett and me can go. There have been no clear boundaries set, but maybe there should be.

She might be completely out of reach, but my body doesn't seem to care. And that's dangerous.

"I had to take a phone call," I blurt out. My voice is strained, and from the way Scarlett scoffs, I know she doesn't believe me.

Out of the corner of my eye, I catch her tipping her glass back and downing her drink. "Right. I'll let you get back to that, then."

I'm taken aback when I reach out for her and grab her wrist, stopping her when she tries to walk away. She swings her head in my direction, and our eyes collide. "Don't go back yet."

She presses her lips together, looking torn. Desperation floods my system and pushes me to get her to stay. I brush my thumb over the skin of her wrist and smile softly.

"Have another drink with me. A real drink. The other two will be fine alone."

"Fine," she agrees. I release a breath. "But a quick one. I don't want to watch the final minutes of the game on a tiny screen."

"You have my word." With a nod, I order her another drink and finish mine off. When I push my empty glass away, her eyes catch the motion.

"You're going to make me drink alone?"

I smirk. "Don't be a bad influence, Scary Spice. I drove us here."

"Banks hasn't been drinking," she states, cocking a brow.

"He would have my car wrapped around a tree if I let him drive. Sober or not."

"He's that bad?"

"He totalled his last car two weeks after driving it off the dealership lot." I chuckle.

She chews on that for a second before saying, "Yeah, I can believe that."

"In any case, I'm not a big drinker. Half a beer and a whiskey is good enough for me," I admit.

Alcohol used to be a coping mechanism when I was younger and not one I would particularly recommend to anyone.

Scarlett eyes me inquisitively, like she knows there's more to what I'm saying and wants to find out for herself what I'm hiding. It's surprising seeing her take an interest in me like this.

"I'm not a drinker either," she says, dropping her eyes to her glass as she swirls the amber liquid around. There's a sadness in her voice that scrapes my insides.

I watch her openly, greedy for more information, but she clears her throat and focuses on the game on the TV ahead of us, shutting me out.

With a nervous swallow, I say, "I meant to tell you earlier, but it's great that you're here. Hockey is your passion; it's not fair for you to punish yourself by avoiding it."

For a moment, I worry if that was the entirely wrong thing to say, but when she turns to me with a small smile, I know it wasn't. My chest swells at the beauty of it, and I become determined to see not only more of those smiles but the full-fledged ones I know will have the power to steal my breath away.

12

Scarlett

I bite back a groan and flop to my stomach, my arms jelly from holding a plank position for so long. Sweat clings to my skin, making me feel disgusting. I probably don't smell all that great either.

"That was the last one. How's the shoulder?"

I glare up at Adam and his stupid perfect smile as he watches me, waiting for an answer. He's leaning against the wall, his arms crossed and bulging beneath his tight black long-sleeve that looks a solid size too small. His lack of sweat and sore muscles has my scowl deepening.

I need some ice and Tylenol before I wind up punching him in the crotch. He's been helping me for a good two weeks now, and even if I can tell that my shoulder is improving more and more with each therapy session, it hasn't changed how aggravating that man can be.

It's not normal for someone to be so happy. It's borderline unnatural.

The only time I've seen him be even remotely upset was at the hockey game a week ago, and even then, he was quick to return to his normal pippy state before I had a chance to dig for much information. As if allowing himself to wallow in the dumps with the rest of us was completely out of the question.

I roll my eyes. "Do you get off on pain and suffering or something? What's with the smile?"

He chuckles lowly and scratches at his jaw. "I get off on a number of things, Scarlett. But pain and suffering? Not my style. I'm smiling because I'm proud of you."

"Oh." *Fucking hell.* What *does* he get off on, then? No. Scratch that. I don't want to know.

"Oh?"

I huff. "Yes, oh. I wasn't expecting that, considering I haven't exactly done anything to be proud of. I won't consider myself anywhere close to where I want to be until I can last longer than thirty seconds in a damn plank."

His brows tug together. "You think you haven't made progress because you can't hold a plank for the same amount of time you could before?" When I nod, he frowns. "That's not fair to you or your healing in the slightest."

"Well, none of this has been fair, so I don't see why I would start caring about that now."

He searches my face, studying it like a cheat sheet for a final exam he can't risk failing. Nerves I didn't even know I had flare at the intensity behind his eyes.

"Your professional career might be done, Scarlett, but that doesn't mean hockey is something that's completely out of reach. Don't give up on your passions and your goals—hell, your entire future—because you were dealt a shitty card in life. Don't let this take everything from you."

Adam pushes off from the wall and stalks toward me. My entire body turns pink and hyperaware of every step he takes. I get up off my stomach and settle on my knees.

"Don't talk like you know me on some deep level, Adam. We're barely even friends."

My dig bounces right off him. He only tilts a brow, looking as if I'm merely entertaining him. "Barely even friends? You wound me, Scary Spice. I thought we were getting to know each other quite well."

Needing to keep my hands busy so they're not flopping in my lap, I thread my fingers through my ponytail. When my fingers get caught in a tangle of curls, I pull a little too hard and wince at the stabbing sensation in my scalp. *Smooth.*

"Are you okay? Does your shoulder hurt?" he asks with a slight tinge of panic in his tone.

I close my eyes for a minute to gain back some semblance of calm before opening them again to find him directly in front of me. He offers me his hand, and I just stare at it like it's about to jump at me.

His laugh is smooth and deep. "Let me help you up."

It hits me then that I'm knelt in front of him, his crotch in my direct line of vision. He's left enough space between us that I don't immediately ignite into a burning ball of mortification, and I almost thank him for that before remembering my knees are still on the ground and my mouth is gaping open.

"Oh my God." It comes out in a rush. With wide eyes, I grab his hand and scramble to my feet. I use my own strength to push myself up at the same time he uses his to pull me, and I go flying. Straight. Into. Him.

A sound of surprise escapes him at the same time I collide with his chest. I barely have time to register just how hard and tense his stomach feels pressed against mine before my chin smacks his collarbone, and he grabs my biceps, steadying me.

"Jesus, Scarlett. Seriously, are you okay? Do you need to sit down somewhere? I can get you a water or some juice—"

"I'm fine." *I'm not, but I would be if you backed up.*

His fingers tighten on my arms, but he doesn't push me back like I'm expecting. I think he just . . . pulled me closer.

I pray that he can't feel how hard my heart is beating in my chest or how it speeds up when our eyes catch and hold despite how badly I try to look away.

Sucking in a shuddered breath, I cautiously press my palms

to his chest under the pretense of using the leverage to back away but find them superglued to the firm muscles instead. I furrow my eyebrows when I feel the frantic, unsteady beating behind his rib cage tapping at my fingers.

I swipe my tongue across my lips and shiver when the pad of his thumb strokes the underside of my arm.

His lips part as his gaze falls to my mouth. The room spins before disappearing entirely. Two words flare to life in my head, repeating over and over until it's impossible to ignore them.

Kiss me.

Adam slides his fingers up my arm and over my shoulder before pausing at the base of my neck. His eyes flick to mine, as if asking for permission to touch me further, and I nod without hesitation. Rational thinking is gone. There's only Adam and me and the tension building and building between us like a ball of electricity waiting to be unleashed.

His eyes flare as he cups the back of my head and tangles his fingers in my hair. The feeling of his fingers gently pressing into my scalp has my knees threatening to give out.

I hold my breath when he mutters, "Scarlett, can I k—"

Three knocks on the door sever the connection.

"Hey, guys. There's someone else on the ice right now, and I think there might have been an—*oh*. Uh . . . I'll just go . . . wait . . . outside. Yeah. Outside."

Like I should have minutes ago, I shove at Adam's chest and stumble back, creating some much-needed distance between us.

"Willow," I breathe. My stomach falls to the floor.

The teenager is as red as a tomato, and I'm not sure I look much different if the pulse in my cheeks is anything to go by. She waves a hand in the air and tries to hide her shock with a forced smile.

"Hi."

I can feel Adam's stare beating into the side of my head, but I can't look at him. God, what is he thinking right now? I swallow the boulder in my throat. I don't want to know.

He clears his throat. "Who's on the ice, Willow? There's most likely a mix-up. Nobody is scheduled to be out there this morning beside you and Scarlett."

"I think it's Rebecca and a girl I didn't recognize. I couldn't tell from where I was standing."

Rebecca is another trainer and someone I haven't spent a lot of time with. She seems nice enough, though. If I was big on making friends, maybe we could have gotten along.

"Alright. We'll get it all sorted out, and you'll be good to go."

I wipe my palms down my leggings and say in a rush, "Actually, I can take her and get it sorted. That okay with you, Willow?" I shoot her a pleading look.

Her eyes widen briefly before she nods. "Yep. Totally okay."

"Are you sure? I—" Adam starts.

I cut him off. "Perfect. Let's go, Willow." I clap my hands together and rush toward her. Grabbing her wrist, I pull her out of the room and into the hallway with my heart in my throat.

Willow tries to keep up with me as I plow down the hallway, asking if I'm okay and what's happening. I don't answer her.

It's not until I'm shoving the women's locker room door open and stepping inside that I release her and some of the tension that's suffocating me.

"Get your skates on," I say, wincing at the harshness in my voice. "Please."

I wait for her to acknowledge me, and as soon as she does, I'm moving frantically around the room, collecting my own skates and everything I need for today's session that I stored in here this morning.

Willow watches me the entire time but doesn't say anything. I would thank her for that if I could trust myself not to blurt out something incredibly embarrassing. Like how I miss the way Adam felt pressed against me or how badly I wish he had planted one on me when he had the chance.

Fucking fuck.

Flopping down on the bench, I drop my skates on the ground

and shove my feet into them, tying the left before the right. By the time I'm done, Willow is waiting at the door for me.

"Ready?" I join her and nod to the hallway.

She smiles, flashing me her teal-bracketed braces. "I am. Are you?"

"Yep." I frown when she starts shuffling her feet. "What?"

Her green eyes are wary. "You could tell me if you're not, you know, okay. I mean, obviously you don't have to since we're not really friends and you're way older than me—"

"Hey," I interrupt. "First of all, I'm not *way* older than you. I'm only twenty-three. And second, you're as much of a friend to me as most people. I'm not exactly the easiest person to talk to, so . . ."

She shrugs. "Me either. I don't have any real friends outside of the girls on my hockey team. But even then, they're what my mom calls surface-level friends. The kind you shouldn't let inside to see the real you but are safe to keep at an arm's distance."

I nod because I know exactly what she's referring to. Unfortunately, I've had my fair share of those people in my life. They're the kind of friends you would chat with in an empty room but never in a busy one. The kind that wouldn't visit or call if you were sick but would rush to hug you and tell you how happy they are that you're okay and how worried they were *after* you've recovered.

Bitterness settles like bile in my stomach. After my shoulder injury and an intensive surgery that was the final nail in the coffin I buried my hockey career in, I can count on one hand the number of teammates who made an effort to reach out and ask how I was doing. It wasn't shocking, not when I already knew none of us were all that close, but that didn't make it hurt any less.

Your teammates are supposed to be the people you can count on to be there for you when you need them, but unfortunately for me, that wasn't my experience in Calgary.

"Your mom sounds like a smart woman," I tell Willow.

"Of course she does. Who do you think I got all my smarts from?"

I arch a brow. "Fair enough. Who did you get your lack of humility from?"

She grins proudly, popping a dimple in her cheek. "That was all me."

My lips curl in a smile. I see a lot of myself in Willow. Maybe that's why I enjoy our lessons so much. It makes me feel like I've accomplished something every time she beats a previous record or crushes a new goal. Like I've used my talent for something helpful instead of letting it waste away. It's only been two weeks, but even in such a short time working with her, I know she's going to go on to do extraordinary things.

I'm just glad I get to be a small part of her journey.

13

Scarlett

I'm pushing a cart down the pasta aisle of the grocery store when Mom halts in front of me. She turns to the wall of pasta bags and boxes and cocks a hip.

"Spaghettini or spaghetti?"

"Is there a difference?"

An audible gasp. "Don't let your grandfather hear you speak like that. You know how he loves our Italian roots."

"That's a stretch. I'm like an eighteenth Italian, Mom," I point out, heaving a sigh.

She looks at me over her shoulder and scowls. "That's because your father muddled your blood."

That gives me pause. The ground shifts slightly beneath my feet.

We don't speak about my father—*ever*. Scratch that, I wouldn't even refer to him as my father at this point. As far as I'm concerned, he's nothing more than a sperm donor. How else would you describe a man who knocked his girlfriend up and then took off only a year after she had the baby? We're better off without him.

However, I'm not sure if I should be concerned about her

sudden slip of tongue. My mom would rather drink dish soap than speak about him.

When I don't answer, she looks back to the shelf, humming. "What about lasagna? I could put the leftovers in the freezer. You can never have too much lasagna. Right, darling?"

"Right."

She picks up a box of lasagna noodles and places them in the cart before continuing down the aisle. I follow behind her with the cart.

"Tell me how work is going," she says while grabbing a can of crushed tomatoes. It falls into the cart with a clang. "How is your shoulder?"

"Slow down. Which question do you want me to answer first?" I chuckle.

"Work first."

"Okay. Willow is amazing. But we've spent most of this week in the gym on the treadmills, and I know she wants to get back on the ice. She's a great sport, though. Barely ever complains about anything."

Endurance training is definitely not her favourite—nor is it anyone's—but she knows how important it is. It won't matter how fast she is if she's down for the count too early.

"She sounds like you." She says it so casually, like it's obvious.

"She's going to be better than me. She nearly already is."

Mom scoffs so loud I worry the shoppers on the other side of the store heard her. "Nobody is better than you. You've always been far too humble."

"It doesn't matter how good I was, Mom. Can we talk about something else?" Preferably before I burst into tears in the middle of this store?

The cart almost catches her heels when she stops in front of me. This time, she flips around and glares at me with a ferocity that makes me wince.

"No, we can't. You are as stubborn as a mule, Scarlett darling.

That shoulder of yours might have been the end of your career, but *you* are the only thing keeping you from still having a successful future. You were meant for far more than just hockey. I wish you would stop thinking less of yourself because you've lost that."

My fingers tingle from how hard I've been squeezing the cart. Her words sink into me, claws splayed, but I shake them off before I lose hold of my emotions.

"We need milk, right? I'll go get it," I say in a rush. Mom starts to protest, but I'm already leaving her and the cart behind.

My head is in shambles as I stalk through the store, keeping my eyes on the floor. I will away the burn behind them.

It's easy for my mother to say all of this. It's easy for *everyone* who has never felt this kind of loss before. Like a piece of you is just gone, disappeared into nothingness, leaving you empty and questioning where to go from here.

It isn't as simple as it seems to just move on. Her heart might be in the right place, but it doesn't really matter.

I quickly grab the milk before heading back. Worry is a prick in my stomach on the way. Mom has been doing fine on her own so far, but the potential of something happening to her when I'm not there is starting to become an issue. I'm half in my head all the time, questioning whether or not she's okay.

I'm almost back where I left her when I hear a male voice. My heart jumps in my chest when I realize it's Adam's friendly vibrato.

"I'm not much of a cook myself, but Cooper is a great help."

"What a sweetie," Mom sings. "My Scarlett has never been much of a help in the kitchen. That is, unless I'm baking. She loves to lick the bowls right clean."

Horrified, I pick up my pace and turn down the aisle. "Mom!" My steps falter when four sets of eyes fall on me. Mom shrugs as if she didn't just say something incredibly embarrassing before turning back to the group of three.

My eyes gravitate to Adam, finding him watching me with a

grin I feel low in my belly. He's wearing a pair of ripped jeans and a plain navy T-shirt with white sneakers. His hair sticks out beneath the backward cap on his head and curls behind his ears.

He looks good. *Really* good.

"Hi, Scary Spice," he greets me, voice soft and welcoming.

"Hey, Adam."

We haven't talked much since Willow caught us doing . . . whatever it was we were doing on Thursday morning. Friday's therapy session was so awkward I was tempted to twist my shoulder the wrong way just so I could finish earlier.

Neither of us made any effort to talk about the day prior, so we just pretended nothing happened. The only thing wrong with that plan going forward is that something *did* happen. And I'm not sure if I can continue to pretend otherwise. Not when even being a grocery cart distance away from him in a crowded supermarket with my own mother as a witness can I keep the air between us from thickening with something I'm too scared to define.

"Scarlett, darling. Have you met Adam's son and girlfriend yet? They were just telling me about their dinner plans."

It's like a bucket of cold water being dumped on my head.

His *girlfriend*? I chomp down on my tongue to avoid saying something I shouldn't in front of his son. Jealousy threatens to tear my insides to ribbons.

It makes more sense as to why he didn't say anything about our almost kiss when he saw me yesterday. Why mention something you so clearly want to forget?

Against my better judgment, I look at the woman standing beside him, one hand on the strap of her purse and the other fidgeting with her thick-rimmed glasses. She's shorter than me and quite a bit shorter than Adam, but it fits her. Her hair is glossy and black and hangs well past her shoulders. She's almost pixie-like. Adam is a giant beside her.

"No, I haven't," I answer with a calmness I sure as hell don't feel. Lowering my eyes, I meet the stare of a young boy with a messy head of dark brown hair and eyes to match. They're Adam's eyes but more curious.

"Scarlett, this is my son, Cooper. Cooper, this is Scarlett. She's a trainer at the rink and a friend of mine," Adam says, and I have to bite back a laugh.

Friends? Not likely.

"Hi," Cooper says with a quick wave. His cheeks are tinted a soft pink that makes him look even more adorable than he already is.

"Hi, Cooper." My smile is more genuine now.

"And this is Beth," Adam says. He's looking right at me now. I can feel it. But I look elsewhere. "Cooper's mother."

"And not his girlfriend. Adam is too far out of my league," says this *Beth* woman.

I try to hide the onslaught of relief I feel with a forced smile, but Adam only laughs, grinning like he knows something nobody else does. If it wasn't already obvious that I didn't like the idea of Beth being his girlfriend, it sure is now. Triumph flashes in his eyes.

Embarrassed that I let myself get jealous over a misunderstanding, my cheeks warm.

"Oh dear," Mom mutters. She runs a frantic hand over the top of her hair, flattening it. "I'm sorry."

Adam shakes his head. "No need to apologize, Amelia. It was an honest mistake."

"My mom doesn't get to spend a lot of time with us, but when she does, that usually always happens," Cooper says.

I flinch. Adam watches me, a silent apology splattered across his face. Knowing that he doesn't have anything to apologize for, I give my head a subtle shake.

I don't know when it happened, but things between us got complicated. And it's for reasons like this that we need to focus on uncomplicating them. He's my boss. My much older boss. Hell, he's standing across from me with his son on one side and the woman he had a baby with on the other.

I don't belong in that lineup.

Steeling my spine, I find something on the cluttered shelves to focus on. A supreme taco kit? Looks great.

"We were actually trying to decide which flavour of ice cream to get for dessert tonight. Do either of you have any suggestions? We can never decide on one," Adam says, swiftly changing the subject.

Mom slaps her hands together. "Call me old-fashioned, but I love strawberry."

"What about you, Scarlett?" There's something in his voice that has me stealing a glance at him. Something that makes goosebumps break out along my skin. It almost sounds like desperation.

"I like cookies and cream."

"Me too!" Cooper cheers, high-fiving Adam. "What's your second favourite?"

I pretend to think about it. "Bubble gum. What's yours?"

He smiles proudly. "Bubble gum. But Dad doesn't like it, so we neeever get it."

"Hey! Don't throw me under the bus. I don't *not* like it," Adam says, his eyes bright with amusement.

"I agree with you there," Mom chimes in.

"You chew bubble gum all the time, though," I blurt out, my cheeks warming.

Adam's eyes find mine. He smirks. "You've noticed that?"

"Only because you're a gum smacker," I say, shrugging in hopes of coming off like I don't really care.

His smirk only grows, and I know he doesn't believe me. We both know he isn't a gum smacker.

"I like regular bubble gum. It's only the frozen stuff I don't like."

I save that information for later, knowing there's no real reason for me to.

"Well, I think we should get a tub of each for dessert," Beth suggests. She's smiling at Cooper, her expression tender. It's obvious she cares about her son deeply, so I wonder why she doesn't see him often.

"Sick!" Cooper exclaims. He spins to face his dad. "That's okay, right?"

"Yeah, kid. That's okay."

Cooper's face lights up. "I'll go grab them now. Be right back." He takes off down the aisle.

"Be quick!" Adam calls as we watch his son disappear. When Cooper turns out of the aisle, Adam offers an apologetic smile to the rest of us. "Sorry about him. He seems to have left his manners at home."

"That's probably my fault." Beth winces.

Mom slashes a hand through the air. "Nonsense. He seems like a very nice young man. Seeing excitement like that is a shot of pure serotonin. We need more of that in the world."

I snort. "Okay, Mom. You're getting philosophical again."

"You're so right, Amelia. It's good for the soul," Beth says.

Good for the soul? *Ugh.*

Adam smirks at me. "How's your soul feeling right now, Scarlett?"

I narrow my eyes. "Like I'm the one who needs two buckets of ice cream."

His laugh is loud and free. It hits me square in the chest, winding me. How can something so simple pack such a punch? I exhale when I realize that maybe Beth wasn't entirely wrong in her statement.

My soul liked that laugh a bit too much.

I clear that thought from my head when Cooper comes running back down the aisle, his arms full of ice cream. Catching his breath, he drops both containers into their cart.

"Quick enough?" he asks Adam.

His dad chuckles and ruffles the top of his head. "Yeah, buddy."

"Oh dear, is that the time?" Mom gasps. She has her watch lifted to about an inch from her face. "If I don't get started on this lasagna quick, we won't be eating until tomorrow morning."

Relieved that I'm being handed an out, I say, "You're right. We should head out now."

"I hate to cut this chat short, but my daughter is right. It was lovely to see you two again and just as nice to meet you . . ." She trails off.

My shoulders drop immediately as I release a shaky breath. I reach for her hand and squeeze it tight, wishing I could push my memories through the embrace.

"Beth," Beth blurts out. Confusion flashes across her face before it's gone again. "It was great to meet you, Amelia."

Mom smiles, but it doesn't reach her eyes. "Right. Yes."

Surprise slams into me when Adam walks toward us and grabs both of my mom's hands, including the one I'm currently squeezing too tightly. Tingles erupt at the point of contact, but it's hard to focus on them when his thumb runs over my skin in long, soothing strokes.

He focuses on my mom with a soft expression. There's no sign of pity or judgment anywhere on his face. My heart rattles my rib cage.

"I look forward to seeing and chatting with you again soon, Amelia. You'll have to let me know how your lasagna turns out." He winks, making Mom blush.

"I'll do one better. Scarlett can bring some on Monday for you and Cooper," she exclaims.

Adam grins. "We would love that. Thank you."

The hand covering mine squeezes once more before moving away. I instantly miss the contact.

"I'll see you on Monday, Scary Spice. Enjoy your weekend."

My reply is far too breathy. "Yeah, see you."

He doesn't move immediately but instead parts his lips like he wants to say something else. I hold his stare and realize I've been leaning forward on my toes. *What the?*

A subtle shake of his head is all I get before he's turning back to his family. I fall back to my heels and swallow thickly.

Beth looks between Adam and me with a silent question that goes unanswered before she and Cooper quickly say their good-byes. They spin their cart around and head down the aisle. Adam places a hand on Cooper's shoulder, and my chest tightens.

"I quite enjoy their company," Mom says once they've cleared our line of sight.

My phone vibrates in my pocket as I nod in agreement. Pulling it out, I read the message on the screen and don't bother fighting the tug of my lips.

Adam White: In case you were wondering, my soul feels a lot better after seeing you.

14

Adam

Despite Cooper's earlier doubts, our chicken casserole is coming together quite well.

I might have had quite the learning curve when it came to cooking once Cooper came into my life, considering I was never taught how to cook a single thing in my entire life and wasn't at all interested in teaching myself, but ten years later, I'm not half-bad.

At least that's what I'm told. The jury is still out on whether that's the truth or a little white lie to make me feel better.

Spaghetti, tacos, and barbecued burgers are the only three things I've successfully mastered, so to speak, but it's better than the cold hot dogs and cereal I started with.

Cooper sidles up beside me and eyes the dish full of layered chicken, rice, and broccoli with suspicion. I set the brick of cheese I was shredding on the counter and push a few curls out of his face.

"What do you think? Edible?" I ask.

He scrunches his nose. "Did you season the chicken?"

"'Course I did." *I think.*

"I didn't see you season it," he says.

"Then why didn't you say anything while it was cooking in the frying pan?"

"I didn't notice until now, looking at it and how plain it looks. It's going to taste like rubber."

I huff a breath. "It won't taste like rubber."

"Yes it will. You always forget the seasonings, and it always tastes like rubber."

"Ouch. Don't take it easy on me because I'm your dad or anything," I mutter.

He looks up at me, batting his thick eyelashes. "I thought I wasn't supposed to lie? Are you saying the rules have changed?"

I press my fingers to my temples and move them in slow circles. "You're going to make me a silver fox years before I'm ready."

"There's always hair dye."

"You have an answer for everything, huh?"

He grins. "Always."

I laugh and push the half-full bowl of cheese toward him before shredding more. "Spread that on the top while I finish the rest."

"Got it, Captain."

"It's Dad, shithead."

A dramatic gasp. "Did you just call me a shithead?"

"Hey, watch your language," I chastise. My lips twitch.

"I can't wait until I'm too old for you to tell me that," he sighs.

I snicker. "You'll never be too old for a good ol' scolding, Coop."

"You need a girlfriend or something."

"What?" I sputter. Talk about coming at me from left field. "What do you know about girlfriends? You don't have one, right?"

He fake gags. "No way."

"Good." I relax. "You shouldn't have a girlfriend until you're at least twenty-seven."

"Twenty-seven?" His eyes go wide.

"Yep. Focus on your music and art for as long as you can with no distractions." I pass him the rest of the shredded cheese and start cleaning up the mess on the counter.

"I'm not interested in girls right now anyway, Dad. I was talking about you," he states, not seeming to want to let this go anytime soon.

Deciding to entertain him, I say, "Okay, so you think a girlfriend will what? Keep me from telling you to behave?"

"Well, if you have another person to focus on, then maybe. But it would be nice for you to have someone else to talk to sometimes. You never go out after work unless it's to see Aunt Ava and Uncle Lee or someone you work with."

Silence falls in the kitchen.

Is he really that perceptive, or have I been that obvious? *Christ*.

It's not like I'm a hermit. I do go out and spend time with other human beings. But maybe he's not completely off base. If I'm not with Oakley and Ava, or Banks and Brie, or even Beth, I'm at home with Cooper. I didn't think there was anything wrong with that, and there isn't, but now that I think about it, I'm realizing that Scarlett has been the only woman in years I've spent time without outside of that small group of people.

The only woman I've *wanted* to spend time with.

The weight of that slams into my chest, winding me. I drop the collection of dirty utensils and measure cups into the sink and grip the edge of the counter.

What does that even mean? She's my employee and someone that I've grown to care about. Sure, we have chemistry. I might have fallen a bit out of touch with women over the last few years, but I'm not dead. And I would have to be not to feel that there's something incredibly palpable between us. Like a live wire connects the both of us.

But that's just sexual energy that sparks between two people who are attracted to each other. And I am incredibly attracted to Scarlett, there's no denying that. From her freckle-covered cheeks and bright blue eyes to her round, tight ass and muscled thighs, there isn't a single thing about her that doesn't drive me fucking crazy.

And if the circumstances were different, maybe I would have acted on that attraction. Maybe I would already know what she feels like beneath me and if that frown of hers disappears when I'm balls-deep and she's coming on my cock.

That's not how this can go, though. Sex leads to feelings, and feelings lead to trouble. I have Cooper to think about now. Even if he does believe I need a woman in my life, I can't risk it right now.

The sound of the front door opening and closing has me pulling back out of my thoughts. My hands are sweaty on the counter when I drop them to my sides.

"Dad?" Cooper asks cautiously, almost timidly.

"You're right, kid. I do need to go out more," I admit. There's no denying that.

"I do like having you around all the time. I didn't mean it like I didn't."

With a sigh, I reach over and rub his back. "I know. You wouldn't know what to do without your old man."

"I can't believe we were at the store and forgot garlic bread. That's the most crucial part of a good dinner," Beth shouts from the front door. Bare feet slap the floor, getting louder and louder until she enters the kitchen.

I quickly put the casserole in the oven and set the cooking timer. Turning to the kitchen island, I watch her place a grocery bag and a bottle of white wine on the counter.

"Did you get the loaf or the slices?" Cooper asks, peeking into the bag. He fist pumps the air before pulling out a thick loaf of bread. "Hell ya!"

"What do you take me for? A rookie?" Beth juts a hip.

Cooper grins and moves to the oven, grabbing a baking sheet from the bottom drawer and getting the bread set up.

Beth turns to me and points to the wine. "Corkscrew? I figured I would pick this up while I was out. You still like wine, right?"

"I do. But I would have been happy to have soda with you."

I don't drink while Beth is around because I don't see the point in teasing it in front of her knowing she shouldn't consume alcohol. It's not a loss, considering I'm not a big drinker.

Regardless, I grab a corkscrew from the drawer before finding a glass and grabbing her a soda from the fridge. After I have everything, I toss her the corkscrew and a can of Coke and set down my glass. Her brows furrow with concentration as she yanks out the cork.

"What were you boys up to while I was gone? It was so quiet when I got in that I thought you might have left," she says while setting the cork off to the side.

I take the bottle from her and start filling my glass. "Cooper was just expressing concern for my social life."

"I told him he needs a girlfriend," he adds bluntly.

Beth laughs. "Welcome to the club, sweetheart. I've been telling him that for the past year."

"And I tell you that I'm fine without one every single time you do."

"And then I tell you that you have too much love in your heart to only give it to the two of us," she sings.

Cooper moves to the sink to wash the grease from the garlic loaf off his hands. When he uses way too much soap, I can't fight off my smile. "Mom has a good point."

"You know, it's usually the kid that doesn't want their parent to date someone new. Why aren't you like a normal kid pitching a fit right now? Where's the 'this isn't fair' argument?"

"I've always been mature for my age."

"Does that mean I can stop asking you to rinse off your

dishes before they go in the dishwasher instead of having to remind you every day?" I ask. He scowls.

"See? This is exactly why you need a girlfriend. I need someone on my side, and Mom is too biased because she's my mom."

Beth watches us with a warm smile that shows she's happy to be here with us, even if this is all we're doing. I lift my glass to my lips and smile over the rim at her.

"What makes you think my imaginary girlfriend would take your side?" I ask him, darting my eyes just in time to catch him carefully pulling a bottle of blue Gatorade out of the fridge. "There's no way that you have a blue Gatorade in your hand. You wouldn't dare try and swipe my flavour, right?"

He gulps and slowly puts it back in the fridge before pulling out a different bottle. "Blue? No. This is orange, old man."

Beth shakes her head. "You are both ridiculous."

"Not ridiculous. Just particular about my sports drinks," I mutter."

"More like greedy." Cooper sniffs. "Maybe a girlfriend could teach you how to share."

I groan. "Enough about a girlfriend, okay? Let me focus on spoiling and embarrassing you with my love."

Beth smacks a palm on the counter. I jolt in surprise, whipping my head to stare at her. Mischief taints her smile. "I nearly forgot to ask what's going on with you and that red-headed woman from the store? Is she the reason you're so against the idea of getting a girlfriend?" She gasps, covering her hand with her mouth. "Are you dating her?"

I ignore most of what she says, fixating on one thing. My voice is low with a warning when I say, "Her name is Scarlett, not 'that red-headed woman.'"

Beth's eyes bulge, and it's Cooper that speaks next. "We'll take that reaction as a yes."

I shut my eyes and take a deep breath. Frustration builds and builds beneath my skin, but it isn't only from their relentless poking. It's also from the flapping sensation in my stomach at the idea of Scarlett and girlfriend being used in the same sentence. Not good. At. All.

"Oh my God," Beth says. Her open mouth does little to hide her surprise. "You *do* like her. I swore I felt the connection between you two but thought maybe I was just making things up. Holy crap."

I narrow my eyes. "Why are you both acting as if me liking a woman is some unbelievable idea? I'm incredibly offended right now."

"So you do like her?" Cooper asks smugly.

"He does," Beth answers for me. They high-five over the island.

I throw my hands up. "I'm not talking about this anymore."

"Because we're right." Cooper initiates another high-five.

"Because my love life is my business and not yours," I correct him.

He doesn't drop it. "And because we're right."

"Cooper," I huff.

"Fine," he sighs, dragging out the word. "But in case you were wondering, I think she's nice. I haven't met a bad person that likes both my favourite flavours of ice cream."

"And how many of those people have you met in your whole twelve years of life?" I counter.

His glare is sharp. "Tons."

"Who, pray tell, are those 'tons'?"

"Adam," Beth interrupts with a giggle. "How long until dinner?"

I raise a brow as if to ask if this is her way of changing the subject.

"We need to know when to put the garlic bread in, right, Coop?"

He nods. "Right."

"Have you guys cut the lettuce for the salad yet?" Beth asks him.

"Not yet."

And just like that, the topic is dropped. If only I could shake my new curiosity about Scarlett just as easily. Instead, I'm left with an itch that I won't be able to scratch until Monday when I see her again.

15

Adam

I SLIDE A STACK OF PAPER INTO THE PRINTER BEFORE COLLAPSING IN my desk chair. It spins in a slow circle as I close my eyes.

There are only a few things I dislike about my job, the main one being the piles of paperwork that collect in my office over the span of a few days. Employee schedules, equipment and item orders, and lesson plans that need approval are only a few examples of what lies across my desk, some covered in red pen while others remain untouched.

Banks has been a massive help since I hired him last year, but there are some jobs that I only trust myself to do correctly. Ava calls it obsessive; I call it wanting to be sure things are done right. It's not that I don't trust Banks to do those jobs—if I didn't, I wouldn't have hired him in the first place—but I just trust myself to do them better. It's my company, after all. For lack of better words, WIT is like my second child. Nobody knows better when it comes to how the company works than I do.

That's why I'm still in my office at half past four instead of picking my son up from an after-school jazz band practice. After making a mad-dash call to Oakley once I realized I wasn't going to be done in time, he was able to convince his three kids to get McDonald's after school to wait for Cooper to finish practice and to bring him home after. There most likely wasn't much convincing needed, but nevertheless, I'm grateful.

It would be easy enough to just bring my work home with me, but that's something I've refused to do since I started this business. My parents brought their jobs home with them, and it separated our family. Tore it apart like thin paper and left the shredded pieces scattered on the always waxed, glistening tile floors of my childhood home.

If I have to spend an extra couple of hours in the office in exchange for a sit-down meal around the kitchen table with my son, where I can hear about his day and whatever gossip a twelve-year-old has to spill, I'll pick slaving away in my office any day.

I scrub a hand down my face and blow out a breath that feels as tight as my chest when my cell phone rings from inside my desk drawer. My head is in the clouds when I pull it out and answer the call without looking at the screen.

"Hello?"

Tyler's smoky laugh scratches my ear. "Hey, man. What's up?"

"Trying to catch up on paperwork. I meant to text you after the game last night, but you guys were phenomenal. The Warriors are making the conference finals this year, no question."

And they deserve it. After losing Oakley the season prior, they were in shambles. It's a miracle they're even making a run for the cup this season at all. Most fans expected it to take another few seasons to rebuild the team to a level that could compete again.

"Thanks. That's the goal, anyway. Got to keep a level head about it still. You know what happens to me when I get a fat ego."

I laugh. "Yeah, you end up slumming it on the third pairing for half of the season. You're a franchise player now, Ty. First pairing or no pairing."

"You sound like my wife."

"Great minds," I note.

He clears his throat. "Speaking of my wife, you're for sure coming to her birthday party, right?"

"Oh, sorry. Did I forget to send a formal RSVP, your majesty?" I tease.

"You did." He's as blunt as always.

I grin and drag the tip of my red pen over next week's schedule, doodling like a kid bored in class. Scarlett's name is in thick black lettering at the top of the page beside her next few shifts, and suddenly, she's at the forefront of my mind again.

I tap the pen on my desk. "Of course I'm coming. Free beer and a boat ride on the ocean? How could I pass that up?"

"See, that's what I told Gray. We might be old as fuck now, but beer, food, and a good time will win us over every time."

"Being older just means we can afford the good shit. I don't remember the last time I had the cheap beer we drank in college." I shiver at the memory of the—for all intents and purposes—beer-flavoured water we would fill our kegs with.

God, it was so much worse in a keg in the sun than it was if we kept it chilled in the fridge. At least if it was cold, it was harder to tell how flavourless it was.

"Cheap beer and expensive wine stolen from your parents' cellar. Those were the days." Tyler sighs.

"You know, somehow, my father always found out about the missing wine. It was never the party he cared about or the puke in the backyard. It was that damn wine where he drew the line." I laugh. "Thinking back on it now, that's definitely why I kept offering it to everyone like it was water from the tap."

"Of course that's why. Your dad was just as big of a prick back then as he is now. Honestly, we should have just drained the whole cellar while we were at it. The asshole deserved it."

"You're right," I agree.

"Speaking of the wrinkled fuck, have you talked to him recently? Are your parents coming to the fair?"

The fair is a yearly event put on by WIT at the end of each

hockey season to celebrate the successes of all my clients. We rent a couple of carnival rides, hire performers, and pig out at the food stands. Brielle has done the majority of the planning this year, with it set to take place on the last weekend of July.

"Hopefully not. There's no reason for them to show up," I say.

A high-pitched scream sounds in the background of the call before Tyler yells, "Oliver! Did you really just put gum in your brother's hair? Right in front of me? Where did you even get gum?"

"Mommy's purse," the six-year-old replies sheepishly.

"Are we supposed to be digging around in Mommy's things, Oli?"

A pause. "No, Dad."

"Go apologize to your brother while I find and tell your mom why we need to shave Jamieson's head."

"You good, man?" I ask once the call goes silent.

He snorts a laugh. "I thought one kid was hard. Oh, how naive I was."

"At least Oli has a friend to grow up with."

"Yeah, so instead of one devil, I get two—ow!" There's a rustling noise in the speaker before Gracie's voice greets me. "Yes, Tyler. Go get the razor, and then you can try your best at shaving our poor two-year-old's beautiful head of curls."

"Me? You mean us, right?" Tyler asks in the background.

Gracie scoffs. "Oh no. I mean you. I'm not going to let him hate me for this."

"But you'll let him hate me?"

"I would prefer him to hate neither of us, but if those are my only two options. Sorry, babe."

I bite my lip to avoid laughing and pull the phone from my ear before turning it to speakerphone and placing it on my desk. It's still hard to believe that just ten years ago, Tyler was pretending not to care about Gracie while she was blatantly pining over him. It was the typical brother's best friend drama that kept them apart but with some bad-boy commitment issues thrown into the mix.

They're both the most stubborn people I've ever met, but somehow, it worked out in the end. A happy marriage and two beautiful children can account for that.

"Adam?" Gracie calls.

I lean my elbows on the edge of my desk. "Hey, Gray."

"Oh, please don't call me that. I found a grey hair this morning. Luckily it was only one, but I'm forever scarred. I'm being aged right before my own eyes."

"Did you rip it out?"

"I did. Imagine if Oakley had seen it. I would never have lived it down," she guffaws.

The devil on my shoulder grins wickedly. "Actually, I have it on good authority that your brother pulled out his first grey hair last year. Ava swore me to secrecy, but I'm willing to take a risk here."

"That dirty cheat. He told me just the other day that he was positive he would never go grey."

I click my tongue. "Naughty boy."

"Thank you for giving me just the ammunition I need the next time he tries to rile me up. I want to say that I owe you one now, but I actually made Tyler call you today in hopes of sooomehow prying a favour of sorts out of you."

My interest piques. "Oh? Gracie Bateman asking little old me for a favour? This must be good."

She laughs. "Well, actually, it's more of a plea than a favour."

"Well, come on. I'm not getting any younger." Quite the opposite, really.

"You know, with my birthday party coming up this weekend and me turning thirty and all, I was really hoping that I would get to meet this Scarlett woman. For personal reasons, obviously," she rushes out, breathless by the end of her ramble.

"Personal reasons?" I chuckle. The only thing personal in that request was in regards to my own personal life. There's only one person who would have gushed to my friends all about my relationship—or lack thereof—with Scarlett, and he is in for a hefty water gun soaking once I get home today. "Let me guess. Cooper?"

A beat of silence before a burst of Gracie's voice scrapes my eardrum. "Maybe. But that doesn't matter! What matters is that you bring her to my party. I promise not to bombard her or scare her away. Just imagine how much fun she'll have on a private yacht, on the Pacific Ocean, under the delicious rays of the summer sun."

I run a hand over the top of my head and swallow the knot in my throat. Would I want Scarlett to come meet my friends? Absolutely. But Cooper is already my plus one, and bringing the both of them together smells a lot like a set-up. Do I want to put them in a position where they can really get to know each other? Where Cooper can start building a relationship with someone who might not be around long term?

"It's not as simple as that, Gray. Cooper will be there."

She scoffs. "And what's so bad about that? From what he told Maddox, he seems to really like her."

Ah, so it was gossip with Oakley and Ava's oldest spawn, then. That can only mean that his parents have quite the rundown as well.

"I don't want him building a bond with anyone I'm not sure will be here for a long time. The last thing he needs is to feel any form of abandonment again like he did with Beth. It wouldn't be good for him," I say. My words hang uncomfortably in the silence that follows.

Gracie softens her voice. "Those are all valid points, Adam. But what about you? Are you just supposed to be alone forever?"

I flinch. "I would prefer not to be. But Cooper comes first. You know that."

"I know this is more Ava's domain and we don't really talk much about this sort of thing, but Adam, if you feel something for this woman, you owe it to yourself to explore that. Cooper wants you to be happy. We all do."

My stomach folds in on itself. I've lost the ability to pretend that I don't have feelings for Scarlett. If even my twelve-year-old son can see it, it's too obvious that I do.

"Having feelings and actually exploring those feelings are completely different ball games."

She sighs, sounding reluctant. "Just invite her to the party. Cooper will be busy with the kids, and it'll be the perfect opportunity to spend more time with her in a non-intimate setting."

"Okay." I give in. My pulse quickens at the possibility of spending time with Scarlett. "I'll invite her. But I'm not promising anything. She could already have plans."

Gracie squeals. "Oh my gosh, yay! I'll add her to the guest list just in case."

There's a knock on my office door that has it opening the tiniest bit. I look down at the watch on my wrist and frown at the time. Nobody should still be here.

"Hey, Gray. I gotta go. I'll keep you posted, okay?"

"Sounds good. Take care, Adam. Love you!"

"Love you too," I reply before hanging up and locking my phone screen. The door pushes open completely, and I go rigid when I see a mess of red curls.

Oh fuck.

16

Scarlett

I'm heading home, nearly at the doors, when Willow comes busting into the arena. She looks around in a panic, her eyes wide and fearful. As soon as she sees me, she pivots on a pair of old, frayed sneakers and runs in my direction.

She's a blur of tight black curls when she crashes into me and wraps her arms around my middle in a surprising hug. My muscles freeze before thawing, allowing me to hug her back.

"Willow?"

Tears dampen my shirt when she presses her face into my shoulder. My brows furrow with concern.

A storm of protectiveness crashes into me, making me tighten my grip on her. Whatever happened to her, I know I'll be the one to deal with it. She's my student, and I've grown to care for her more than I thought I would. Especially in only a couple of weeks of knowing her.

Willow has that way with people, I guess. She's special. I knew that the moment we met.

"What happened?" My voice is gentle, cautious. She shakes her head and swallows loud enough I can hear it. "I can't fix what I don't know, Willow."

"I don't want to give up hockey. It's all I have," she whispers.

I blink, confused. "Why would you have to give it up? You don't. We love you here."

Her arms drop, and she stumbles back, swiping angrily at her swollen eyes. "It doesn't even matter. I don't know why I came here."

"Hold on," I rush out when she turns to look at the door, like she's debating whether or not to take off. "You came here to talk, right? So, let's talk. Don't run off."

"I don't know why I came here."

I nod. "Okay, then let's figure it out. But not in the open like this. Come on." Grabbing her hand, I lead us through the halls in search of the staff room.

When we reach the glass door, I unlock it and lead us inside. Willow looks around the unfamiliar space with slight approval.

It's a nicely decorated room with a leather sofa, a few armchairs, and a small kitchen decked out with a full-size fridge and one of those fancy toaster ovens. There's a pricy coffee machine on the counter that I've been too scared to use in fear of busting it and a spinning carousel of mugs with cheesy sayings.

Willow heads right for the mugs before bursting into a fit of laughter. I'm both happy to see her smile and concerned as to what could have made her switch up so quickly.

When I move to stand beside her, I look at the cup in her hands and growl, "Adam."

It's a matte-black mug with a pair of devil horns above the words *If Lost, Return To Scary Spice.*

"He loves to piss you off, huh?" she asks, setting the cup back on its hook.

"If riling me up was an Olympic sport, Adam would be the one with all the gold medals, not me."

I sit on the couch and pat the spot beside me. Willow releases a long breath but joins me.

"We're not going to talk about Adam and his hobbies right now, though. You're going to tell me what's going on with you and why you think you have to quit hockey."

Willow grabs her knees and squeezes. "My mom can't afford to pay for my lessons. She never could, but I was tutoring a few rich kids before school, during my lunch breaks, and after school whenever I could to pay half of the fees, but now that school's out, that's not an option.

"Her job has cut her hours again, and between me and my three other siblings, even if I could find another job, she wouldn't be able to pay the other half anymore. She isn't sure if we'll be able to afford for me to even stay on my hockey team for next season."

My heart constricts. *Shit.*

"That's . . ." I begin.

"Horrible?" she finishes. "Yeah. I can't not play hockey, Scar. And I don't know, I guess I came here because out of everyone I know, it's you who would be able to understand."

"Because I've lost it all." God, those words hurt. It's like pouring vodka in an open wound.

I collapse into the couch and rub at my face. How am I supposed to give advice to someone when I can't even deal with my own problems? I'm probably the worst person in the world to come to with this, but I think I might be the only option for Willow. That means I can't sit here and wallow in the castle of pity I've built for myself over the better part of a year. It might be too late for me to make a comeback, but it sure as hell isn't for her.

"You're not done, Willow. Far from it. If you think there's any way Adam would let you walk out of here before you're ready, then you truly have no idea the kind of guy he is or how good you are."

When she stares at her feet in silence, I continue.

"Did you know that he sought me out and hired me just to train you?"

Her head whips in my direction. "No."

"As soon as he knew I was in town, he brought me in and even offered to help me with my shoulder if it meant that I would work for him. He did that because he wanted the best for you, and even if I'm no longer out there winning gold medals, that's exactly what I am."

My eyes go wide as I realize what I've said—or accepted, really. Willow's lips spread in a small smile.

I clear my throat. "Anyway, my point is that there's no way you're giving up hockey. We will figure something out." It's a promise in its purest form.

A mix between doubt and hope spreads across her face before she nods once. "Is he still here? We should go talk to him now before I leave and lose my edge."

"Your edge?" I laugh, earning myself a glare. "Right. We wouldn't want you to lose your *edge*. He was still in his office a few minutes ago." We get up off the couch and leave the room.

"Did you really take the job just to work with me?" Willow asks when we step into the hallway. The main lights are off now that the rink is closed, leaving only the dull automatic ones to light the path.

"Adam told me how good you were, and I said yes. I haven't regretted that decision once."

At least I haven't when working with her. Adam, on the other hand? It might have crossed my mind a couple of times. More so lately than before, though I think that stems from a completely different problem.

"Okay," she murmurs.

"So, you have three siblings? Boys or girls?" I ask and cringe at my attempt at small talk.

I'm not one to ask about someone's personal life. Most of the time, I don't see the purpose of getting to know someone that isn't going to be a constant in my life for a long period of time. It seems unnecessary to build bonds with temporary people.

Yet with Willow, I want to get to know more about her. And I think that's because we've already created a bond that I don't want to break, regardless of if its permanence. We're so similar it's almost uncanny. I see myself in her and want to give her the best chance of success. She deserves it.

"Two older brothers and a younger sister. I'm the third child. Do you have any siblings?"

"No. I'm the only one. I think it was a blessing that way, though. I was hard enough on my mom without adding another kid in the mix."

"Yeah, my second oldest brother is the same way. My mom always said that if she knew how much of a shit he was going to be, maybe she wouldn't have kept popping out babies."

That makes me laugh. "He's a real handful, then."

"Just yesterday, I had to pick him up from the skate park after he got into a fight and hit some kid in the back of the head with his board."

"Okay, yeah, I can see it. So, what, you're the designated bail buddy?"

She snorts. "Yeah, you could say that. Luckily, hockey usually keeps me pretty busy, so I get out of it a lot of the time."

"Well, if you ever need a bail buddy or anything, I . . . uh, I could be that for you."

Willow looks at me and grins. "That would be awesome."

I smile back. "Okay."

As soon as Adam's office door comes into view, Willow halts, coming to a sudden stop. I look at her curiously.

"What's wrong?"

She chews nervously on her lip. "Do you think you could go in first? Warm him up a little?" My eyes go wide, and then hers follow. She rambles her next words in a hushed voice. "Okay, that's so not what I meant. I'm so nervous I have no control over my words. Please forget I said that. I mean, unless that's something you want to do? If so, please feel free. I'll just wait out here and put headphones in or something."

"Willow, stop talking. Please." My cheeks feel as warm as hers look. "I can go in and talk to him first."

Yeah, simple enough. It's not like what I'm thinking about now is all the ways I could "warm him up."

She sighs in relief. "Okay. Thank you."

"Just stay close or something. I'll come get you when I'm done talking to him."

After she gives me another nod of confirmation, I leave her where she's standing and continue the walk to Adam's office. As soon as I get close, I hear his voice through the crack in his door. An involuntary shudder moves through me before a woman's voice joins his.

"Okay. I'll invite her. But I'm not promising anything. She could already have plans," he says. I lean forward a bit.

Who is he talking to? And what are they talking about?

I swallow the questions in my throat and knock on the door a bit harder than necessary. He quickly says goodbye to the woman he was speaking to and hangs up but not before I catch him throw out the L word.

Bile churns in my stomach, and I lose my balance, stumbling right into the door and pushing it open. Adam's eyes are alert when they meet mine.

"Scarlett," he says. Are those nerves in his voice? If so, what the hell kind of conversation was he having to be nervous about?

"Hi. Is now an okay time to talk? I can come back. You sounded busy."

"I'm never too busy for you. Come in." He gestures for me to enter, and I do, opting to leave the door open.

I cross the room and sit in one of the chairs in front of his desk. Adam steps around his desk and sits on it, facing me. He folds his arms and grins.

"I'm surprised to see you're still here. You usually leave right at four."

"Yeah, something came up. Or someone, I guess."

His eyes flash with interest. "Is everything okay?"

"It's Willow," I sigh. "She found me when I was leaving. *God.*

She was crying and hugging me, and I had no idea what to do or say."

A warm hand brushes my knee, and I find Adam watching me intently with a look I can't decipher. It makes my heart beat erratically.

"Slow down," he urges softly. "Why was she crying? Tell me how to fix it."

"She can't afford this place anymore. Her family probably won't be able to afford hockey at all next season. You need to help her. She can't lose this. Please don't let her go," I plead. My chest constricts, and my lungs clutch onto the air inside of them like it's the last taste of it they'll ever have.

"What changed? Is it something I need to be concerned about?"

I shake my head. "I don't think so. She didn't seem worried about anything but hockey. Her mom's job cut hours, and from what she told me, they're barely holding on as it is."

He blows out a long breath and, without breaking eye contact, says, "Okay. I'll help her."

"What?" I gasp. The corners of my mouth tug, and before I realize what's happening, I'm grinning at him. "Are you sure? Do you even know how you'll do it? You don't have to decide today."

Adam's smile sears my insides. "It seems as though I would do anything you ask me to, Scarlett. Especially when that smile is my thank you."

17

Adam

I don't know why I just told her that, but I do know it's the truth.

Even now, as her blush-coloured lips pull up in a beaming smile that I feel coiling itself around my heart, I accept that I'll do anything and everything she wants just to see her look at me like that again.

Like I've done more than simply agree to help a phenomenal athlete continue her training regardless of finances.

My confidence is bubbling like soda in a can that's been shaken a few too many times, and I use it to my advantage. If I don't ask her about Gracie's party right now, I risk the possibility of chickening out.

"Actually," I start and sigh in relief when her smile only wavers with silent curiosity. "I was already planning on asking you about this before you walked in here—actually, it's what I was just talking on the phone about, so know this has nothing to do with Willow or my choice to help her. But there's a birthday party that I'm going to this weekend, and I would love it if you came with me."

I don't bother clarifying that it doesn't have to be a date

because I think that's exactly what I want it to be, as unorthodox as it might be.

Scarlett's eyes go wide, and her lips slowly fall. I feel sweat break out on the back of my neck before I reach back and rub it away. Eternities of silence is what it feels like as I wait for her to answer.

"Is this a date?" she finally asks. There's no immediate repulsion in her words, so I'll take that as a good sign.

"That's up to you, Scary Spice. Date or not, I just know I want you there with me."

A beautiful flush works up her neck and spreads to the tips of her ears. "So, if I said it could be a date . . ."

"I wouldn't complain in the slightest."

A stray curl slips from behind her ear when she looks away, and I fight the urge to reach toward her and twirl it around my finger.

"But there's no pressure. As long as you come with me, I don't care what you're coming as—date or friend," I add.

Her eyes meet mine again. They're more reserved than they were just moments ago, and I frown. "What kind of party is this? I don't have much dating experience, but I'm pretty sure having a first date around a large group of people isn't exactly ideal."

"So, it would be a date?"

"Did you listen to anything else I said?"

"Yes. And I know it's a bit unorthodox to have a first date surrounded by all of my family and friends . . . actually, you're right. That sounds far less appealing when I say it out loud. Friends, then?"

I try to ignore the pang of disappointment that label brings and slip a smile on my face. I mean, come on. What man in his thirties brings a woman to meet his family on the first date? I inwardly wince. Maybe I am a bit rustier in the dating world than I thought.

"I don't do well with big crowds. I'm not exactly a people person," she says.

"Luckily for you, I am. Let me worry about the schmoozing."

She lifts a brow. "I find it hard to believe you're okay with dating someone who would rather find a quiet, empty room to sit alone in than gossip with the girls."

"Dating? How presumptuous of you, Scarlett." I smirk.

Scarlett glares daggers at me. She jumps to her feet, huffing. "You're infuriating."

I grab her wrist and gently pull her toward me. There's still feet of distance between us, but I've become sucked into her orbit. Her skin is warm and smooth beneath my fingertips. I revel in the hitch of her breath when I run my thumb over her wrist bone.

"I'm sorry. I know what you meant," I begin. She stares down at my hand around her wrist. "And to put it bluntly, I don't give a flying fuck if you want to sit in a quiet room and take a break. Tell me you want to go, and I'll come with you. Tell me you want me to stay, and I'll keep up appearances for the both of us. Personally, I'm partial to option number one. I'm sure there are plenty of things we can do to keep ourselves occupied in the dark."

Her eyes travel up the length of my arm and torso before finding mine. They flare with a fierce heat that makes my dick stir.

"I came in here for a reason," she says breathlessly.

I release her wrist and slowly, cautiously, touch her fingers. When she doesn't pull away, I slip them between mine and test the way it feels to hold her hand. "Tell me you'll come with me this weekend."

"You're sure you want me there? This is your last chance to change your mind."

"Absolutely. Without a doubt."

"And this has nothing to do with you helping Willow? Because she's outside your office right now thinking her life is about to end."

I tighten my grip on her hand. Scarlett's protectiveness of

Willow is becoming one of the most stunning things about her. "You could tell me to shove my offer up my ass right now and I would still do everything in my power to help that girl."

She gifts me a small smile. "Then yes. I'll come."

Triumph blares in my ears, but I try to silence it. Yes, I might want to throw my arms up and shout a quick boo-yah, but there is a concerned sixteen-year-old waiting for me to tell her everything is going to be okay.

"Then let's go find Willow."

Scarlett

Mom rubs her hands down my arms for the third time in a row before stepping back and placing the tip of her finger to her chin. She squints her eyes, examining me.

"Well?" I ask, ignoring the urge to rip out the small hoops in my ears. I don't remember the last time I wore earrings, but I doubt I like them any more now than I did then. "Do I look private yacht worthy?"

She smiles. "You look beautiful."

"Really? Because I feel like one of those makeup dolls I had as a child."

I let Mom pull my hair up into a braided ponytail and put more makeup on me than I've worn since my high school graduation, although that's not really saying a lot. I never had the time to put much effort into my appearance when I was playing hockey, but even if I did find the time to try, it would have been for nothing once I began to sweat at practice. I'm a complete novice when it comes to knowing how to use half of the stuff on my face right now.

My legs are clad in a pair of jean shorts with a rip in the front left pocket, and an oversized, cropped tee hangs off my shoulders. Mom tried to force me into a sundress she found in the back of my closet, but I was quick to shut that down.

If I was going to let her paint my face, then I was going to choose my outfit.

"Well, it doesn't matter. You still look great regardless," she states.

I smile and reach forward to give her a hug. "Thank you."

She returns the hug eagerly, and I soak up the affection for a few seconds longer than necessary. My stomach is still a mess of nerves when we break apart, and I wipe the beads of sweat off the back of my neck.

"You look nervous, my darling."

I choke on a laugh. "Really? What gave me away?"

I've been nervous since Adam asked me to come to this party. It's been a week of awkward hellos and high-strung anticipation. Not to mention the sexual tension that's grown to the point it's impossible to ignore whenever we're alone.

We've had three therapy sessions since Monday afternoon, and each one gets worse. I've started contemplating bringing extra underwear in my gym bag just to change into afterward because of the effect he's started to have on me. Even the slightest brush of his fingers is enough to send me into a lustful haze.

Whatever has grown between us has to be affecting him, too, because ever since Tuesday's session, he has made extra sure not to touch me at all. Instead, I've been repeating the same exercises on my own each day.

It's obvious we need to figure out what's going on with us before it starts to hurt my progress, but the thought of talking about this with him is enough to send me into a panic.

Adam isn't like the other guys I've been with. Being with him would be complicated. And complicated scares me. Especially with where my life is at the moment. Yet regardless of all of that, I can't get him out of my head.

I'm screwed.

"Do you want a shot of tequila before you go? Maybe you need a bit of warmth in your belly to calm the nerves," Mom suggests.

"Thanks, Mom. But I'm driving."

She clucks her tongue. "Why isn't Leo coming to pick you up? This is a date, is it not?"

"I'm going out with Adam today, Mom. And I told you this morning that he had to pick up his son from a band practice. I offered to meet him at the dock."

When realization doesn't dawn on her, she frowns deeply. It pulls at the lines in her skin.

"Right, of course. I'm sure you did, sweetheart," she whispers.

I place a hand on her shoulder and kiss her forehead. "Would you like me to help you get settled before I leave?"

"Yes, I think that would be great."

I nod and steer her in the direction of her yellow armchair in the sitting room. She has a view of her side garden from the window across from the chair, and I've caught her sitting there watching the butterflies a few times this week.

Once I have her situated in her chair, I place an eating tray beside her and head to the kitchen to grab her a glass of lemonade. A few moments later, I'm turning the television on and locking the back door.

"My phone number is on the fridge. If you need anything, and I mean anything, Mom, please call. I can always send over Mrs. McConnell from next door if I can't get back here soon enough."

She swipes a hand in the air and grabs the TV remote from the side table. "You worry too much. I'm not eighty and incapable of taking care of myself. Go have fun with Leo, and I'll see you when you get back."

I close my eyes and hold back the onslaught of emotions that flares to life when she says Leo's name again.

"I will," I say, pressing a kiss to the top of her head. "I'll lock the door on my way out. I love you."

Mom looks over her shoulder at me and smiles. "I love you more, my darling."

I watch the TV screen as it changes from the news to a crime show before turning around and heading for the door.

18

Scarlett

I've never been on a boat before. But this mansion on the water is not how I expected to lose my boat virginity.

The yacht towers over the boat dock, all bright lights and loud music. Three levels of glass and sleek white walls. The walkway to the boat comes from inside and touches the dock just enough for me to feel semi-confident stepping onto it.

My stomach swirls with nerves as I continue to stand on the dock, rubbing my palms back and forth across my shorts. I can see a group of people on the second level, but I don't recognize anyone.

Adam told me he would meet me on the dock at four, and when I checked the time inside my car, I was only a couple of minutes early. Now I'm wishing I had waited and given myself a quick five-minute pep talk.

I'm about to pull my phone out of my pocket to check if he's texted me at all when a high-pitched squeal captures my attention. I lift a hand over my eyes and squint at the back of the boat to try and focus on the woman speeding in my direction.

She's an image of bouncing blonde hair and pink sparkles as she makes quick work of the distance between us. The toes of her white stilettos touch the bridge that hangs over the water when she stops.

"Scarlett? It has to be you!" She waves enthusiastically, smiling from ear to ear.

For such a tiny woman, her presence is huge, attention demanding. Intimidating.

"Hi," I say.

"Oh, my God! Am I the first one to notice you?" When I nod, she claps. "Yes! This is going to be amazing. Come on over here. The bridge is safe, I promise."

Uncertainty pricks my mind, but I force myself to step onto the metal contraption anyway. With quick movements, I cross the gap and step onto the boat. It doesn't so much as budge, which shouldn't surprise me but does.

A small hand grabs mine, and I jolt in surprise, pulling it out of the woman's grip just in time to see her lips form an O shape.

"Oh shit, I'm sorry. You have no idea who I am, do you? Dammit, Adam." She looks at me apologetically. "I'm Gracie. The woman who doesn't know when to keep her hands to herself. I'm so sorry about that. I'm just too excited to have you here."

I relax slightly. "It's okay. Happy birthday, by the way."

"Thank you so much. It's so beautiful out today, isn't it? You brought a bathing suit, right? I swear, if that shithead didn't tell you to pack a suit, I'm going to throw him off the top deck."

"He did. It's in here." I awkwardly pat the bag slung over my shoulder.

Her eyes light up. "Perfect. Come with me, I'll introduce you to everyone."

Darting my eyes to the dock, I grow uneasy when I still don't see any sign of Adam.

"He should be here soon," Gracie says, reading my mind. "I can wait with you here for him if you want. Or I can leave you to wait alone."

"God no," I blurt out, my eyes growing in size. "I mean, we

don't know how long he's going to be, so . . ." And I really don't want him to find me sitting here waiting for him like I can't handle his friends alone for a few minutes.

Understanding flicks across her features. She smiles warmly. "Got it. Let's get to it, then."

I hike my bag higher on my shoulder and follow her toward a staircase off to the side of the first level.

"I hope you like kids," she says when we start up the stairs. "There's about ten of them where we're going."

"I can't say that I don't not like them. I didn't really grow up around kids."

She laughs. "Fair enough. They'll all be too busy with themselves anyway. When I left to check if you and Adam were here, they were shooting each other with Nerf guns."

"One of my old teammates had a son who always brought those with us on road games. I'm pretty sure I still have a bruise on my thigh from getting shot with one at close range."

"I believe it. Cooper and Maddox, Oakley and Ava's oldest son, are really the only ones who can use them properly, but the younger kids love to try and keep up."

When we reach the top of the stairs, I look around in awe.

The room opens up completely, with a living room, bar, and kitchen tucked in the back corner. The living space has a massive rounded couch and several leather armchairs, all the same beige colour as the walls. It looks and feels like luxury, and I'm still not sure how I feel about being here.

Besides the shouting voices of the kids I spot running on the deck through the open wall beside the kitchen, it's silent. Too silent. My attention is pulled to the crowd of people staring at us —or, more specifically, at me, and I gulp.

Gracie stands close to me and gently touches my arm. "Everyone, this is Scarlett. Scarlett, this is everyone."

"Hi," I croak, waving.

"Want to get any vaguer, Gray?" someone asks her from across the room.

"Right," Gracie giggles. "Let me try this again. That's Oakley and Ava over there." She points to the two people sitting at the bar.

A noise of excitement comes from the brunette sitting beside Oakley. Having met the retired NHL player a handful of times over the past few years during charity events or volunteer activities, he's a familiar face in a crowd of unfamiliar ones, and I latch onto the small slice of comfort that brings me.

His arm is slung over the shoulders of the woman beside him, and I quickly place her as his wife, Ava. She has a calmer aura about her than Gracie does but still wears an expression of barely contained joy as she stares at me.

"I'm so happy to meet you," she gushes, clasping her hands together.

Oakley speaks next, his words ultra-calm in comparison to the two girls I've just met. "It's great to see you again, Scar. Thanks for coming."

I smile at them both while Gracie points to the couch. There are two large men sitting on opposite sides of a dark-haired woman. One of them has a large hand placed high on the thigh of the woman beside him.

"My husband, Tyler, is on the end there, and the guy who looks about ready to slip his hand up his pregnant wife's dress is his brother, Braden. Sierra is the poor woman getting felt up beside him."

I choke on a laugh, and both men hop off the couch. Braden, the stockier of the two men, reaches down to help Sierra up. Tyler rounds the couch and walks toward his wife with a grin while my jaw falls open.

It's just now clicked in that Tyler is Tyler Bateman, the best defenseman in the hockey league right now.

Oh, shit. Am I sweating?

He moves to Gracie's side and kisses her cheek before looking at me. "It's nice to meet you, Scarlett. We've heard great things."

Sierra walks closer to the rest of us and places a hand on her slightly rounded belly. "Your hair is amazing. Is that your natural colour?"

"Oh, yeah, it's natural," I answer. Subconsciously, I push my hair back.

"Scarlett with the fire-truck-red hair, huh?" Braden asks. Sierra glowers at him.

"It's a name I'll never forgive my mother for," I say honestly.

Braden bursts out laughing, and everyone else quickly follows. I smile slightly, feeling a bit more relaxed.

"Braden can be a bit of an asshole sometimes, Scarlett. Just a fair warning," Tyler says.

I focus my attention on him and find myself overrun with questions I want to ask him. Like what was it like to enter the league undrafted? Did it make his experience harder compared to Oakley's? Or was it similar?

Suddenly, a hard chest brushes my back. My breath hitches at the contact, but I don't move away. Instead, something has me leaning against the hard wall of muscle behind me and relaxing completely for the first time since I was in my car.

A large hand grips my hip, squeezing as hot breath warms the back of my ear. "You're looking at Tyler like you idolize him. It's making me jealous."

Goosebumps pebble my skin. "You're late."

"I know. I'm sorry," he whispers.

The pads of his fingers press deeper into my hip when he pulls me flush against him. The feeling of him pressed against me has my head spinning. I shudder and try to focus on the group around us.

I'm aware of how this looks, but despite that, I can't get myself to move away like I know I should. All I can think about is how perfectly I fit against him and that I've missed him since the last time we saw each other.

Someone in the group whistles, and it acts like a shock to my system. I take a step forward, and Adam's body heat disappears, his hand dropping.

"That was hot," Braden says. I find him fanning himself.

"You're embarrassing us," Tyler grumbles, staring at his brother. He offers me an apologetic smile. "See? What did I say? An asshole."

Braden scoffs. "As if we weren't all thinking it."

"That's the difference between you and everyone else. We thought it but didn't say it," Ava scolds.

My cheeks have to be just as red as my hair right now. They feel like they're moments away from bursting into flames.

I can feel Adam's eyes on me, but I can't get myself to look at him. I'm tempted to jump off the side of the boat and swim to the dock.

Turning to Gracie instead, I ask, "Where's the bathroom?"

After she tells me, I place a smile on my face and excuse myself.

Adam

SCARLETT'S PANICKING.

I turn to Braden and, for the first time in all the years we've known each other, have to hold myself back from punching him in the face.

"What the fuck is wrong with you?" I growl.

Ava gasps, but I only focus on Braden. This protectiveness is new for me—terrifying, even—but all I know is that I don't ever want to see that look on Scarlett's face again. Especially not because of someone I consider family.

"If you're going to punch him, Adam, please do it somewhere the kids won't be able to see," Gracie sighs.

Braden whips his head in her direction. "You're kidding me, Gray. I don't deserve to be punched."

"I would have already knocked your teeth in," Tyler pipes up.

Braden snorts. "That's because you have the restraint of a toddler."

I give my head a shake and ignore them all as I follow after Scarlett. My fingers are still curled at my sides, and this feeling of desperation is nearly suffocating. I'm desperate to get to her and make sure she's not completely freaking out.

For someone who doesn't like meeting new people nor social gatherings, I can't imagine being called out in front of a group of unfamiliar faces in an uncomfortable environment is very settling.

If I wasn't late, maybe this wouldn't have even happened, but I try to push that thought away. Scarlett is a big girl, and from what I saw when I arrived, she was handling herself just fine.

Her strength and confidence is what drew me to her in the first place. It's one of my favourite things about her.

With how demanding my life is, I need someone that can handle themselves but also knows they can lean on me when the pressures of everything gets too much. She's exactly that.

The bathroom door is locked, so I knock twice. "Scary Spice?"

"Leave me here alone to die of embarrassment."

I laugh. "Not happening. Can you let me in?"

A huff and then the clicking of the lock. "Say one wrong thing and I'm kicking your ass," she grumbles.

"No pressure."

I turn the handle and open the door. She's leaning against the vanity, her palms flush to the sides. When she turns to look at me, I swallow.

Fuck, she's stunning.

I only got a good look at the back side of her when I got here, and as fantastic of a backside as it is, it pales in comparison to the front.

There's black lining her eyes when they meet mine, and it makes the blue in her eyes appear even lighter than usual, like glacier water. The makeup surprises me after seeing her without it every day for the past couple of months, but she looks beautiful. She always does.

Scarlett blinks a few times, long, thick lashes fluttering before a sound of annoyance escapes her. I watch with intrigue as she reaches up and pulls her eyelashes off before doing the same with the other eye and then setting a clump of lashes in the sink.

"My mother made me wear those. They feel like caterpillars on my eyes."

"Good to know."

She rolls her eyes before looking away. "You didn't have to come after me. I just needed a minute."

"Yeah, Scar, I did."

She's staring at her feet when she says, "That's the first time you've called me Scar."

I lift my brows. "And? Do you approve?"

"Anything is better than that ridiculous nickname of yours."

With a teasing smile, I shut the bathroom door and lean back against it. I cross my arms. "Okay, we're completely alone now. Admit you don't hate the name as much as you let on."

She turns her head. Our eyes lock. "Why would I do that?"

"It would make me happy."

"It's a good thing your happiness isn't my concern, then."

I push away from the door and swallow some of the distance between us until we're standing opposite each other. The bathroom isn't all that big, and I quickly realize how much closer we are than I anticipated. Still, I don't back away.

"No? 'Cause for weeks, yours has been at the top of my priority list."

Her breath skips. The shirt she's wearing hangs off her right shoulder, leaving her skin bare, exposed to the greed in my eyes. Before I can stop myself, my thumb is swiping across her collarbone, tracing the outline of a crowd of freckles.

"I love how many freckles you have. It's like you're covered in stars," I whisper.

"Your imagination is impressive," she replies, slightly breathless.

I shake my head and trail my touch up the side of her neck. Her pulse thumps beneath my fingertips. "There's nothing imaginary about you or the way you make me feel, Scarlett."

"Adam," she starts. Her voice trails off when I slip my fingers through her hair and palm the back of her head, tilting it back so our lips are a breath away.

"I'm a patient guy when it comes to things I really want, so I'll wait for you to admit to yourself that you feel the same way I do, because fuck, Scarlett. There's no way you don't."

Her eyes flare. "It's not that easy."

"Not yet. Just give me some time to convince you that it can be."

If there's one lesson I've learned over the course of my life, it's that the best things never come easy. You have to work your ass off for them, and Scarlett might just be the best one I'll ever come to know.

"I'm too old to play games when it comes to the things I want, and I want you and everything that comes with you," I confess.

She chews on her lip. I'm not surprised to find reluctance heavy in her stare.

"Let me try something," I plead. I free her lip from between her teeth and swallow a groan at how soft it is. Her nod is barely there, but I catch it.

I bring my mouth to hers in a kiss that threatens to send me to my knees. Her lips part on a gasp, and I fight back a smile, knowing it's affecting her the same way.

Her hands brush my chest in a way that hints at her curiosity.

It's like she wants to touch me but isn't sure if she should. I tighten my fingers in her hair and deepen the kiss while grabbing one of her hands and spreading her fingers. With her hand open, I press it to my chest and hold it there.

Her touch is electric, addicting in the same way adrenaline is.

A gruff noise escapes me when her other hand joins the first. They start moving up my body, and I nip at her bottom lip, unable to hold myself back the more she touches me.

The tension between us has finally exploded, leaving us buzzing in the aftershock. Scarlett opens her mouth for me, and I get my first real taste of her.

When she moans against my lips, the final bit of my restraint snaps in half. I drop my hand from her hair and grip her hips before lifting her and setting her on the vanity.

Stepping between her spread legs, I slip my fingers beneath the bottom hem of her shirt and hold her waist. She's all warm muscles and smooth skin, and my head swims with need for her.

I ache to bring her closer but know better than to push my luck.

It's her that breaks the kiss, pushing me back and closing her eyes. Her chest rises and falls just as fast as mine does.

"What am I supposed to do with all that?" she snaps, suddenly furious.

I can only grin, staring at her swollen lips. "Remember how you just felt when you think about the possibility of you and me. Maybe it will help clear some things up for you."

"You make everything sound so easy."

I sober up. "I know. There's a lot for you to think about. Just know that I'm ready to talk about it when you are."

"And if I tell you that you're wrong? That I don't feel what you think I do?"

I squeeze her waist one last time before releasing her and stepping back. Grabbing the door handle, I say, "If you lie to me, then we'll be here again. Only it won't be your mouth I'm kissing."

19

Scarlett

Hours later, I can still feel Adam's mouth pressed to mine. I can still taste him and smell the woodsy aftershave on his jaw. My lips tingle. My core aches for more.

Confidence, skill, emotion—it was the perfect mix of all three.

I've never been kissed like that. Like the other person wouldn't be able to breathe again without knowing what my mouth felt like pressed to theirs. It was passion and hunger and desperation, and as shocking as it was to be on the receiving end of a kiss like that, I should have been expecting it.

Adam and I are electric. We always have been. It was only a matter of time before we blew a fuse.

It's just a shame I can't lose myself in that connection like I want to. Not yet. Not when there is still so much to figure out. Both with myself and what a relationship with Adam could mean. What it could bring.

Speaking of what it could bring. Cooper's voice is what pulls me out of my thoughts. He and Maddox are currently chasing after Noah, Oakley and Ava's second-born son, and Tinsley, Braden and Sierra's daughter, with a handful of water balloons.

"You stand no chance against us!" Cooper yells and launches

one at the tiny legs of Tinsley. She squeals when it explodes and the cold water soaks the bottom of her poofy pink dress.

Cooper's floppy brown hair hangs in his face, brushing his eyes. His grin is a testament to how happy he is, and I find myself smiling too. He's so similar to his father in the way his feelings are so boldly shown. They don't fear their emotions. Not the same way I do.

Tinsley's giggle is pure child happiness as she jumps on her mom's lap and holds on to her for dear life. "No more!" she yells.

"That's cheating," Maddox grunts.

The oldest of the Hutton children is already near his mother's height and has a scowl that could intimidate a grown man. Hell, I know it's already intimidated me. His eyes are the same piercing shade of green that both his parents have, and his hair is a soft brown that's cropped close to his scalp.

He's only ten and already screams mischief and trouble. I hope his parents are prepared for the hell he's going to bring when he gets older.

Not long after Tinsley cuddles up on Sierra's lap do the other kids turn to leave, clearly not bothered too much by the five-year-old's decision to sit out the rest of the game. The only kid that stays is Noah. He lingers beside Sierra's chair with his arms folded and an adorable scowl on his face as he faces the rest of us. He's taken up the position of Tinsley's bodyguard, it seems.

"You know, I've dyed my hair so many times over the past few years, but I've never tried red," Gracie hums from the chair on my right. I can tell she wants to reach over from her pool chair and touch my hair but decides against it, choosing to touch her own instead.

"Red is overrated," I reply.

"It's so beautiful, though. Unique too," Ava adds.

There's a vibrance to her green eyes that is either from the number of fruity, alcoholic drinks she's had today or just from pure enjoyment of our conversation. It's probably the first option.

"Sure. It's great until you spend most of your school years being asked if every freckle on your face represents a soul you've taken. It didn't help being named after a shade of red either." The two girls stare at me, looking equal parts surprised and intrigued. I suck air through my teeth. "Sorry. A bit bitter, I guess."

"Don't apologize. You know, I actually remember that stereotype from when I was in school," Ava says.

Gracie frowns. "If I hear Oliver saying anything like that to one of his classmates, I'm going to kick his ass."

Ava makes a noise of agreement. "Same with my kids. Maddox's best friend's sister has red hair a bit darker than yours, Scarlett, so I hope he knows better. I'm sure if Braxton heard him making fun of her sister, she would kick his ass for me, though."

"Doxxy and Braxy sitting in a tree!" Tinsley starts to sing before Maddox shouts over at us.

"Don't, Tiny!"

Gracie giggles. "His cheeks are so red."

"Young love," Ava says on an exhale.

"Just wait until it's your Adalyn blushing over the thought of a boy," Sierra teases, running her fingers through her daughter's hair.

Oakley's scoff is loud and comes from the direction of the inside of the yacht. He's making quick work of the distance between himself and Ava, a bottle of beer in his hand and a scowl spread wide on his face.

"Not happening until long after I'm dead," he says.

Tyler and Braden follow after him, but I don't see Adam.

Instead, I feel his presence slide up behind me seconds before two large hands cover my shoulders and squeeze. I lean back into his touch.

His lips brush my ear when he bends over and presses his jaw to the side of my head. "Give me your hand."

Confused, I reach behind me and give him my hand. I gasp when something cold meets my palm. Pulling back my hand, I stare at the dewy water bottle.

"Figured you might be thirsty," he whispers before leaning back, his lips grazing my hair along the way.

My stomach is a mess of flapping wings. "Thank you."

Another shoulder squeeze, and then he's no longer hovering over me. A frown threatens to form.

"What are we talking about?" Braden asks a beat later, distracting me.

I focus my stare across the deck and see him bypassing Noah and scooping both his wife and daughter up in his arms before sitting in Sierra's chair and putting them both on his lap. Sierra leans her head on his chest and smiles.

Oakley flops down on the lounge chair on Ava's other side. "The unspeakable," he grumbles.

"You know, big bro, I think your son gets his grumpy attitude from his old man of a father," Gracie pokes.

"And where do you think I got my grumpy attitude from? Oh, that's right, I spent too much time with your husband," he replies coolly.

Tyler chuckles, and I watch the interaction with a weird appreciation. This group has an interesting dynamic, but it's almost comforting in a way. I didn't expect this casual, playful attitude from either Tyler or Oakley. Not after watching them on the ice for so many years being the exact opposite.

It almost makes sense, though. Adam could never be around people who didn't at least shine half as bright as he does.

It makes me wonder why he's so adamant about spending time with me.

My muscles grow taut when Adam sits down on the end of my lounge chair, between my feet. He keeps his attention on the conversation happening around us but slowly places one hand flat on the cloth material of the chair and the other on my shin. His fingers splay across my skin before slipping to the underside of my leg and cupping my calf.

I inhale sharply when he lifts my leg and sets my foot in his lap before starting to dig his fingers into the taut muscles of my calf. A quiet moan slips from my mouth when he digs deep and kneads a particularly sore spot. The sound has his head whipping in my direction. His eyes are fire when they meet mine.

I'm aware of the conversations happening around us, but it's all static.

His throat stretches with a swallow before he's scratching at his jaw and running a hand over his hair. He's becoming fidgety, and all I want is for his hand to move up my leg and settle between my legs, on the wet fabric that never had the chance to fully dry from our time in the bathroom before becoming soaked again.

"Dad, you brought extra clothes, right?" Cooper asks.

I nearly jump out of my skin when he appears beside my chair, looking bored. If he cares at all about his father touching me, albeit just my lower leg, he doesn't show it.

Adam seems to care a lot more because he casually sets my leg back on the chair and removes his hand, placing it in his lap.

"Yeah, bud. I have a bag in the living room on the second level. I can show you," he says quickly.

I can't ignore the pang of disappointment that's bloomed in my stomach as I watch him get up and start to lead Cooper off the deck and inside the sitting room.

Once they've disappeared, I force myself back into the conversations going on around me. The guys appear to be in a heated discussion about who they think is going to win the cup this year, and regardless of the Vancouver defenseman sitting with them, Oakley and Braden show interest in Minnesota, the team the Warriors will be up against in the final round of the playoffs.

"I'm not saying the VW will lose. I'm just saying they're up against a harder team than they've faced so far in these playoffs, and without a consistent, reliable goaltender. I'm a Warrior until I die, but I'm not going to lie and say they're the best team in the league right now," Oakley says.

"You guys have already proved the shit-talkers wrong, Ty. You've made it to the final round with a backup tendy at best and a lacking defensive core. Without you, we all know there would be no VW in the finals," Braden adds. He's sporting a supportive smile, but it bounces right off Tyler's frown.

He looks at Oakley and says, "Minnesota has a history of choking against us. You know that better than anyone."

"The last time Oakley and the Warriors went up against Minnesota in the playoffs, they didn't have Orlo on their team. They went up against an aging defense well past their prime and a goalie right out of the draft."

I don't realize I've spoken until after the words hit the air. Everyone goes silent as my spine steels.

Braden blows out a low whistle and settles in his chair, tightening his arms around his girls.

Tyler turns to me, his eyes narrowed. He doesn't look angry but curious. Like he's not sure what to make of what I've said.

"Orlo might be a great player, but he's not the entire team, and the team is lacking this season," he states.

I cock my head. "They're also not playing with a backup-level goalie who's pushing through an undisclosed groin injury."

Tyler blanches. "Where did you hear that?"

"Nowhere. It's just obvious." I shrug.

"Our goalie is fine," he lies swiftly.

"Lie to me if you want, but it won't change the fact you can't afford to be cocky."

"She's right," Oakley says. His posture is stiff. "You've made it this far to win—don't let your superficial view of the opposing team cloud your judgment."

Tyler swallows that advice like you would a big pill with no water. He nods once, and the conversation dies. I almost feel guilty for butting in, but when Oakley shoots me a smile, I let it go.

"I think I just fell in love with you, Scarlett," Gracie says quietly, leaning over the arm of her chair.

A laugh swells in my chest before exploding out of my mouth. And when the other girls join me, I don't bother trying to stop.

20

Adam

I wake up the morning after Gracie's party and flinch at the pain in my throat. It's swollen and raw, and my nose is stuffed. I lift a hand to my chest just to make sure there isn't a giant's foot pressing down on me and shudder a breath before coughing.

"Fuck," I whisper, dropping my hand back to the bed.

The sun streams in from the slit in the middle of my curtains, and I wince when a headache springs to life in the centre of my forehead. I squeeze my eyes shut and call out, "Cooper!"

I'm not even sure if he's still home. I don't have the strength to try to find my phone and check what time it is, so I'm pretty screwed if he's already off at school.

Shit. Work.

"Cooper!" I shout again and feel a jolt of relief when I hear a set of rushed footsteps slapping the floor in the direction of my room.

A moment later, my bedroom door is pushed open slightly, and Cooper's head peeks through the crack. His eyes go wide when he sees me sprawled across the bed, dripping sweat and coughing up a lung.

"Are you dying?" he asks, walking toward me.

"Feels like it. But no. Don't think so."

"You look like you are. Should I call Mom?"

I shake my head. "No. But you can grab my phone for me, please. What time is it?"

"Almost eight. I was about to leave for school."

Double shit. Eight means I'm missing Scarlett's therapy session. My stomach sinks.

He rustles around in my nightstand before placing my phone in the hand I've flopped over on the sheets. The screen is way too bright when I lift it over my head and attempt to find her name in my call history.

"Let me help," Cooper says before taking the phone again. "Who do you want me to call?"

God, he's such a young man already. Pride hits me like a freight train as I smile at him like a loopy idiot.

His eyebrows pinch when he notices me watching him. "Stop looking at me like that. It's scaring me."

I want to laugh but think better of it. Instead, I croak, "Call Scarlett. Tell her I didn't mean to just not show up and that I'm sorry. Then call Banks and tell him he needs to go to WIT ASAP."

Brielle would have taken my absence as a sign to get the arena open and ready on her own, but there's too much that needs to get done for her to do on her own until this afternoon when Banks is supposed to get there.

I watch through watering eyes as Cooper steps out of the room and disappears from view. A raspy breath escapes me before I throw my arm over my eyes and sniffle. This is a nightmare. It's been years since I've gotten sick, and even then, I don't remember it ever hitting me this hard.

It's probably from being around so many kids yesterday. Kids are infection-spreading little buggers.

My curiosity sparks, and I begin to wonder how Scarlett is doing. Is she sick too? If she is, who's taking care of her? I would love to think Amelia is, but something tells me that Scar might fight against that idea.

I must drift off to my thoughts because I wake a few minutes later to Cooper holding a tiny plastic cup of cough syrup to my mouth and urging me to drink it. I do, and after taking a couple of pills out of his hand and taking them too, I drop my head back to my pillow and fall asleep again.

Scarlett

I DOUBLE-CHECK the address Cooper sent me and swallow past the nerves in my throat. The house in front of me is everything I thought it would be.

Tall peaks, large windows, and grass as green as it is in commercials. There's life spilling from every chip in the sidewalk and a ball-sized dent in the garage door. The porch is small but in perfect condition. Actually, the entire house is in perfect condition. It's well cared for, well-maintained.

A hockey net is tucked beside the back gate, between his house and the fence that separates Adam's yard from his neighbours. There aren't any flowers or shrubs, but there's no need for them. The house is warm and welcoming as it is.

The deep-blue-coloured front door opens, and Cooper waves at me anxiously. I lock the doors of Mom's car before tucking the keys away and jogging up the sidewalk.

"Hi, SP," he says, grabbing my hand and guiding me inside. "Dad's in his room. I gave him the medicine you told me to, and he fell right asleep."

"Good." I nod before pausing, looking at him curiously. "SP?"

"Yeah, it's short for Scary Spice."

"Wouldn't it be SS, then?"

He cocks his head. "I guess. But it doesn't sound as cool. SP sounds more badass."

"Are you allowed to say badass?"

He looks up at me curiously, and I stare back, a bit uncomfortable being alone with him. Not because he's not a nice kid, but because I have no idea how to act around him. My experience with children is almost non-existent.

"I have a question," he blurts out.

I swallow. "Okay."

"Do you not like kids?"

I fumble with a response. "Uh . . ."

There's a determination in his gaze that reminds me of his father. "Because I'm not a kid. I'm twelve."

"I thought you were no longer a kid when you turned thirteen."

"Well, I guess. But I'm mature for my age."

I nod. "Right."

"So, do you like my dad?"

"You like taking people by surprise." I laugh tightly. What am I supposed to say to that?

"I want you to like my dad because he likes you."

My cheeks get hot. I look everywhere but at the kid watching me. "He might like me, but you don't even know me. Why do you want me to like your dad so much?"

He lifts a hand to his chin and contemplates that for a few beats before smiling proudly. "My dad hasn't had a girlfriend since before I was born, and I think it would make him happy. Plus, you're cool. Dad showed me some of your hockey games on YouTube, and you were pretty good. Is it true you won a gold medal at the Olympics, or did he lie to make you seem cooler?"

Okay, there's a lot to unpack there. "First, he's *never* had a girlfriend? How is that possible? And yes, I did."

Cooper's eyes light up with victory, and I mentally curse myself for showing my cards. "He tells me he's been too busy, but I think he just hasn't found someone he likes enough. That's why I think you should date him."

"And what do you know about dating?"

He balks. "Gross stuff. Like kissing and holding hands."

I can't help but smile at the way he curls his nose in disgust. "That's it?"

"I'm only twelve, Scary Spice."

"Okay, we have to stop with that nickname," I huff.

He grins. "Too late. We love it."

"You might love it, but I do not."

"Maybe you'll grow to love it like you will my dad."

My breath hitches. My answer comes out on a shaky exhale. "Maybe."

"Maybe almost always means yes," he states, throwing a celebratory arm up in the air.

Suddenly, my skin prickles with awareness. His presence is heavy and grabs my attention as effectively as if he had said my name. I turn my body toward the hallway and gasp.

"Maybe means maybe, Coop," Adam says, his voice scratchy.

He leans against the wall, his arms hung at his sides. I swallow hard, and my eyes trail the length of his body of their own accord. His chest is bare, leaving all of the sweat-slicked, tight muscles completely exposed. My gaze snags on the trail of dark hair leading from between his top two abdominal muscles, down the other five rows, and below the elastic band of the briefs and tight pajama pants hugging his hips and thighs.

My mouth dries up when I flick my eyes lower and find a more than impressive-sized bulge between his legs. I'm pretty sure it's getting bigger the longer I stare at it—

"Scarlett."

I sputter a cough and look up, finding two dark brown eyes burning into me. His nose and cheeks are red. "You should be in bed," I mumble.

"Take me to bed, then." He says it like a dare. Like he doesn't think I will.

Clearly, he has no idea just how bad I want to do exactly that.

"Please help him," Cooper pleads, touching my arm. "I have to go to school before I miss too much."

I cautiously place my hand over his and say, "Yeah, I'll help."

His smile warms my chest. "Thank you." Turning to his dad, he grimaces. "Stay in your room. I'll see you after school."

"Yes, Doctor," Adam croaks.

Cooper heads for a room with a closed door before slipping inside and disappearing. A second later, another door slams shut.

"I didn't know he was going to ask you to come here," Adam says when silence envelops the house. His eyes are drifting shut when he presses his head to the wall.

I move quickly toward him, scared he'll pass out right there and I'll have to drag him to bed. "I figured. Come on, you shouldn't be out of bed."

He opens one eye to look at me when I reach his side and grab his forearm. Despite being sick and sweaty, he still smells good. A realization that makes my mind wander to a place it really shouldn't right now.

I heave his arm over my right shoulder and brace myself when he leans some of his weight on me. "You'll have to tell me where to go."

"Down the hallway, last door on the left," he whispers.

Nodding, I take slow steps down the hall, making sure not to jostle him around too much without knowing the state of his stomach.

There are multiple picture frames and awards hung on the wall. Cooper's school pictures fill most of the frames, but there are a couple with familiar faces. We pass one of Cooper and Adam from what looks like years ago. Adam has a small Cooper on his shoulders, and there are large smiles on both their faces. Cooper's tiny arms are in his dad's hair, pulling it up like he's using it as reins.

My heart swells.

"You're a good dad," I say.

His gaze penetrates my cheeks. "You think so?"

Risking a glance at him, I gasp when our faces are closer than I expected. His breath tickles my nose. The memory of our kiss has me looking at his mouth.

"Yeah, Adam. You're pretty great." I don't know if I'm talking about his parenting or something else.

His fingers caress my shoulder, making me shiver. "You're so beautiful. I don't ever want to stop looking at you," he whispers.

His words do something to me. They stroke a part of me that before Adam had been hidden for as long as I can remember. The same place he nearly touched when he kissed me in the bathroom yesterday, God, everything changed on that damn yacht.

"Then don't stop looking at me."

His lips twitch. "Okay. I won't."

"Come on. We need to get you back in bed, sicky."

As if reminded that he's sick, he nods, swaying slightly.

Once we're in his room, I pat along the wall for a light switch. As soon as I find it, Adam's words stop me from flipping it.

"Leave the lights off. My head kills."

"Okay."

I let him try to pull us through the dark room while I look around, taking in as much of his space as I can.

A large window sits across from the door and above a large dresser. Adam's king-sized bed is on the far side of the room, fit with two nightstands on either side. My toes sink into a plush rug at the end of the bed when he stops us.

Curious, I find his face in the dark. The light that peeks out from the bottom of the curtains highlights his jaw and the scruffy hair that covers it. My fingers tingle with the urge to reach up and see how it would feel against my palm.

"In bed," I order, attempting to give him a small nudge.

His eyes don't waver from mine. They're full of something that turns my insides to mush. "Will you join me?"

I suck in a breath. "In your bed?"

A nod. "I won't be able to sleep knowing you're in my home and not beside me. Keep me company. Please."

His arm falls from my shoulders, and his hand grabs mine. Our fingers tangle together, and I lose the battle I knew was impossible for me to win.

"Okay. Let's get in bed."

21

Adam

I GET IN BED AND PULL THE BLANKET I DISCARDED EARLIER UP TO MY waist. The corner of the room is too dark to see the expression on Scarlett's face, but by the lack of movement on the opposite side of the room, it's easy to tell she's nervous.

"Want a pillow wall?" I offer, patting the empty space beside me.

"I don't need a pillow wall," she says defensively.

"Then come here. I want to feel you beside me."

My throat is so far beyond sore there's no point in keeping my mouth shut now. Especially not when I'm about to have her here, in my bed.

"I mean that in a non-creepy way, I swear."

It was an impulsive decision to ask her to join me in my personal space—something I haven't done in over a decade—but I couldn't help myself. Cooper might have gone around me to invite her here with hopes of trapping us, but this might be the one time where I appreciate his sneaky ways. He handed me a chance here to spend some time with her.

Alone.

There's no way I'm going to give that up. Just having her in my house, talking to my son like she's known him for far longer than a few weeks, had my heart rattling in my chest like it wanted to burst free and go to her.

"Stop talking," she grumbles.

The sheets rustle beside me before the bed dips and she crawls in beside me. Her perfume invades my senses, doing more to help this stupid cold than any medication has.

My eyes are heavy as I turn on my side to face her and fold the pillow under my cheek. I can hear her breathing, and with a bravery that I don't expect, I reach out to touch her arm. Following the length of it, I close my hand over hers.

Her fingers are slim and smooth and fit between mine like they were made to do so. I bring our hands to my lips and graze them over her knuckles.

"Thank you for coming," I say softly.

Scarlett turns her head in my direction. Her breath fans my face. "I was already planning to come by after work once I got your address from Brie. You didn't show up this morning, and I was . . ." She trails off.

"Worried?"

Her swallow is audible. "Yeah. I was worried. You've never missed a day before, and you don't seem like the type not to message ahead of time if you were going to."

"No, I'm not that type of guy," I agree. The way she seems frustrated with her worry for me has me asking, "Does it bother you that you were worried about me?"

"I shouldn't worry about you," she says.

"I shouldn't worry about you either. But I do, and I don't want to stop."

Scarlett doesn't say anything. Instead, she inches closer to me and squeezes my hand. The extra contact does wonders to distract me from the pulse between my brows and the pressure in my nose, but it's still not enough.

I roll to my back and release her hand, pulling my arm up and resting it on her pillow, just above her head instead.

"Come here." It's both a plea and a demand.

My heartbeat skyrockets when she moves close and curls into my side. Her cheek presses to my chest, and her arm moves slowly, carefully across my abdomen.

"Tell me something, Scarlett. Something I don't know about you," I murmur.

Her words are the last thing I hear before the darkness closes in.

"I didn't think I would ever be able to replace what I lost, but because of you, I think I have."

MY EYELIDS FLUTTER open when a soft touch brushes my hair back. A cold cloth is set on my forehead, and I moan at how good it feels against my hot skin.

"Lean up for me, Adam."

I push up enough to swallow two pills and drink some water before falling back to the mattress. "Scar," I mumble, despite the burst of pain in my throat.

She shushes me. "Go back to sleep."

"Don't go. Stay here."

I feel her lips touch my cheek. "I'm not going anywhere. You've won. I'm here."

Her words confuse me, but I only nod, content with her confirmation at the moment.

"Okay. Good night, baby," I murmur before falling back asleep.

22

Adam

"Ten more seconds!" I shout over the loud clap of the weighted ropes hitting the floor. Over and over, Scarlett throws them in the air before bringing them back down again.

Her shoulder is doing phenomenally well. It won't ever be back to what it is, but after the past eight weeks of physiotherapy, I think she's almost as good as she'll ever be again.

The ropes she's lifting aren't the weight she's used to—far from it, really—but I think she's just happy to be doing something different today. Something that is a testament to how hard she's worked to heal and how far she's come.

Sweat drips from her face and is soaked through her tank top, leaving a wet patch beneath the neckline. There's almost a hint of a smile on her face that has me beaming with pride.

"Good! Drop 'em."

They fall to the floor. She tosses her head back and takes long inhales. "How did I do?"

"Perfectly, Scar. You were perfect. You've come so far since we started."

She smiles, pushing the matted pieces of hair off her forehead that have escaped her bun. "I had help."

"No, that was all you. I just stood here and barked orders."

"Just take the compliment, Adam. I don't give them away often."

There's a twinkle in her eyes that hits me deep. "If you insist. *Thank you.*"

She nods, then starts to chew on her lip, looking lost in thought. It's only a moment later when she blurts, "I want to go on the ice."

"Okay. I can unlock it for you."

"No. I mean with you. I want to . . . I don't know. Maybe we could shoot a couple pucks around or something. I really fucking miss it, Adam. I want to do more than just stand there and watch. I want to grip a stick in my hand and line up a shot before I forget what it feels like," she rambles, fidgeting with the hem of her shirt. "I'm ready."

Fuck. Watching her overcome a hurdle that's burdened her since her injury might just be the most beautiful thing I've ever seen. I want to storm across the room and kiss the rest of her doubt away.

"You will never forget that feeling because I won't let you. Hell, you won't let yourself, and this only proves that. If you want to play a one v. one game out there, we'll play a one v. one. If you want me to stand in front of the net and pretend I have any goalie talent whatsoever, I can do that for you too. Anything, Scarlett. I can get Brie to open the arena, and we can stay on the ice all day if you want."

She blinks rapidly. "You're serious?"

"Of course I am. Get your skates, and I'll meet you there."

"Great, yeah. I'll be quick."

My mouth quirks as I take backward steps to the door, watching her grow more flustered the longer we look at each other. Once I'm in the doorway, I wink. "See you soon."

I'M BENDING the blade of my stick over my thigh when the rink doors slam shut. I whip my head around to see Scarlett walking toward the opening in the boards, her custom black-and-yellow skates on and a stick fairly similar to mine in her hand.

"Is yellow your favourite colour?" I ask, staring curiously at the yellow tape wrapped around the top section of her stick.

She simply stares at me, unimpressed. "Were you expecting it to be black?"

"I mean, now that you mention it." I smirk.

"You're hilarious," she deadpans.

She sets the blade of her stick to the ice and leans to the side. Her eyes flick to the fresh tape on my stick. "Is red your favourite colour, then?"

"It is as of late."

"Why?" She narrows her eyes, almost as if my answer offended her.

A smile parts my lips. "Isn't it obvious?"

She shakes her head.

"Because, Scarlett. It reminds me of you."

"Oh," she mumbles, her chest flaring with the pinky-red colour I love.

I skate toward her, not stopping until our skates touch. Her blue eyes are wide as they stare into mine, both surprised and intrigued. I lift a hand and twirl a loose curl around my finger. It's as smooth as silk and just as springy as I remember.

"You turn the perfect combination of red and pink whenever I touch you. It does things to me," I admit. As if to prove my point, the tips of her ears flush. "Where else are you pink, Scarlett?"

Her breathing stutters, and she leans toward me. My stare drops to her lips while my hand moves to cup her cheek. I brush my thumb across her cheekbone.

"I want to kiss you again. But I won't."

"Why not?"

I bend my head and bump her nose with mine. "Because when I do, I'm not going to stop. And you're not ready for that."

With that, I pull back and slowly skate a safe distance away from her. She doesn't move from the place she stands, and I use the break to pull myself back together.

I told her I was patient, and I'm willing to be. But that doesn't mean it isn't killing me not to have her already. I've long since accepted that the way I feel about her isn't going anywhere. On the contrary, it's only getting stronger every day. There's no point in fighting it anymore.

I'm hers for the taking. All I can do now is hope that she doesn't leave me out to dry.

It's a risk bringing her into my life, but what Gracie said to me on the phone really stuck. I've put my personal life on the back burner for ten years now. Cooper is not only my son but my biggest cheerleader, and if he's okay with this and the risk it brings, then I should at least try to be too.

He's already begun to grow a bond with her through his own meddling, and knowing he likes her and wants her to reciprocate those feelings for me is a bit of comfort in this wild unknown.

"I'm going to dinner after tonight's playoff game with Leo," Scarlett says from behind me. My shoulders tense as a prickly feeling comes to life in my stomach. *Jealousy?* "If I get more pucks in the net than you do, from let's say, the blue line, would you come with me?"

I spin around and find her in the exact same position as earlier. "And if you don't beat me?"

Her grin is wicked. "I will," she states. The two simple words go straight to my cock as it hardens in my briefs.

"After you, then, Big Baller. Best of what? Fifteen?"

"Works for me."

Scarlett skates around me and grabs the bucket of pucks we usually keep off to the side of the ice by the handle before bringing it over. Dropping the bucket in front of me, she kicks it over and begins to separate them into two piles with her stick.

Once there are two piles of fifteen pucks, I take a few glides back, making room for her to line herself up. She pulls a puck from the pile and moves it back and forth across the ice a few times before stilling it.

I watch, nearly in awe, as she wraps her fingers around her stick and, in one swift movement, pulls it back and swings it forward, slapping it against the puck.

She sends it flying, and a second later, it sinks into the centre of the netting. A huff escapes her.

"That's not where I was aiming."

I turn to her in disbelief. "Dead centre isn't good enough?"

"No," she says before collecting another puck and taking another shot, this time swapping her slapshot for a wrist shot.

Again, her form is perfection. She snaps the shot, and the puck hits the top left corner of the netting.

"Better," she notes.

"I didn't think you could get any sexier, but I was wrong. Very, very wrong."

She peeks at me over her shoulder, brows raised. "Are you a puck bunny, Adam?"

I grin. "When it comes to you, I think I could be just about anything. But Adam the Puck Bunny does have a nice ring to it, don't you think?"

"Sure." She takes another shot and sinks her fourth puck. "Maybe I'll make you a custom cup with your new nickname on it to replace the one you made for me."

"You found it?" I had that cup made weeks ago. It's about time. "Is it still in one piece?"

She shoots two more pucks into the net. "I debated throwing it into traffic, but the road to get here isn't busy enough. I would have been standing in the ditch for hours."

A brash laugh escapes me, echoing off the walls. Scarlett gifts me another one of those rare, wide grins, and it pierces my chest.

She looks ahead of her again before lining up and sending off the remaining pucks. All but one makes it inside, and even though I knew I wouldn't win when I agreed to this bet, the alpha inside of me is a bit grouchy knowing he's going to lose.

"Ready?" she asks me, a hint of something mischievous in her tone.

I skate up beside her and lean in, kissing her cheek. "I think so." Gripping my stick, I turn to the side and grab a puck. "What time is dinner? I have to see who can watch Coop for me, even though he'll probably ask to go home with Maddox after school anyway."

"Eight," she says. I nod while winding up my first shot and slapping the puck at the net. When it pings off the top bar and scatters off the boards, Scarlett snorts. "Cooper and Maddox seem pretty close."

"They're the closest in age. If we're going to get into specifics, the entire group is very close, but the Hutton clan are the closest thing to family we have. We spent a lot of time with them when Cooper was really young."

Two more shots. Two goals.

I can feel her curiosity from where she stands behind me.

"You're not close with your parents?" she asks.

My next shot is harder than the others and completely misses the net. "No. We're very different people."

"They're grumpy? Rude? Glass half-empty types?"

I turn to her and release a breath. She's staring at me like she wants me to cut myself open and bleed every single one of my secrets out on the ice for her. Little does she know all she'd have to do is hand me a knife.

"All of the above with a sprinkle of unsupportive and a dash of stuck-up."

She winces. "Yeah, that would do it."

"They're not a part of my life anymore. Cooper deserves better."

"So do you," she says, her voice so soft I barely hear it. I hold myself back from closing the distance between us and pulling her in my arms. "Some people don't deserve the time of day, and from what you've told me, it sounds like they're those people. The sun's too bright to be cast out by gloomy storm clouds."

My heart thumps against my rib cage. "Are you calling me the sun, Scarlett?"

She rolls her eyes, but the action does little to hide the warmth in them.

"Yeah, Adam. You're the damn sun."

23

Scarlett

Leo is already waiting at a booth in the back corner of the pub when I arrive.

The Minnesota Woodmen just won game two in the final round of the playoffs, evening the score to one for both teams. The mood in the pub is a mix between frustration, anger, and a small flutter of happiness from the few MW fans.

Having the home team lose at their own arena in their city sucks. This was their chance to come up with two before heading to Minnesota, but instead, they gave their advantage away.

Even though I'm a VW girl at heart, I can't pretend like I didn't scream a bit too loud when Leo scored the final goal and sealed the win for the Woodmen.

"Letty!" Leo calls from the booth. He's standing now, waving his hand in the air as if the pub is too crowded for me to see him.

I sidestep a guy in a Bateman jersey with green paint all over his face when he falls off his stool and mumbles drunken words that I don't understand.

He's going to feel that in the morning. Along with a mountain of hockey-induced frustration.

Leo's grin is cheek-splitting when I reach the booth. "Look at you. You're glowing." His arms are wrapped around me in seconds, squeezing me in a bear hug.

I roll my eyes and hug him back. "It's sweat from how hot it is in here."

He places a kiss to the side of my head. "I actually found it quite cold."

"That's because you're a Woodman in a Warriors bar. I was expecting to find you pinned to the wall and being used as a dartboard."

Leo pulls back, laughing that same belly-warming laugh that always seemed to free me from a losing-game funk. His soft brown eyes twinkle under the hanging lights above us.

He hasn't changed much since the last time I saw him—maybe just a bit bulkier, considering the training regimen he has to follow. His hair is still that light blond colour that reminds me of wheat fields, and his dimples are still deep in his cheeks when he smiles.

"It's safer for me here than at a bar celebrating the Woodmen win. At least here, everyone hates me too much to come ask for an autograph."

I snort a laugh. "Good point."

We both sit down, me on the bench opposite him. There are already waters on the table and a giant plate of nachos in the middle.

"I see you eyeing them up, and yes, they're for the both of us," he says. A smirk pulls at his mouth. "And Adam, of course."

My skin heats. "Don't start."

"Start what? Poking you for information about your boss? I would never."

I grab a bunch of loaded tortilla chips and shove them in my mouth. Chewing slowly, I watch Leo lean forward, looking like he's getting ready to dig into a conversation I know will make me uncomfortable.

"I'm a bit offended that you haven't mentioned Adam in any of our phone calls or texts since you started working at

WIT. Then all of a sudden, I get a text asking if it's okay that he comes to dinner? You threw me for a loop, Letty, and now you don't want me to bug you about it? Nu-uh. Don't think so."

I swallow the nachos and take a drink of water before slowly setting the glass back down and meeting Leo's stare. Despite his words, he doesn't look upset. Just curious.

"Why don't we start with catching up? Not talking about Adam."

"Sure." He shrugs. "Well, I've been playing hockey, working out, and sleeping. What have you been doing other than trying not to bang your stupid-hot boss and coaching a sixteen-year-old prodigy?"

"Okay. Point taken," I grumble.

I've never been annoyed with how often Leo and I talk, but right now, I'm far beyond it.

He frowns. "Actually, tell me about your mom. Now that I think about it, you've been a bit sticky with me about that topic."

Ice spreads through my chest. "She's getting worse."

"Shit, love. How much worse?"

"I've been looking at in-home caretakers for when I'm at work or doing anything, really. She's been forgetting more and more. Two days ago, our neighbour found her standing on the curb wearing her nightgown and yelling at one of the teenagers in the house across the street, accusing him of sleeping around on her daughter."

It was mortifying having to get home from work and apologize to everyone in the neighbourhood for the disruption, especially the teenager at the forefront of her wrath. He did look a lot like my high school boyfriend, Bradley, so I can see how she put two and two together to equal five.

It makes it worse that she doesn't remember doing it. There's nothing I can say or do to help her. She can't just get better. This will never go away.

"It's exhausting. And I feel guilty for having this . . . anger and frustration in my heart. It's not like I'm the one suffering with the disease. What do I really have to complain about?"

Emotion burns behind my eyes when Leo reaches across the table and covers my hand with his. I tip my head back and blink to try and clear the film from my vision.

"You're allowed to feel exactly how you are right now. Yes, it's not you with the disease, but you're suffering also. You're watching your mother lose herself, knowing there isn't anything you can do to stop it. Never feel like you can't hurt too. You're human, Scarlett, and humans feel. It's our greatest gift and our worst punishment," he murmurs.

"Fuck," I whisper. A tear escapes before I quickly swipe it away. "You should have been a therapist."

He squeezes my hand. "Nah. You're one of the few people I care about enough to talk like this with. My sensitive side is very picky about who it shows itself to."

"Maybe that's why we get along so well."

"You're probably ri—shit," he curses, something to the left of me catching his attention. Surprise flares in his eyes before he squeezes my hand once more and looks at me, releasing my hand. "Letty, your man is on his way over here, and from the venom in the glare he's shooting me, I'm guessing he noticed your tears."

"What?" I whip my head to the side and gasp at what I see.

My mouth goes dry—sand in the desert dry. Adam's scowl does little to distract me from the rippling of his biceps beneath the sleeves of his black T-shirt or the bulging veins in his forearms as he jams his hands in the pockets of his blue jeans and clenches them.

Like that time in the grocery store, he's wearing a hat on backward. Pieces of curly brown hair peek out beneath it and curl behind his ears and at the base of his neck. My fingers twitch, wanting nothing more than to push his hat off and run through his hair.

By the time I grab hold of myself, he's already standing at the table, towering over us. His eyes are no longer two angry pits of dark brown; they're steaming cups of hot chocolate.

"What's wrong?" he asks, voice tight with concern. My tongue lies limp in my mouth when he lifts my chin with his finger and presses it with his thumb. "You're crying."

"Hello to you too, Adam," Leo sings.

Adam spins on him with wild eyes. "You do this?"

I reach out and press my palm to the rigid muscles of his jaw. Adam stills. "I wouldn't have been sitting here if he had. I'm okay."

He turns to me again, blinking. "Why were you crying?"

"Leo was letting me vent about what's going on with my mom. We hit a sore spot."

There's no point in hiding it, nor do I really want to. Adam won't judge me.

"Sweetheart," he breathes. His eyes are focused again as he watches me.

"Sweetheart?" Leo echoes.

This time, both Adam and I turn to him.

"You're going to get your ass beat," I say.

"Adam wouldn't do that to me. He wouldn't risk ruining all the work he did healing me all up after my injury."

"I wasn't talking about Adam."

"Yes, I would."

We speak at the same time.

Leo crosses his arms and grumbles, "Cute."

"Wanna scoot over, or should I pull up a chair?" Adam asks me.

I instantly move to make room for him. He sits beside me, his large body taking up most of the bench. Our thighs are pressed together, arms brushing. My body is one giant spark.

"So, Adam. Who are you cheering for to win the cup?" Leo asks after taking a sip of his water.

Adam settles his arm on the back of the booth. His fingertips brush my shoulder.

"If it were any other team up against you, I think I would cheer for the Woodmen. Can't betray my team, though."

"Fair enough. Letty is the same, no matter how many times I try to convert her."

Adam's eyes beat into my cheeks. "Doesn't surprise me. She's about as headstrong as they get."

"I'm right here," I mumble. The plate of nachos in front of us looks cold, but I pick them apart and slip a few into my mouth anyway.

"How long have you two known each other?" Adam asks.

Leo answers for me. "Since co-ed. We were, what? Twelve?"

I nod. "Yep. Couldn't get rid of him."

"So rude, Scarlett." Leo sighs dramatically.

An involuntary shiver works through me when Adam starts tracing patterns on my skin with his fingers. My stomach fills with flapping wings.

"How has it been working with my Letty?" Leo asks. I could smack him at the possessive claim. He's trying to spark a reaction from Adam, and from the slight tensing of his body against mine, it's worked.

"Scary Spice is the best trainer I have. She's phenomenal at everything she does. I have yet to work with anyone who has half the coaching potential she does."

The sincerity and awe in Adam's words pull my attention. Our eyes meet, and a breath is pushed from my lungs. I've always wondered what it felt like to be looked at the way he's looking at me right now.

Like I'm the only thing he sees.

"Thank you," I breathe.

He gives me a half smile. "It's the truth. Don't thank me for that."

"I don't know where to start: Scary Spice or whatever the hell kind of connection just happened between you two," Leo starts. He pokes the toe of his sneaker to my shin before standing up.

"You know what we need? Shots. I did just win a damn playoff game, after all. Be right back."

Leo takes off to the bar while I choke on a laugh. Adam grins and tucks a curl behind my ear. He leans close and says, "You look beautiful."

"You look good too."

His grin somehow grows. "You don't plan on eating cold nachos all night, right? Let me get you something else."

"Yeah, they're pretty bad. The waitress hasn't come around since I got here, though. Leo probably told her to leave us alone until we wanted to order something."

He looks around the pub, most likely for the missing waitress. "I'm surprised he wanted to go out in public tonight. The glares coming at our table are a bit harsh."

I catch one from an older guy wearing a Warriors practice jersey and smile dramatically at him. "Leo doesn't care about stuff like that. He wouldn't want to spend the night of a massive win stuck in his hotel room."

"I can respect that. Oakley and Tyler are the same way." Adam turns back to me, locking his eyes with mine. "What are you doing after this?"

I blink. "I was going to go home."

"Is there anyone watching your mom?" he asks gently. His concern makes my chest swell.

"Mrs. McConnell is spending the night because I didn't know how late I would be. She's a sweet lady. I feel bad asking her to watch my mom, though. It's one of the reasons I've been looking into getting the help of a professional."

He cups my shoulder and brings me closer to his side, staring out at the pub. "How has that been going? If you need any help, I'm here. You don't have to do this alone."

A small smile pulls at my mouth. "Thanks. It's been going okay. I'm meeting a few potential caretakers next week."

"You're a good daughter, Scar. Don't forget that."

My conversation with Leo flies to the front of my mind.

Everyone but me seems to think I'm doing the right thing and have a right to feel how I do. I just wish it was as easy to believe what they're saying as it is to think they're just trying to make me feel better.

"Who's watching Cooper tonight?" I switch the subject.

"At Oakley and Ava's. He's sleeping over." His words are deep rumbles.

"Oh."

A heavy weight seems to settle between us. It's almost like that by knowing neither one of us has a reason to go home early, a door has opened, leaving us contemplating shutting it or walking through.

"Yeah. I made sure my night was completely open," he says softly.

God, my pulse is racing. What am I supposed to say to that? Shit, some of the things he says completely strip me of all my defenses.

"Good news, guys!" Leo shouts. I snap my eyes to him when he bounds toward us with a tray of shot glasses. "We're going out tonight. I just got the details from my captain." He drops the tray on the table and picks a shot up before shooting it back. "Hope you're ready to celebrate pro-style."

I risk a glance at Adam to find him already looking at me with soft, warm eyes. His calm energy helps to stifle the anxiety pumping through me.

"Looks like we found our plans," he says.

24

Adam

I haven't been to a club since I was twenty-three. That was ten years ago, yet Sinner's is the exact same as I remember it.

The air is musty, rich with sweat and marijuana. My shoes stick to the cocktails on the floor, and bass-heavy music thumps from the speakers.

The only difference between now and then is that for the first time in my life, I'm tucked behind a thick red rope at the back of the club with a woman I'm helplessly falling for and a group of intoxicated hockey players who might just take home the cup.

Eight players of the Minnesota Woodmen are spread about the VIP section, expensive bottles of tequila and vodka in their hands and a plethora of women in their laps.

Leo is currently drinking straight from a bottle of Don Julio while Scarlett and I sit squished together on a leather couch, watching them with wide eyes.

The music isn't quite as loud in the back section, and for that, I'm extremely grateful. It wouldn't be possible to talk to Scarlett if it were too loud.

I lean toward her and say, "Leo's going to throw up."

"He has a surprisingly strong stomach."

"Nobody has a stomach that strong."

She snorts a laugh. "You're probably right. Tequila is a silent killer. How does the saying go? Tequila makes her clothes come off?"

I stretch my arm along the top of the couch behind her and grin. "Is that how you handle tequila, Scar? Do your clothes come off?"

"Maybe."

I swallow hard, sobering up with her honesty. My tongue shrivels up in my mouth at the thought of her stripping down for me. Suddenly, I have the mind of a horny teenager.

"Someone get this babe a tray of tequila shots, then!" one of the players from a few seats over shouts, seemingly overhearing our conversation.

His eyes are on Scarlett, a carnal spark in them that has me flushing with annoyance. The arm I had behind her falls directly to her shoulders.

"Not happening," I snap at him.

As soon as the guy gets up and staggers toward us, I recognize him from the scar along the right side of his face. Asher Clodelle is a third-line grinder with an attitude problem. He and Tyler have gotten into it twice already in this playoff series.

Scarlett sighs, annoyed by him, and I can't help but smile at that.

"If you're not into her, man, let me try to score."

Despite the revulsion sparking in my stomach, I keep my face cool, calm. "Say shit like that again and you won't have a dick to 'score' with afterward."

He looks taken aback, as if someone telling him off is a rare occurrence. The sad thing is it probably is. His hands fly up in front of him. "Shit, sorry. I didn't know you were together."

Scarlett subconsciously turns her body toward me. My heart jumps.

"Clearly," I mutter, cupping her shoulder, brushing her skin with my fingertips. She shivers against me. I lower my voice to a murmur only she can hear. "Come dance with me."

I never dance. Never have, never thought I would want to. Maybe it's the possessiveness I feel in my bones or the energy in the club, but all I want is to have her pressed against me, her body heat fusing with mine.

She turns and looks up at me. "I'm a terrible dancer."

"Me too. Let's be terrible together."

I smile, relieved when she nods. "Fine. But you can't laugh at me."

"You have my word."

I get off the couch and offer my hand for her to take. When she slides her fingers across my palm and links our fingers, I accept the sparks that break out beneath her touch like an old friend.

We head for the security guard standing watch at the entrance to the VIP section and wait as he unhooks the rope and lets us through.

As soon as we step onto the dance floor, I'm hit with a wall of nostalgia. The last time I was here, I was coaxing Beth away from Gracie and into an alleyway, where she told me I was a father. The next day, I was alone with Cooper, and Beth was admitted to a psychiatric hospital.

I don't realize I've stopped walking until I feel Scarlett tug on my hand before coming to stand in front of me. Her closeness has me wanting to pull myself from my thoughts, but I seem to be locked in them.

An onslaught of emotions crashes into me, threatening to knock me on my ass. It's not that I haven't accepted what happened and how it changed my life forever. But it's different being here, knowing this is the place where everything changed.

In a way, it was on this dance floor where my life really began. What happened turned me into the man I am today, and maybe I'm a bit naive or way too fucking hopeful, but there's a part of me that wonders if I've come full circle. If being here right now with Scarlett is what helps turns me into the man I'll be tomorrow.

"Adam?" she shouts above the noise.

I swallow the emotion in my throat and bring our linked hands to my chest, holding the back of hers to my pounding heart. There are too many things I want to say to her that I can't. Not yet and definitely not here.

Instead, I flash her a smile and bring her hand to my lips, kissing it. "Let's dance."

She stares at me for a few moments, not convinced, but relents with a mouthed *okay*.

We walk a bit further into the crowd before I lift our hands in the air and spin her around. She grins, releasing a giddy laugh that burrows itself in my memories.

I stare down at her with an open gaze, letting her feel every single thing I do. Taking her in my arms, I palm her waist and drag my thumbs over the hem of her shirt. It lifts, and our skin touches.

We're getting closer with each thump of the bass, until our bodies are pressed together. Her eyes flare with desire as we sway to the music, and the proof of how attracted I am to her digs into her lower stomach.

It's only the second time we've touched like this—if the yacht bathroom really counts—but I need it to not be the last. She feels perfect against me, like she was made to fit in my arms.

Her eyes drop to my mouth when I lean forward and rumble a warning "Careful."

An eyebrow twitches. "Careful?"

I press the rigid outline of my cock against her and hold her still when she tries to swirl her hips. Her breath hitches, forcing me to stare at her parted lips. They look as soft as I remember.

"I haven't touched a woman like this in a long time, Scarlett. Make sure this is what you want."

She doesn't hesitate. "Touch me, Adam."

I release a breath, slipping my hands beneath her shirt and holding her bare waist. "Not here, in the open like this."

Suddenly, nerves flash across her features. She stays silent.

"What's wrong?" I ask.

"Can we go outside?"

Worry has me nodding quickly and pulling her through the crowd and out the front doors. Once we hit a wall of fresh summer air, she relaxes a bit.

I lead us away from the club and to the side of a neighbouring building. We're still close enough to faintly hear the music but far enough there's nobody else around.

She stops in front of me, and I slip a hand through her hair, holding the back of her head, forcing her to meet my eyes.

"What's wrong?"

Her cheeks are pink, and I'm not sure if it's from the heat in the club or something else.

"It's so stupid."

"Nothing that upsets you is stupid to me."

"It's just been a . . . long time since I've been intimate with anyone. I don't want to do anything wrong," she admits, her voice timid.

I blink. "Are you a virgin? Because that's not something I would judge you—"

"No!" she rushes out. "Not that there's anything wrong with that. It's just not . . ."

I must look as confused as I feel because she blows out a harsh breath and shuts her eyes. "This isn't something we should talk about on a sidewalk in the middle of the night."

"Okay, then let me take you to my place. We can talk there."

She opens her eyes. "Are you sure?"

I brush my thumb across her cheekbone and nod. "Of course. Text Leo and let him know I have you so he doesn't worry while we hunt down my car."

"Okay," she agrees before I drop my hand to my side and shove both in my pockets.

While she texts Leo, I move to the side and will my body to calm down before my erection rips a hole in my jeans.

I FLIP the light switch on in the entryway and kick my shoes off, watching as Scarlett does the same. The air is tense between us, and even though she's been in my home before, it feels vastly different this time.

Easton comes bumbling in our direction, his ears flopping with each step. Scarlett drops to her haunches and starts to give him chin scratches.

"He's going to fall in love with you," I tease.

She looks up at me, smiling. "He's sweet."

"Cooper trained him. He did a pretty good job of it too."

"You hear that?" Scarlett asks the big pile of panting fluff. "Your dad says you're a good boy."

"Sometimes a good boy," I correct her before moving around the two of them and further into the house. Turning into the kitchen, I grab us each a bottle of water and untwist both the caps. The time above the stove says it's just before midnight.

Scarlett enters the kitchen a few moments after I do. "You didn't drink tonight," she notes.

I shrug. "You have more of an effect on me than any amount of alcohol would."

"When you say things like that, I want to be a different person. Someone who can say the same things back."

Her admission surprises me. I walk toward her and hold out one of the bottles. She takes it eagerly, bringing it to her mouth and drinking half of it in one go.

"I wasn't always like this, Scary Spice. And I don't need you to be anyone but who you are. Who you are is precisely why I say these things."

"If you weren't always like this, then what were you like? How does young Adam compare to you now?"

She spins around and leans back against the counter. Her

fingers are tight around her water bottle. I stand beside her, copying her stance.

"I was someone who didn't bother learning a woman's name before taking her to bed and drank bottles of my father's expensive wine just to piss him off. I was the guy crushing on his best friend and nearly ruining his entire relationship with her over it. I was half the man I am today."

She blows out a long breath. "I don't even know where to start with that. I mean, you were into Ava? Like Oakley's wife?"

I laugh, looking at my socks. "You pieced that together pretty quickly. But yeah, I liked her. Thinking back on it now, it definitely wasn't what I thought it was. She was, and will always be, my best friend. I was just a pissed-off teenager choosing to cling to someone who made me happy and reading all of the signals wrong."

She hums in understanding. "Why were you so angry? I'm guessing it has to do with why you busied yourself with drinking your father's booze."

"My parents weren't around much. I rebelled to get attention, but even that didn't work."

"I'm sorry," she says.

"Don't be. I've had thirty-two years to get over it." I take a drink from my bottle, desperate to soothe my dry throat. Talking about my parents never gets easier. Betrayal is a lot harder to get over when it's your family. "Were you a rebel growing up?"

"Right," she scoffs, crossing her arms. "I didn't even really date. It was all hockey, hockey, and more hockey. There was never time for boys or partying."

"Well, you weren't missing much. Boys don't know how to treat a woman. That's a man's job." I waggle my eyebrows.

"If that's the case, I guess I should head out and go find one."

I suck air through my teeth. "That was cold, Scar. Ice-cold."

"Ice-cold is my specialty. They called me the Ice Queen in Calgary for a reason."

"Calgary breeds assholes like they're scared they'll eventually run out. I hope you didn't take it seriously."

After having that brief interview with one of Scarlett's old teammates, Lilliana, and witnessing how she talked down to my woman, it's easy to imagine the environment back on that team. The thought of Scarlett being spoken to like that on a daily basis upsets me deeply.

"I didn't really care. I wasn't there to make friends."

I frown. "They should have been your friends, though. Teammates are supposed to be like family."

"I am what I am, and not everyone likes that. If I wanted to be all sunshiny like you, I would."

I spin to face her and cup her head in my hands. She stops breathing for a second before releasing a slow breath and blinking up at me with curious eyes.

"You don't feel cold, Scarlett. If I'm the sun, then you're my warmth."

25

Scarlett

HIS WORDS SEVER THE LAST OF MY SELF-CONTROL.

With my heart in my throat, I lean up and press my lips to his.

It's not a gentle kiss. It's greedy, an attack of pent-up frustration and a connection deeper than anything I've ever experienced. I inhale his groan and give him one of my own.

His hands slip through the curls at my nape and tilt my head to deepen the kiss. Flutters erupt everywhere. Under my skin, in my belly, between my legs.

When his tongue parts my lips and sneaks inside, I press my hands to his chest and curl my fingers in his shirt, desperate to gain some stability as lust and desire rock the world beneath my feet.

Our bodies couldn't be closer, yet that's exactly what I want. Suddenly, I drop my hands to the bottom of his shirt and slip them beneath it. I gasp when I feel the hard, hot skin of his abdomen. Curiosity gets the better of me as I start to explore Adam's body. Coarse hairs tickle my palms when I brush my fingers along the thick ridges running up his stomach.

He rips his mouth from mine when I lightly scratch at the line between his abs. His eyes are dark, blown with desire.

"You're killing me, Scar," he rasps.

I nod subconsciously but can't bring myself to stop touching him. Instead, I drift my hands further up his body, brushing the sharp nipples on his pecs and then back down again.

His hands fall from my hair and incite a sigh from me when they sneak beneath my shirt and begin to creep higher and higher. My heart jolts when his thumbs brush the underside of my bra, rubbing back and forth but never slipping under.

"You were going to tell me something. That's why we're here," he murmurs against my lips.

I shake my head once. "It doesn't matter anymore." *Not when you're touching me like this.*

He breaks the kiss then, leaning back the slightest bit. "It does. It matters. I won't take advantage of you."

"You wouldn't be. I just don't care anymore. I want you to keep touching me like this."

His expression morphs into one of pain. "I will. I'll touch you all fucking night once you tell me."

My words come out in a frustrated rush. "I don't just orgasm. Okay? When I do, it . . . I get messy. God, this is embarrassing."

Adam's eyes fill with intrigue. "How often does it happen? Every time?"

"Mostly when I'm really turned on," I answer sheepishly. My skin is on fire. "There's no real telling it will happen until it does."

"That's the sexiest thing I've ever been told, Scarlett. You shouldn't feel embarrassed about that."

In one swift movement, he has the cups of my bra yanked down, exposing my breasts. My nipples are pinched between his fingers as he gives them a gentle pull.

My back arches, forcing my chest further into his hands. "I can try to hold back. Not every guy likes it," I gasp.

He hums low in his throat and drops his head to murmur in my ear, "Don't you dare hold back on me. I want everything you have to give me."

Lust is thick in my blood, blocking out the pesky nerves I felt at the club. My answer is easy, instant.

"Okay. I won't."

He's on me a second later. His mouth closes around my pulse point at the same time we're spinning. My back hits the fridge with a force strong enough to rattle the contents.

My shirt is pushed up over my breasts and discarded before my bra is unsnapped and tossed to the ground. I'm so turned on my muscles are weak, and my head lolls to the side as he slides his mouth down my throat, his tongue gliding along my skin, tasting me.

"If I slip my fingers inside these tight leather pants, will I find you as gone for me as I am for you?" he asks gruffly.

Another wave of arousal crashes into me. My fingers curl, and I nod. "Yes."

"I've been wanting to taste you for weeks," he continues.

My thighs squeeze together as I lean back against the fridge and reach for his neck. When my fingers intertwine behind his head, I force him to meet my pleading stare and whisper, "Then taste me."

A rumble builds in his chest. "I'm not taking you for the first time in my kitchen."

Adam doesn't give me a chance to be disappointed. Not when he grabs me beneath my thighs and starts carrying me in the direction of his bedroom. I wrap my legs around his waist and whimper when the bulge in his jeans brushes my clit.

The room is dark, and we don't bother flicking on the light, letting it seep in from the hallway instead. I drop my face to his neck and attack the sensitive skin with my own assault of kisses as he leads us to the bed. The smell of his cologne and aftershave makes my head swim. I curl my fingers in his hair and sigh.

He sets me gently on the edge of the bed, and I make quick work of crawling my way up to the top. My legs fall open, and my chest lifts and falls rapidly as I watch himself disappear into the ensuite bathroom.

When he returns, it's with a thick black towel in his hands.

My breath falters when I meet his stare at the end of the bed. He's looking at me like he would drop to his knees and worship me if I gave him the chance. Like he wants to devour me.

My mouth falls open when he reaches behind his head and pulls off his shirt, tossing it to the side before moving to pop open the button of his jeans.

He's over six feet of pure muscle and confidence as he stands there, his jeans undone and hanging open, his chest bare. The affection in his eyes calls to mine, forcing it out of hiding. Adam deserves to feel the full depth of my feelings for him, even if I'm still trying to figure out what they all mean.

"What are you doing?" I ask as he continues to stand there, the hint of a smile on his lips.

His eyes hold mine. "Looking at you in my bed. The last time you were here, I was out of my head. I couldn't fully appreciate it."

I swallow. "I did. I mean, I did appreciate it. Being with you like that."

"Yeah?"

"Yes. I would appreciate it more if you came over here, though."

He doesn't need me to beg. In a beat, he's left in only a pair of black boxer briefs. I gulp when I focus on the thick, rigid outline of his cock.

"If you keep looking at me like that, this will be over way quicker than either of us want," he warns me.

Spreading my arms out on the blanket beneath me, I watch him get on the bed and move toward me. Once he's hovering above me, I arch my back in an attempt to get closer, greedy to feel him against me again.

His fingers brush a few stray curls away from my face as he kisses me. Once, twice, three times, before pulling back and moving down my body.

He drops his head and sweeps his lips across my stomach.

His scruff scratches my skin, but it only adds to the pleasure. The towel he brought from the bathroom is swiftly placed below me before a hand moves to cup one of my breasts.

"Adam," I choke out. My core is pulsing with anticipation. The buildup is threatening to make me spiral out of control. "Please don't tease me. I—I feel like I'm going to combust."

He blows a breath against the skin below my belly button before leaning back on his knees and slipping his fingers beneath the waistband of my pants.

"Tell me what you want me to do, Scarlett. Tell me what you like."

I shake my head furiously. "Anything. I just need you to touch me."

He yanks on my pants, and I lift my hips to help him free me of them. Once they're gone, I'm left in only a thin black thong. It's plain, boring, and not the least bit sexy, but from the way Adam's staring at them, looking like he wants to tear them to shreds, I start to think that maybe he doesn't care what they look like.

I inhale sharply when he brings the tip of his finger to the damp spot between my legs and ever so softly brushes a line from bottom to top.

"Shit," I hiss, fighting to keep my legs from closing and rubbing together to soothe this new ache.

"Your panties are soaked, baby," he says in awe.

"Good catch, Captain Obvious," I mutter.

He chuckles lowly before hooking two fingers under the side of the fabric and moving it to the side, finally exposing me. I shiver when the cold air hits my wet skin.

"Christ," he groans, leaning between my legs and pressing a light kiss to the tuft of red hair I keep trimmed above my pussy. "You're beautiful here too."

My eyes roll back when he slides down to his stomach on the mattress and uses two fingers to spread me open for him. He drags his tongue flat up my centre, from bottom to top, before drawing slow, teasing circles around my swollen, aching clit and closing his mouth around it, sucking once.

I whimper, fisting the mattress. Adam makes a pained sound and smooths a hand over my calf before throwing it over his shoulder. He pushes impossibly closer to my pussy and, for lack of a better word, completely ravishes me.

It's been years since a man touched me like this, and even then, it was never anything like this. This feeling of passion and raw need is completely new to me, but as I fist the sheets on either side of me and clench my leg tighter around Adam's head, I let myself fall completely into it.

"You taste even better than I imagined," he growls against my wet flesh.

When a finger slips inside of me, I cry out at the intrusion, in both surprise and relief. "Yes," I gasp.

"You like that?" he asks. When I nod anxiously, another finger joins the first. "What about that? More?"

"More."

A third finger slides inside, and when Adam curls them to stroke the soft spot inside of me, I turn my head to the side and bite down on my lip. My thighs quiver, tightening to the point of pain.

"That's it, baby. Just relax and focus on how good it feels."

He laps at me like a starving man, alternating between flicking my clit with his tongue and sucking it into his mouth until I'm begging for the climax I can feel building and building inside of me.

"Back up," I beg him when a twirling sensation sparks between my legs. My fingers curl around the bedding tight enough the tips throb.

When he only speeds up his movements and focuses on the beckoning motion of his fingers against my G-spot, I try to move back and away. He looks at me through his eyelashes and shakes his head once before placing his free hand flat on my stomach and holding me in place.

It's only when a high-pitched moan escapes me that he delivers one final lash to my clit and pulls his face from my pussy. As my climax slams into me, my vision darkens, and I reach for him, digging my nails into his arm.

"*Fuck yes.* You're doing so good. Let me have it," Adam groans, continuing to stroke my walls even as liquid soaks into the towel beneath us and possibly even wetting him.

My eyes are squeezed shut as my orgasm slowly dies.

"You're amazing, Scarlett," Adam rumbles, placing soft kisses all over my thighs and hips.

The words are enough to have me opening my eyes. I find him looking up at me with a bold hunger. There's a wet spot on his boxers, but I don't think that's from me.

"We're not done, are we?" I ask on a breath. The thought alone has my gut sinking. I'm far from ready to be done.

"No, Scar. Not until I wring another orgasm from you and feel the way you quiver and scream for me when my cock is inside you."

26

Adam

My cock has never been so hard. Hell, the slightest breeze from the AC has me throbbing in my underwear.

Scarlett lies in front of me, splayed out and bare on my bed. The image of her like this would have been enough to invoke such a carnal desperation inside of me on its own, but after just watching her hit a high so powerful she nearly soaked a towel, I'm barely holding on to my sanity.

"Promises, promises," she whispers, staring at the near-painful erection stretching the material of my boxers.

I arch a brow and palm my cock, stifling a groan at the promise of relief. "Your sarcasm is going to get you in trouble one day."

Her lips twitch. I pull the towel out from beneath her and toss it to the side. Dropping my hand, I move my face between her legs, licking her from bottom to top, not able to stop myself. Her taste explodes on my tongue, and I lap at her again and again until her fingers are threaded in my hair, urging me back.

"I need you inside of me, Adam. *Now.*"

"Needy girl," I chastise lightly, flicking her clit with my tongue in punishment. "I haven't had my fill of you yet."

I swirl my tongue around her opening and slip it inside as she gasps, "*Please*. Please just fuck me."

Hearing her beg is enough for me. I pull back and frantically shove my boxers down. I'm reaching into my bedside drawer to grab a condom when she wraps her fingers around my wrist, stopping me.

"I'm good. I haven't had sex in a long time, and I was tested on the team. I've had an IUD for years."

"I haven't been with anyone for a long time. And I was tested after the last time I was. Are you sure it's okay without one? I'm happy to wear one." Even if the idea of being inside of her with no barrier makes my cock grow impossibly harder.

Scarlett nods and pulls on my wrist, bringing me back to her. I settle between her legs, so close to being inside of her yet still too far, and take her thighs in my hands before using my grip to yank her toward me. We're so close I can feel the heat of her pussy trying to draw me inside.

Her breasts bounce with the movement, and I bite my tongue to hold back how much I enjoyed that. In a tight grip, I take my cock in my hand and slowly stroke it as she watches with laser focus. Her tongue wets her lips, and I groan, low and long.

"Fuck, baby. I want your mouth around me so bad. You want that too, don't you? My cock in your mouth? On your tongue?"

Her eyes spark. "I do."

I watch her push up on her hands before reaching one out toward me and pushing mine away. She drags a single fingernail up the entire length of me, and I shiver, my eyes rolling back.

"You're bigger than anyone I've ever been with," she admits, almost in awe as she wraps her fingers around my thick cock.

"You can't say stuff like that to me right now," I grunt.

I nearly lose it when she starts to line me up with her pussy and presses the tip to her slick flesh. Meeting her lust-blown gaze, I start to slowly push inside, careful not to hurt her as she stretches around me.

She keeps her fingers around me until I bottom out. Only

then does she pull her hand back and place it on my shoulder, grounding me.

"You don't feel real," I choke out.

Her silk walls flutter around me, squeezing me so tight it only makes holding on to my self-control that much harder.

I want to pound into her so hard she screams my name for the entire fucking world to hear. I want to claim her as mine and keep her here for the rest of her life. She turns me into a barbarian, yet I don't hate it.

"I'm real. You're real. This is real," she whispers.

There's something in her eyes that steals my breath, something that shifts the world around us until I'm on unsteady ground.

Scarlett reaches for me with her other hand and grips me like I'm the rope keeping her from drifting out to sea. She squeezes her eyes shut when I pull out and thrust back inside of her hard enough for the headboard to smack the wall.

"God, yes," she sighs, tossing her head back.

I move up her body and rest my hands on either side of her head before falling to my forearms. Our lips brush, and I thrust again, this time hearing the way her breath skips and feeling her heart thump inside her chest.

"You're mine, Scarlett. When are you going to accept that?"

She answers by kissing me. Her ankles lock behind my back, keeping me buried inside of her. "I already have," she whispers against my lips.

My entire body shudders. I pull back, forcing her ankles to drop, and slam back inside. She cries out.

"That's right. You're. Mine," I groan.

I pick up tempo and slip a hand between us to play with her clit, needing to set her off for me again. My orgasm is already building, threatening to sweep me under when I shift my hips and start to fill her even deeper, brushing the soft spot I became acquainted with earlier.

"Need you to come with me, baby. Need you to give me everything."

"I'm trying," she whimpers.

It's like everything we've said holds a double meaning. I can't sort through it all right now. Scarlett is everywhere. She's in everything. I'm drowning in her, and I don't want to come up for air. I couldn't if I tried.

"I know. Just give me a bit more. Give this to me right now."

She brings her hand to my jaw and holds me where I am, with my lips grazing hers and our breaths intertwining. Nodding, she lets herself fall.

My name tears from her throat as she comes, squeezing me tight, her walls pulsing. I follow right after her, reaching that peak with her name on my lips and slashed across my soul.

I pump into her a few more times as I come before stilling, out of breath. I look down at Scarlett, overflowing with feelings I haven't felt before.

She meets my stare with one that looks similar but more reserved. A knot forms in my stomach at the thought of her pulling back from me again.

I lean down and kiss her once before pushing back to my knees and sliding out of her. Despite my recent mind-blowing orgasm, the sight of my cum seeping from her swollen pussy is enough to make my cock twitch.

I grab the towel from the bed and use it to quickly clean her up, careful with how sensitive she must be.

"I'll be right back," I say softly, getting off the bed and bringing the towel with me to the ensuite. I hear a faint humming noise and smile.

Flicking on the bathroom light, I toss the towel in the laundry bin. After washing my hands, I'm about to head back when I catch my reflection in the mirror.

I turn my body and grab the edge of the counter. There's something different in the way I look, and it doesn't take me long to realize what it is.

I've seen the same expression on the faces of every single one of my friends.

It's love. A form different than the one I'm used to.

The feelings churning inside of me fit into place. They click.

There's a stupid grin on my face when I finally leave the bathroom. I reach the bed, and somehow, my smile only grows.

Scarlett is still in the same position she was when I left, only her eyes are closed and her swollen lips are parted on a yawn. She makes a soft mewling noise before opening her eyes.

Noticing my smile, she asks, "Yes?"

"Nothing," I say, shaking my head. I might have finally accepted the extent of my feelings, but the odds of Scarlett doing the same are most likely pretty slim. "I just like having you in my bed. In my space at all, really."

She must be exhausted because I don't get a smart-ass comeback to that. Instead, she lets me pull back the blanket for her and slips beneath it, her head hitting the pillow instantly. I cover her with the blanket and watch as she smiles at me before turning to her side, facing the empty spot.

It only takes me a moment to get to my side before I'm crawling in and turning to face her. Her eyelashes flutter as she looks at me.

"You have a tattoo," she says on a yawn. The tips of her fingers brush my side over the small script that lives on my skin. "It's Cooper's name."

I hum. "I got it when he was five."

"There's a story with you and him." It's not a question.

Brushing my knuckle over her jaw, I say, "There is."

"Tell it to me," she whispers, eyes half-open.

I swallow and nod. There isn't a single thing I wouldn't tell this woman, even if what she wants to know is something not many besides my closest friends know. Not because I hide it, but because it's not something others need to know. It's personal, not only to me but also to Beth.

However, it's something Scarlett needs to know. It's a piece of me that I don't mind sharing with her.

"I've known Beth since I was in elementary school. She had a similar family life to mine, and I took it upon myself to befriend her. I kept the mean kids away and, as we grew older, would make sure to do things like drive her home from school or listen to her rant about whatever was bugging her.

"Eventually, her friendly feelings toward me turned into something I couldn't reciprocate, and when that upset her, I decided it was best to separate ourselves. We didn't have any contact with each other after that, until university came around."

I pause, and Scarlett nods in understanding. Her eyes are more open now, more awake.

"The first time I saw her again was when Ava spilled coffee all over her in a Starbucks. It was an accident, but Beth was more outspoken then and took it as something it wasn't. It started a feud between them, and even though I was curious about the new Beth, I kept my distance."

"Until you didn't?"

I nod. "Until I didn't. I was a hormonal college guy who thought with his dick more than his head and ended up sleeping with her. More than once. Then she disappeared. She dropped out of school, and I didn't hear from her until three years later."

Scarlett's fingers tense around my hip. "What?"

"Yeah. It was three years after our last time together that she found me at Sinner's and told me I had a son. She was having a manic episode, and . . . it was just really scary. She was yelling for me in the middle of the club and going at it with Gracie because she couldn't find me. That's when I found out she was diagnosed with bipolar disorder shortly after she had Cooper.

"Her parents didn't take the pregnancy well, and with a dad who works for the mayor, they all but forbade her from telling anyone about it. Even me. They thought it would make them look like fools that their daughter got pregnant by a guy who didn't want her. Beth spent her entire pregnancy locked away in her house and the following two years struggling with her new disorder and raising a baby alone."

Scarlett's hand has crept up to my waist, and her grip is tight. She blinks away a film of tears in her eyes.

"That must have been a nightmare for her," she whispers.

"It was. I'm just happy Beth came to me when she did. God, Cooper was in the car that night. I was half out of my mind after the bomb she had dropped on me, but I remember as clear as day following her to her car and looking in the back window. He was asleep in his car seat, his little head leaned to one side. There was a small blue blanket tucked over his lower half, and he had it clenched in his tiny fist. I thought I was going to pass out on the curb."

"Adam," Scarlett whispers and uses her thumb to brush the wet skin beneath my eye

Despite the sudden tears, the ghost of a smile pulls at my lips. "I knew instantly he was mine. Not only was the timing perfect, but he looked just like me. He still does. We got a paternity test just to be safe, but the results weren't surprising."

"He's your mini-me. I noticed as soon as I saw him the first time," Scarlett says, smiling.

I kiss the palm of her hand and intertwine our fingers. "I know you have more questions, but Beth will probably want to be the one to tell you everything else. Some of it isn't for me to tell."

Scarlett nods before leaning toward me, our mouths a hair apart. "You're a good man and a great dad, Adam White. I'm lucky to know you."

Her words pierce my chest. I press our lips together and pull her as close to me as she can get. Wrapping her up in my arms, I hold her tight and pray that this won't be the only time I get to have her this way.

It's too late to go back now.

27

Scarlett

I WAKE UP FEELING LIKE I'VE SPENT THE NIGHT UNDER THE summer sun.

A heavy arm is draped over me, and my legs are sandwiched beneath a hairy one. I'm warm. Secure. Adam is a protective barrier between me and the world right now, and I want to stay here for as long as I can.

I'm only an inch away from the edge of the king-sized bed, and that only makes me stifle a laugh so I don't wake him. A pinky-orange colour glows beneath the blackout curtains covering the window, so it must be very early.

Adam's breath fans my hair, and I can feel his lips pressed to my head. A smile breaks out on my face. The memories of last night replay in my mind. Everything we did, everything I felt, it's all burning inside me.

I'm falling in love with him. That much I can't deny. Now, what do I do with that? What does all of this mean going forward?

All I know for sure is that I need to figure my shit out sooner rather than later. I've been putting my future on the back burner for too long now, and it's become a weight tied to my ankle, pulling me down.

I can't continue to drown when I have someone offering me a life jacket.

A deep rumbling noise escapes the cuddle bug behind me as his arm tightens around my side and he pulls me even closer. I laugh, letting him move me however he wants.

"How long have you been up?" he asks, sleep thick in his tone.

"Long enough to realize that you're not only a bed hog but also a serious cuddler."

He chuckles. His lips meet my ear and then the skin below it. "I had to make sure you couldn't get away in the middle of the night."

"I'm only here because I didn't want to have to wiggle against the massive boner digging into my ass right now and wake you up before I could disappear." I push back against said boner and let his pained groan settle between my legs.

He splays his hand across my stomach and tries to still me. His voice drops to a growl. "If you don't stop, it will be doing a hell of a lot more than just digging into you."

I shiver and, with a boost of confidence I don't recognize, reach behind me and grip his bare shaft. He hisses through his teeth.

"Don't tease me with a good time, Adam."

Suddenly, he's pulling my hand from his cock and slipping his fingers between my legs. I lift my leg to make room for him and let my head loll to the side when he swirls one around my opening and pushes it inside.

"You talk a big game, baby. But we both know you'll fold as soon as I touch you."

I want to argue, but words fail me. Instead, I have to hold myself back from begging for more. Adam has an alpha male side that I did not see coming. One that only lifts its head when we're like this, completely lost in each other. It makes my stomach turn to goo and my pussy soaked.

He pulls his finger from my pussy and uses it to rub my clit. "No argument?"

"You know I don't have one," I grind out and push myself further into his hand, desperate for him to give me *more*. He pulls his hand away completely instead. "Adam, pl—"

The broad head of his cock pushing inside me steals my breath and my words. He slides in easily with how wet and ready I am for him and curses my name when he fills me completely.

"Your pussy—*shit*—it feels like fucking heaven," he grunts, beginning to thrust. "Stretched around me nice and tight."

"You're huge," I gasp. "That's why."

He reaches around me to grab my breast and pinch the nipple between his splayed fingers. "No, Scarlett. It's because it was made for me. It was made to take this cock."

My eyes roll back. "And you were made for me."

His thrusts falter. His voice isn't commanding or thick with desire when he speaks next. It's warm, almost nervous. "Yeah? You're right. I was."

I squeal when he rolls me to my stomach and settles behind me. His hands palm my ass cheeks before spreading them and pushing inside me again.

"Oh, shit," I curse, burying my face in the pillow.

The new position has the tip of his cock hitting my G-spot and my clit brushing the mattress with each thrust. When he places a hand on my lower back, I look at him over my shoulder and find his eyes on me, burning so bright with a hefty cocktail of emotions.

His brows tug in with his pleasure as our eyes lock and hold. I cry out when his pace slows and becomes harder, each thrust sending me jolting forward. I'm nearly there, and he realizes it with a groan.

"Give it to me, baby. Give it all to me," he half pleads, half orders.

I drop my head forward and claw at the sheets as his words

push me over the edge. Stars burst behind my eyes, and sounds escape me that I can't hold in.

"Fuck, you make the prettiest sounds when you come."

A full-body shudder racks through me as he continues to pound into me. The sound of slapping flesh is enough to pull me out of my orgasm-induced brain fog.

"I want you in my mouth," I rush out.

He doesn't hesitate to pull out and stroke himself while watching me fumble to my knees and crawl to him. I'm desperate to have him in my mouth, and when I replace his hand with mine, bringing him to my lips, the groan he releases says he's desperate for the same thing.

I swirl my tongue around the tip, collecting the mix of our flavours before sliding it down his smooth shaft, down to the base. He gently gathers my hair and pulls it from my face.

"Put it in your mouth, baby."

He doesn't have to tell me twice. I push him past my lips and slide down the length of him, only stopping when I can't take him further. Wrapping my fingers around whatever I can't fit in my mouth, I pump my hand in time with every rise and fall of my head.

"That's it. So fucking good."

His praise encourages me to take him deeper, hitting my gag reflex. I sputter, and spit leaks from the corners of my mouth.

"Christ. Not going to last much longer. I'm nearly there," he chokes.

The grip on my hair tightens, but he doesn't push me. He lets me take it at my own pace, even if he's dying to fuck my mouth.

I hollow my cheeks and suck him harder each time I reach the tip. Using my other hand, I touch his balls, cradling them in my palm and rubbing the smooth skin beneath them with my thumb. His groan tears through the room.

"Where?" Adam asks suddenly. I look at him through my eyelashes and blink, answering him with a hard suck. "Dirty fucking girl."

I hum around him and fight off a smug grin when that's the final thing to set him off. As soon as he whispers my name like a curse and presses his fingers into my scalp, he fills my mouth.

Only after I've swallowed everything he's given me do I pull away and suck in gulps of air, trying to catch my breath. The hands in my hand move to my cheeks as he pushes forward and captures my mouth.

It's a deep kiss, one that carries the weight of appreciation. I smile against his lips before pulling back and falling backward on the bed.

"Did you know that you have a filthy mouth, Adam?"

He tips his head back and laughs loudly. "I do. And you seem to like it."

I shrug, smirking. "It's like you have an alter ego. It's kind of sexy."

"Only kind of?"

I watch him fall to the bed beside me and turn to face me. His eyes twinkle, even in the dark.

"Mm. I'm too tired to search for another compliment," I mumble, shutting my eyes. "What time is it, anyway?"

The bed dips before the sound of him digging around his side table fills the room. "Seven thirty," he says.

My eyes shoot open. "Crap. I thought it was earlier." I nearly throw myself out of bed and wander around the dark room, grabbing pieces of clothing off the ground and attempting to put them on. "Where did I put my phone?"

More rustling. "Your pants?"

"No pockets."

"Kitchen?"

After tugging a shirt over my head that smells like Adam, I find the door and peel it open before rushing into the hallway. It's much brighter out here, and I have no trouble finding the kitchen. My phone screen is lit up when I spot it on the island.

Grabbing it, I see a photo of my mom on the screen. I frantically answer the call.

"Hi, Mom. Everything okay?"

Adam must turn the coffee machine on behind me because it makes a hissing sound before liquid begins to drip into the pot.

"Where are you? You missed curfew, young lady. You're lucky I didn't call the police," she chastises me like a child.

Like a child.

My inhale is warbled. Fear sinks its jagged claws into my chest and twists. How do I deal with this? This has never happened before.

When a strong chest meets my back and two strong arms bracket me, I fall back into the embrace.

"Where is Mrs. McConnell, Mom?"

"She came over for coffee, and then I sent her home. It's far too early for company, anyway. Silly woman."

"You're right. I'm sorry I'm not there. I'll be home soon," I say cautiously.

"Where are you, Scarlett? This isn't like you."

Adam presses a gentle kiss to the side of my head when I speak again. "I stayed at a friend's house, but I'm coming back right now."

Mom clucks her tongue. "Yes, you are. I'll see you in a little while, then."

"See you," I whisper before hanging up and calling Mrs. McConnell. I don't allow myself to focus on anything else.

She picks up on the second ring. "Hello?"

"You just left my mom alone?" I ask, my voice louder, more brash than I wanted. She gasps, and instant regret digs deep in my gut.

Adam places his hand over the one holding my phone and gently slips it from my grasp. I let him bring it to his ear and tell my neighbour what's going on, knowing that I'm nowhere near the right headspace to talk to her.

Placing a hand to my chest, I close my eyes and let Adam's conversation with the older woman turn to static.

The reality of my mom's disease is heavier now than ever.

She's been getting worse every day, but this is just another sign that I can't do this on my own.

She deserves the best help she can get, and I'm beginning to realize that isn't me. With my job at WIT being the only real source of income we have now that she can't work anymore—even just helping out at the greenhouse a few hours a day is too much as of late—I can't afford to quit and stay home with her again.

Shit. How is me working at the rink going to change after what's happened? I'm going to have to get another job. I can't keep working for Adam. He can't be my boss.

My heart feels like it's cracking. I've grown to love my job. I love working with Willow and getting to see her growth with each session. I love my mornings with Adam and the smiles he sends me whenever our paths cross throughout the day. *Oh, God.*

"What a mess," I say on an exhale.

Adam, done with the phone call now, moves his hands to my shoulders and squeezes. "Mr. and Mrs. McConnell are going back over to your house now to check on your mom. They're going to call back after they speak to her."

I spin around and press my face to his bare chest before slipping my arms around his waist and holding him tight. He blows out a breath and hugs me back.

"I have to go home now."

"You do. I'll take you there."

"My mom keeps getting worse. I need help," I admit.

Adam rubs my back in slow circles. "Then let me help. Tell me what to do."

If only it was that easy. I have no doubt Adam would fix anything that dared upset me if given the chance. That's just the kind of guy he is.

"I have a few meetings planned with some in-home caretakers. I just need to set a day to do it. I need to pick someone as soon as I can."

"Do you want me to come with you? What day do you need off? I can clear us both," he offers.

I shake my head. "Don't do that. As much as I would like you to be there with me, that only brings us to my other problem."

He stiffens. "What problem?"

"I can't be your employee anymore, Adam. I can't be with you and work for you at the same time. It won't work," I croak. Emotion stings my eyes, and I blink to try and push it away.

"You barely work for me, Scarlett. You work for Willow and any other skater that comes to WIT needing a trainer with your skill set and experience."

"It wouldn't feel the same as it does now. And what would everyone else think? That you're sleeping with your employees now? I can't damage your reputation like that, and I don't want to lose you. Me quitting is the only option."

He releases me and takes a step back. His eyes are guarded. I want to reach for him but chicken out, letting my arms hang limp.

His voice is strong, almost angry. "Fuck my reputation, Scarlett. It means nothing compared to you. And everyone knows you got your job because of how fucking amazing you are on the ice. Because of the glow you get every single time you clap for Willow and every medal you've earned and record you've beaten. You got your job because of how much you deserve it. You're not losing me."

"I got it because I was the only all-star athlete lounging around without a career and in need of a reason to leave the house." The words feel wrong, like I don't fully believe them anymore.

He runs a hand over his hair and over his jaw, tense with frustration. His eyes flick around his kitchen.

"You've spent months at WIT, and I've watched you fall in love with what you do there. When I met you, you wanted nothing to do with hockey. You thought you had lost everything with your injury—the same injury you've pushed yourself to heal from, in case you've forgotten. Dammit, Scarlett. This is your second chance. It might not be what you expected, and yeah, you won't ever win another Olympic medal or score another season-winning goal, but does all that really matter? Does it matter when you've found something else that makes you feel the same rush? The same feeling of success? Of happiness?"

His words are perfectly aimed bullets of truth. Each one sinks deep.

A sob-like sound escapes me, drawing his gaze. Our eyes clash together, his suddenly soft as he says, "It's time you stopped hating yourself for what happened and started to shift your perspective. Your glass isn't half-empty, baby. Not anymore."

28

Scarlett

Adam's words linger heavily in the air.

Everything he said is true. He threw a hard slap of reality right at me, and I'm reeling from the burn left behind.

It's not a bad burn but one that won't go away easily.

He was right when he said I hated myself for what happened. I did. And I still do blame myself for the how and for the why, but not for what happened after. I can't—not anymore.

I know that if I had been paying more attention during that game, I wouldn't have missed the player headed right for me. I wouldn't have gotten thrown into the boards, and I wouldn't have hurt myself. But it was me that chose to come home, and after everything that has happened in the past few months, I would make that choice over and over again.

If I hadn't come home, I wouldn't have known my mother was sick. I wouldn't have been able to help her, and I would have missed out on the time I've had with her.

If I hadn't come home, I wouldn't have met Adam. Or Cooper, or Willow. I wouldn't have found a love and a passion for helping athletes like Willow.

My shoulder was never going to get back to what it was.

Regardless if I had stayed in Calgary and continued my therapy after my surgery with my previous therapist, I would still be where I am today. Only I wouldn't have learned what was out there, waiting for me to find.

I can't say that I'm not still sad. Not still disappointed. How could I not be? I will never get another chance to accomplish something very few have.

The difference now is that I think I can live with that. I can use it to motivate me to be better, to push myself when I need to. The memories will always be there. It's just time to make new ones.

A weight lifts not only from my shoulders but from my soul. It took months to get to this point, and now that I'm here, I feel like I can breathe again.

My mom shouldn't spend the few good years she has left remembering me as the broken girl who lost everything and gave up. She should remember me as the one who got up after falling and found a reason to run.

"You really want me to stay at WIT?" I ask softly, finally breaking the silence in the kitchen.

Adam doesn't hesitate before answering me, eyes shining as sincere as I've ever seen. "Yes. Do you want to stay?"

"Yes." *Desperately.*

"Then tell me what I can do to make you feel more comfortable with staying. If working with athletes makes you happy, I don't want you to stop. Especially not because of me." He winces and clears his throat. His eyes dim, like someone flipped a light switch inside of him. "If a relationship with me would take this chance from you, then say the word and I'll walk away."

"What?" I stare at him with my mouth gaped. A cold flush slithers down my body before it's replaced with a surprising sense of frustration, aimed right at Adam. The words run out of me. "And what about your happiness? When are you going to start putting yourself first? You are worthy of getting everything you want too, Adam. There aren't always sacrifices you need to make for other people."

I catch him off guard, and it takes him a few seconds to recover. Once he does, he laughs. He actually laughs. I scowl hard, only making him laugh harder.

"I already have been putting myself first. Don't you get it? The risk I took letting you meet my son, my friends, getting to know *me*—that was my way of putting myself first."

I swallow. "Then why are you prepared to have done all of that for not—"

He shakes his head. "Don't finish that sentence. You need to listen to me, Scarlett Carter, because as much as I love you, sometimes you make me want to shake some sense into you."

It's like someone's reached inside my chest and taken hold of my heart. My next inhales are wobbly, unsteady. *What?*

Adam closes the gap between us and takes my cheek in his hand. His eyes shine, no longer dim. They burn bright as he traces my Cupid's bow with his thumb.

"From the moment you stepped into my office, you swept me up in a tide of grumpy comebacks and frowns that I ached to see flip. I became obsessed with learning more about you, so I did just that.

"I've learned that you only ever drink black coffee because you actually like how bitter it tastes. I know that you always tie your left skate before your right because that was your pre-game ritual and you can't break the habit. I know you can't brush your curls because when you do, they turn to 'fluffy strands of frizz,' and I know that you have a heart too big for your chest. Shit, baby, I haven't been able to stop learning things about you because I am so incredibly in love with you that I can't.

"And it's because I'm in love with you that I would put my own happiness aside to make sure you got everything you wanted in life. If you wanted me to walk away from this—from us—and have you report only to Banks, I would arrange it right now, even if I shattered myself in the process. If you told me right now to find you another job in another province, hell, another fucking country, I would do it if it meant you didn't lose something you love doing again."

Tears drip down my face faster than he can wipe them away. I reach for his hands and cover them with mine. He presses our foreheads together and bumps my nose with his.

"I know you would make the same sacrifices for me that I'm prepared to make for you. That's why you were going to quit, because you were willing to give up something you love to be with me," he finishes softly.

"You're the most annoyingly happy person I've ever met, but I went and fell in love with you anyway," I reply, releasing a mangled laugh. Adam smiles before it grows to a full-fledged grin. "You are incredible, Adam, in every way possible. I didn't think I was ever going to find anything that made me feel the way hockey did, but I found something better instead. I love my job. But I love you more."

These words feel right. They feel like they've been waiting to be said for a while, but I was too full of self-loathing and disappointment to notice them.

"It feels so good to hear you say that," he breathes before covering my mouth with his in a bruising kiss.

I loop my arms around his neck and pull him closer, kissing him back with an urgency that says everything I haven't been able to put into words.

This man loves me, despite my flaws and my less than appealing personality. Somehow, we just fit. We were drawn together like magnets from the moment we met. There was no stopping this.

We were inevitable.

ADAM PULLS open the passenger door of his car for me as I step out. The summer sun roasts my neck and shoulders, making me wince.

He takes my hand and links our fingers together before shutting the door. I exhale a wavering breath and try to collect myself before we head toward my house.

"I don't know what to prepare myself for," I admit.

"Do you want me to come inside with you?" He brushes his thumb back and forth across the back of my hand.

I shake my head. "I don't know how she'll be once she sees me. It's probably best if you don't come in." Even if leaving his side is the last thing I want to do right now after what happened this morning.

We didn't spend any more time in the kitchen after our kiss. Mrs. McConnell called shortly after we broke apart and told us my mother was okay. She was disoriented, confused, and embarrassed, but she was okay.

After hanging up, Adam had pecked my lips once more before ushering us back to his room. He helped me find my clothes and, after we were both dressed and ready, drove us here.

My mom's car is still at the pub from last night, and despite my reluctance, Adam insisted he'll bring it to my house tonight. My pulse hasn't steadied in hours, and I can't help but realize what an odd feeling it is to be so unapologetically obsessed with someone like this.

Adam nods in understanding, although I can tell he wants to push me on it. "Are you ready?"

"I have to be, right?

"No. You just have to try to be. This isn't an easy responsibility to carry, but you've been doing so well already under the weight of it. I'm here to help now, and once we find a caretaker, they'll help too. You can handle this, Scarlett. I know you can."

"Thank you," I whisper, the use of the word *we* not evading me. His words fill me with enough confidence that I start to lead us to the house. "What time do you need to pick up Cooper?" I ask to distract myself.

We've reached the garage when he says, "After lunch. He most likely isn't even up yet."

"A late sleeper, huh?"

Adam laughs. "Yeah. I think he's still catching up on all the sleep he lost when he was a toddler. The kid loved to play cars at two in the morning."

"Let me guess, you got up and joined him every morning?"

"Every single time."

I sneak a glance in his direction once we reach the porch to find him staring inquisitively at the flowerpot housing one tall sunflower. "I made that in third grade," I tell him.

The pot was once a bright orange colour with puffy white clouds and my name scrawled across it, but after years of weather damage, the pot is chipped, and the paint is dull.

"Mom's kept it on this porch ever since. I'm pretty sure it's housed every variation of flower known to man over the years."

Adam looks at me, smiling. "She loves you. Adores you, really. It's beautiful to see."

My heart clenches. "Yeah. She does. I feel the same about her."

He squeezes my hand, and I realize we've been standing, stalled, at the bottom of the porch stairs. "Come on, Scary Spice. It'll be okay."

"It will," I repeat, steeling my spine.

We step on the first step together before doing the same with the second. Too soon, we're in front of the door.

"I'm going to wait in my car for a few minutes, okay? If you need me, just come outside or call me. I won't leave until you tell me to," Adam says when I grab the doorknob. Our hands are still linked.

"I don't want you to go," I whisper, a lump building in my throat. I'm not sure if it's fear, but it sure tastes like it.

His expression is sure, decided. "Then I'm not leaving. I'm staying here with you."

I want him to stay too badly to keep insisting that he go, so I don't. Instead, I open the door and lead him inside.

29

Adam

Scarlett is practically vibrating with nerves as we step past the front door and move inside her home.

There are low, quiet voices coming from the left of the entrance way, and that's where Scarlett heads first. I follow after her, staying close but not too close, and breathe in the smell of flowers that seems to be in every room.

Their home is small but well-kept. It's cozy and welcoming, like somewhere you would want to go to relax and be alone. There aren't many family photos on the wall. Instead, they seem to be kept on a corkboard on the wall above a bin of yarn. Several photos are tacked to the board, and I make a promise to myself that I'll remember to come look at them all when we're done here.

Scarlett leads us to a small sitting room off the entrance that houses a moss-green armchair with a tall back and thick armrests, along with a tall lamp tucked in the corner, a television on the wall that's playing what looks like a Hallmark movie, and an array of plotted flowers scattered along the walls.

We find Amelia staring out the big circular window beside the chair, looking out at a lush side garden.

"Mom?" Scarlett breathes. She sounds both relieved and scared, and I hate that I can't do more for her.

As much as I try to be there for her, I'm completely out of my depths with this. I'm a fish out of water when it comes to sick family members. Or family at all, really. Or at least I am when we're speaking of blood relation.

There's nothing I can do or say other than offer her my support in everything she does from this point forward.

Amelia sucks in a breath before spinning around to face us. Her cheeks blossom with a blush when she notices me beside her daughter, our hands connected and our fingers linked.

"Oh my. Look at you two. I can feel the love from here," she sighs.

Scarlett's mother is dressed in an ankle-length, pale pink nightgown with dainty white slippers on her feet. It's clear she wasn't expecting me, but I'm both happy and relieved that she's not upset with the surprise.

"Good morning, Amelia. It should be a crime to look so beautiful so early in the day," I compliment her, smiling wide. "You're making the rest of us look bad."

Scarlett laughs softly as her mom brushes me off, blushing. "You're going to give this old woman a heart attack, Adam."

"You're hardly old," Scarlett says.

"Well, my wrinkled ass cheeks say otherwise."

"Mom!" Scarlett shrieks at the same time I burst into laughter.

"You're a natural comedian, Amelia," I say, shooting her a quick wink.

Amelia looks innocently at Scarlett. "Was it something I said?"

"Yes," my girl says while I say, "No."

Scarlett turns to me, exasperated. "You are not helping."

With a grin, I tug her close and whisper, "Sorry, baby."

"Yeah, right."

"Adam, you wouldn't mind if I stole my daughter for the rest of the day, would you?" Amelia asks, almost shyly.

She's watching our interaction with intrigue and probably has a million questions to bombard her daughter with. Scarlett looks up at me and nods reassuringly.

I meet her stare and squeeze her hand, as if to ask if she's sure, and when she mouths a simple *yes*, I believe her.

"Of course not. I have a son to pick up in a couple hours and a festival to finish planning for next weekend, so I'm sure I can keep myself busy," I say.

Amelia's eyes flare with excitement. "A festival? I haven't been to one of those in years." She looks at her daughter. "Are you going, my love? Would you take this old lady with you?"

Neither of us tells her that it's an annual event and has been for the past eight years. Scarlett smiles at her mother. "Of course, Mom. Everyone from WIT will be so excited to meet you."

Amelia arches a brow. "You've talked me up, have you? That's my girl."

"She adores you, Amelia. Truly," I share.

When Amelia gives me a smile that looks far too sad for someone filled with so much happiness, Scarlett inches closer to me and says to her, "What do you say I make some lemonade and we go sit on the back deck? I'll tell you all about the festival, and you can tell me about your night. Deal?"

"Deal, my love," Amelia replies gently. She comes at me with a hug before I have a chance to realize what's happening. I'm only just returning the gesture when she whispers, "Thank you. Thank you for taking care of her for me."

She pulls back quickly after that, and I'm left with a dry mouth, words a foreign concept. Her smile is sincere when she squeezes my arm and disappears through an archway I assume leads to the kitchen.

Scarlett moves to my front and places her hands against my chest as her eyes meet mine. "I actually think having you here helped. She had no choice but to try and get past her own emotions. Your flirting worked."

I smirk. "That wasn't flirting, Scary Spice. You're the only woman in a decade that's been on the receiving end of my flirting. That was me being honest. Think I've won her approval?"

"You've had her approval since the moment she ran into you with a plant in her arms."

I place my finger beneath her chin and tip her head back the slightest bit. "Good. Although I would have been here whether I had it or not. This just makes it less awkward."

And with that, I kiss her goodbye.

MADDOX AND COOPER are inhaling stacks of pancakes at the table when I enter the Huttons' kitchen. Noah is drawing on a small kids table a few feet over, and Adalyn is sitting on Ava's lap beside the two boys.

Addy is the first to notice me, her green eyes lighting up. "Dam! Dam!"

The two boys look over at me as Noah says, "Adam, Addy. He's Adam."

His sister stares at him, unblinking. "Dam."

"Sure," Noah grunts before going back to his colouring.

"Hey, Dad," Cooper says through a mouthful of pancakes. He quickly drinks his orange juice. "You're early."

I look at my watch. "It's eleven. And I'm here to go over festival plans with Ava. Not dragging you home just yet."

Ava plants her elbow on the table and sets her face in her hand. "We were expecting you to be here much later."

"Much, *much* later," Oakley adds from behind me. He claps my shoulder before walking around me and to where his wife and daughter sit.

Adalyn grins and waves her hand excitedly when her dad

kisses the top of her head and tugs gently on the tiny tuft of hair at the top of her head. "Daddy!"

"Hey, baby girl," he murmurs before bending down to kiss Ava's head. She looks up at him with a smile.

"When are we picking up Braxton, Dad?" Maddox asks while swiping a finger across his syrupy plate and bringing it to his mouth.

Oakley flops down in the chair beside him. "When do you want us to pick her up?"

Cooper snorts a laugh, and Maddox pinches him under the arm. "Ow!"

"After lunch," Maddox says.

"Wow. I get it. You'd rather spend time with a girl than with me," Cooper sighs.

Maddox shrugs. "She's funnier than you."

"She smells like flowers." Cooper scrunches his nose.

"I like how flowers smell."

"Since when?"

"Since I decided I like flowers."

"Oh, what a coincidence."

"Shut up, Cooper."

"Make me, Doxxy Poxxy."

Cooper cries out when Maddox shoves him off his chair, and he falls to his butt. I stifle a laugh behind my fist when Cooper reaches up from the ground and grabs Maddox by the arm, pulling him to the floor.

They continue to poke, pinch, and hit each other as Ava sighs and looks at me, exasperated.

"God help us all when they get old enough to do serious damage to one another."

Oakley laughs. "I don't think we'll be waiting too long for that."

"Especially not when they seem to love beating on each other," I add.

"Great," Ava huffs.

"Gweat," Adalyn repeats. Her mom curls an arm around her and bounces her leg.

"You'll stay away from the boys when you get older, right? For my sake? Maybe you'll like music like your brother Noah," she says, sounding far too hopeful.

The toddler shakes her head and points to the two boys now spread out on the floor, catching their breath. "Play!"

"Music's mine," Noah states, not looking away from the drawing in front of him.

"Music isn't yours to guard, bud," Oakley tells his son.

Noah ignores him.

"Anyway," Ava says. She looks at Oakley and then down at the girl in her lap. "Adam and I should get started on these plans."

Oakley pats his lap and grins at Addy. "Come here, sweetheart. Let Mom go help Adam."

Not needing to be told again, the toddler dives toward her dad, giggling like crazy when he grabs her and sets her on his lap.

Ava stands and grins at me. "My office?"

"Sure."

"Have fun gossiping. I expect to be updated on everything after," Oakley shouts when we disappear down the hallway.

Ava snorts. "He's just as bad as a teenage girl."

"I don't know, the boys seem to be worse gossips than any girl I knew growing up."

"Good point."

Ava's office door is open, so we walk right inside. There's no need to turn the light on with the amount of sun shining through the massive floor-to-ceiling windows.

I sit on the cream leather couch and stare out at the uninterrupted view of their acreage and the peace within it. Their closest neighbour is a half-hour drive away, leaving them the privacy they deserve after so many years under the media's thumb.

Ava sits beside me, curling her legs beneath her. She's watching me expectantly, and I chuckle.

"What do you want to know first?"

"How was dinner?"

I scrub a hand over my jaw, thinking of how to word what I'm thinking without just blurting out the first thing that comes to mind. There's only one thing I can focus on right now.

Ah, fuck it.

"I love her."

Ava sucks a breath between her teeth. Something sharp pricks my chest when her bottom lip quivers and her eyes mist over.

"Don't cry, O," I plead.

She leans toward me and shoves at my arm. "Don't tell me not to cry, you asshole. You should have known this would happen when you decided to tell me that."

"You're right. I just . . . I can't not say it, you know? I'm so full of it that I feel like I could explode at any time. I want to tell everyone," I admit. Ava nods in understanding. "She's it for me. I'm sure of it."

"Oh, Adam," she whispers. Her eyes shine with more than just tears. Pride, happiness, love. So many emotions swirl together to create that shine.

"I didn't think I was going to tell her so soon, but I did. She was talking about quitting WIT, and it just burst out of me. The thought of her leaving—I never want to feel that panic again."

"What did she say back?"

My pulse lurches. "That she loves me too."

Ava curses. "And here I go. Hand me the tissue box on the table behind you, please." I do, and she starts ripping them out before wiping under her eyes. "What happens next? Please don't tell me you're going to take things slow because I'm not sure you can get much slower. It's been months already."

"There's still a lot to figure out. We didn't have time to talk about what happens next," I say.

"Why not?"

I lean forward with my elbows on my thighs and look at her. "Her mom is sick. Scarlett is trying to figure out how to help her, and I need to find a way to make her feel comfortable with working for me still. I also need to talk to Cooper. Beth too."

"Work is easy. Let Banks handle payroll. Have her stay at WIT, but don't be her boss. It's about time Banks took on more responsibility anyway."

"You think it will be that easy? She'll still see WIT as my company, therefore making her my employee," I say.

Ava hums quietly. "I think if she wants to make it work as badly as you do *and* wants to keep her job, she'll accept that."

"She also thinks us dating will make me look bad."

"Nothing could make you look bad. You're too damn friendly," she states confidently.

"You'll have to tell her that the next time you see each other."

She laughs. "I think you can handle convincing her you'll survive the ridicule. As far as everything else goes, let her focus on her mom while you get your ducks in a row.

"Cooper likes her, and he's old enough to understand what she means to you and what your relationship would bring to the family. He just wants to see you happy, and I'm sure once you sit down and talk about everything with him, he'll tell you the same thing. As far as Beth goes, you don't need her approval, if that's what you're after. Your personal life is just that when it comes to her. Personal."

I sit back and rest my head on the couch back. Staring at the ceiling, I ask, "What would my relationship bring to the family, though? Would Cooper be okay with a sibling one day? What would it mean if we got married? Cooper thinks he knows what would happen and what it would mean, but until it's a reality, I'm not sure he could ever properly understand. They barely know each other."

Ava grabs my shoulder and squeezes. "It would only mean that there is one more person in his life who loves him and his dad. They might not be close now, but give it time. They've never had the time to really get to know each other. I know I bugged you about it, but you should take your time with this if that's what you feel you need."

"He's everything to me, O. I just want him to be happy."

"I am happy, Dad."

My head turns at the sound of Cooper's voice. Panic has words escaping me.

"You worry too much," he adds, entering the office and flopping down on the chair across the room.

Ava squeezes my shoulder again before getting up. "I'll go grab us a couple drinks."

I nod and watch her scurry out of the room, closing the door behind her. Looking at my son, I find him examining the room.

"How much of that did you hear?" I ask.

The part where I mentioned someday marrying a woman or having another damn kid? They're both premature possibilities, things Scarlett and I haven't talked about yet, amongst a thousand other things. Having Cooper in the conversation already was not my intention.

He looks at me timidly. "Pretty much everything. I didn't mean to eavesdrop, though. I'm sorry."

"It's fine, Coop." *Maybe this is for the best.*

"Do you really love her?" he asks, catching me off guard, but despite that, I don't hesitate to answer.

"I do."

"And she loves you back?"

"She does."

He smiles. "I told her she would learn to love you. Just like she will learn to love her nickname."

I huff a laugh, remembering the day I heard him tell her that. Granted, I was half-lucid, but I remember her whispered "maybe" like she had said it against my lips.

"You're okay with us loving each other?"

"If it makes you happy, then yes," he says. "I want to spend more time with her to make sure she's cool enough for us, but yeah. I'm okay with it."

"You're a great kid, you know that?"

He grins and lifts his chin. "I know."

"Now, come give your old man a hug before he starts crying."

Cooper starts laughing, and I smile, shaking my head as he crosses the room. My son is everything I could have asked for.

I'm the luckiest dad on the planet.

30

Scarlett

I HELP MOM OUT OF THE CAR, AND SHE LOOKS AROUND US IN AWE. "Oh my. This is more than I imagined."

I tighten my grip on her arm, feeling the same way. WIT's festival is in full swing and busier than I thought it would be. There are crowds of people as far as I can see, and I'm sure the inside of the arena looks the same.

A carousel ride, rows of food trucks, and more carnival games than I could count on both hands fill the field around the arena. I know how hard Adam and Brielle have worked on the planning for this event, and judging by the turnout, it looks like all the late nights have paid off.

Adam has been so busy over the past week that we haven't seen each other outside of our stolen kisses in the break room and coffee exchanges in the morning. He likes the fancy stuff that requires me struggling with the espresso machine, but his grin each time I bring it to him in a mug with a cheesy saying is worth the effort. The thought has me tightening my grip on my purse, conscious of the gift I have for him inside.

I miss Adam. Spending this week apart after everything that happened last weekend feels like some sicko's type of torture.

My brain has been working in overdrive to try and figure out exactly what comes next.

I know what I want, and that's Adam and Cooper in my life and the job I love. It sounds simple, easy, but that would be naïve of me to believe. It will take some effort—a lot of it—but I've never been scared of hard work. Not when the reward is well worth it.

"We shouldn't be surprised. Adam never does anything half-assed," I tell Mom. She laughs beside me.

"No he doesn't," she hums, starting to pull me away from the car. Her excitement makes me happy, knowing how hard it's been for her lately. "He certainly doesn't love you half-assed. That man loves you exactly how a woman should be loved."

My chest heats as I walk with her into the crowds. "Mom, don't start."

"I'm only speaking the truth. You've found what I couldn't, baby. I can't begin to tell you how happy that makes me, knowing you'll be taken care of once I'm gone."

The ground tilts, and I nearly lose my footing. "Stop talking about yourself as if you're on death row. You've always been one for dramatics, but let's keep them to ourselves for today, yeah? You're not going to die anytime soon."

The smell of cotton candy and popcorn has never been more putrid than it is now. My mood has soured exponentially in the past two minutes. Mom never would have spoken about something like this so out in the open a few years ago, but now she can't help it.

"You're upset with me," she notes when we pass a group of teenagers huddled around a whack-a-mole game.

"I'm fine," I say tensely.

There's a break in the crowd, and I spot Ava, Gracie, and their husbands working a merchandise stand. I'm about to turn around and hide, knowing my attitude is about as grim as Death himself, but freeze when Ava spots me. She throws her hand in the air and shouts my name, in turn ensuring that everyone around us notices me as well.

"Shit," I mutter under my breath before throwing on a smile and pulling Mom in their direction. "No more talk about death, please," I beg her.

She throws on a bright smile. "A little faith, my love."

Right. My bad.

"Scarlett!" Gracie greets me excitedly when we reach the table.

"Hi, beautiful." Ava beams at me.

"Hey, guys," I say, smiling slightly. Mom tugs on my arm, and I quickly introduce her to everyone. "Mom. This is Gracie, her husband, Tyler, and then Ava and her husband, Oakley. Guys, this is my mother, Amelia."

"It's so great to meet you," Oakley says warmly.

Tyler smiles at her, and everyone tells her how happy they are to meet her. Mom eats it up, the little attention lover.

"Aren't you a lively group. It's a pleasure to meet you all," Mom gushes.

As she starts to schmooze, I eye the table in front of the group with interest. It's full of hockey gear speckled with the Vancouver Warriors and Minnesota Woodmen logos. Names of the players have been written on the tape labelling the items, and I grab a puck with Leo's signature scrawled across the middle.

"What is all this stuff?" I ask. "Is Leo here?"

"I saw him around earlier. He dropped off some of his team's gear about an hour ago," Oakley says.

"And this is a bunch of stuff from the Warriors and the Woodmen to sell to raise money for Adam's new program," Tyler adds.

My brows tug together. "What new program?"

Ava quickly jumps in. "The one for athletes who can't afford private training. He's been working on it for a few weeks now. You didn't know?"

"No."

This has to do with Willow, I know it does. Fuck, Adam and his massive heart are going to be the death of me. If I wasn't already in love with him, I would be now.

Tyler shouts in pain, and I look at them to find Gracie pinching his underarm. "Way to go, loose lips," she scolds him.

He scowls. "I didn't know it was a secret."

"It's fine, guys," I say. They look reluctant, but I shrug. "Really, it's okay. I'm sure he was planning on telling me when it was official."

Mom scoffs. "Of course he was going to. Adam doesn't seem like the type to keep secrets."

Ava is quick to defend her friend. "He really isn't."

My appreciation for her grows.

"I know," I set Leo's signed puck back on the table. "Where is Adam, anyway?"

"Last I saw, he was waiting for Beth with Cooper. He's probably close by," Tyler says.

Ava rounds the table and grabs my hand. "I can help you find him if you want."

I don't pull my hand away as I turn to Mom. She's not paying any attention to me, too busy chatting with an enthusiastic Gracie about what colour she should paint her toes tonight.

"Gracie's got her. She won't let her out of her sight," Ava adds a beat later.

I find myself nodding before we're moving through the crowd. Looking back again, I glance at Mom and smile at the carefree look in her eyes. She looks truly happy.

Facing forward again, I ask Ava, "You offered to take me because you wanted to grill me, right? The best-friend special?"

We pass two dunk tanks, and I choke on a laugh when I see both Braden and Leo each sitting above a tank of water, waiting to take a swim. Sierra is handing out balls to the kids in line, a sneaky smirk on her face as she looks at her husband and winks. A second later, she rushes toward him and slams her hand on the target, sending him falling to the water, sinking deep.

Ava laughs. "Guilty. I didn't get the chance during Gracie's party."

"Go ahead. There isn't much to tell, but I'll try."

"I doubt that—oh, there! Let's sit on that bench. My feet are killing me."

We swerve toward a wooden bench in the shade of an overgrown tree and sit. It's a bit away from the chaos of the festival, which I'm grateful for.

Ava crosses one leg over the other and turns her body to face me. "You know, when I first met Adam, he couldn't go ten minutes without saying a sexual innuendo or making fart noises in the library. He's single-handedly responsible for the dirty jokes Oakley says, thinking he's an absolute comedian."

I snort a laugh. "That must feel like a lifetime ago."

"It does and doesn't. Adam is one of those guys that you can't shake. Once you let him in, you don't want to let him back out again. He's just always there, like family."

"Yeah, I've begun to realize that."

She twists her mouth, as if she's thinking about what to say. Like she wants to make sure everything she says is perfect.

"He worries about Cooper," she begins. "He would do anything to see that boy smile, like I'm sure you know. I worried that he would let that control his life. That he would never want to risk that smile for anything, even his own happiness. I can't even tell you how happy I am that he didn't let that stop him from chasing you. I've honestly never seen him like this before."

"Like what?" I ask quietly.

"In love."

A flush rolls up my body as I look down at my hands. It's silly to feel nervous about this, but this is Adam's best friend. The woman that, at one point, he thought he wanted to be with romantically. It's a different feeling having her tell me this—trusting me with this.

I clear my throat and gather my confidence as I say, "Look, I'm not like Adam. I'm not someone who can find the good in every situation or smile when I'm feeling like shit. I have utterly no first-hand experience with children, and I may not have the kind of success in my career that he does, but I do love him. And I want to be with him. I want to get to know Cooper with the hope that one day he'll grow to care for me in the way I'm beginning to care for him. I know it won't be easy and that I'm probably too young to want all of this, but it doesn't matter to me. All I know is that Adam is the person I want to be with, hopefully forever, if he doesn't kick me to the curb before then." I choke on a laugh.

Ava huffs and wipes under her eyes with her thumbs. "You and Adam are both going to kill me with the stuff you say about each other. But I need you to understand something that I fought for years to believe myself."

She sniffles and blinks before saying, "When you find someone who loves you as much as you love them, your differences don't matter. The person that you think is too good for you fell in love with *you* for who *you* are. If they wanted someone different, they would have gone and found that person. And your age? Fuck it. Society has engrained it in our heads that it's wrong for people in their twenties to know what they want instead of getting drunk at parties and making mistakes, when that's not true at all. I was planning a wedding and getting pregnant when I was in my early twenties, and I don't regret those decisions in the slightest. You are who you are regardless of your age. Just because you're more mature and at a further point in your life earlier than others doesn't make it wrong. Adam doesn't see it that way either."

Her reassurance strikes deep. A feeling of contentment sinks over my shoulders, and I exhale a slow breath. Having her cut down insecurities I didn't even know were there, lurking in the shadows, has me reaching over and hugging her.

She hugs me back instantly. "He's not going to let you go

now. Not as long as he's breathing, anyway. You're theirs, and ours, no matter what."

"Thank you," I whisper.

She laughs lightly and squeezes me once before releasing me. "You're welcome. Now, let's go find your man. I'm sure he's losing his head not knowing where you are."

31

Scarlett

There have been several times in my life when I've wanted to find my father and shove my successes in his face. The first time my skates hit Olympic ice, the moment I had a gold medal draped over my neck, and now as I search for the man I love at a festival that he put on for the community and every athlete in the city because his heart is just that big.

I wonder what he would say if he could see how happy I am—how much I've accomplished in such a short time. Yet there's also a small part of me that doesn't want to give him that pleasure.

After growing up being showered with so much love from my mom and then getting to witness the love Cooper receives from both his parents, I know my father wouldn't be worthy of witnessing my successes.

Beth faced an adversity that not many of us could say we would have dealt with the same way. She risked everything for Cooper, and even though it almost broke her, it didn't stop her from doing what she knew was right.

That's the kind of parent we all deserve. And that fact alone helps break me out of my thoughts long enough to catch said woman standing off to the side beside a corn dog stand with her phone clutched tightly in her hands.

Her eyes are wide and frantic, and I turn to Ava, saying a quick "be right back" before jogging toward Beth. A feeling of protectiveness hits me when I register the fear on her face.

"Beth! Hey," I say when I reach her. Her head snaps up, and some of the tension on her face disappears when she spots me.

"Oh, Scarlett. Hi."

"Are you okay? Have you seen Adam yet?"

She shakes her head. "I haven't been able to reach him, and I'm late for my date with Cooper."

I put a cautious hand on her forearm and try to reassure her with a smile. "I'm looking for him too. Ava thinks he's inside with Cooper and forgot his phone in his office. We can find him together if you want."

"That would be great, actually. Thank you."

I shrug. "It's not a big deal. I don't do well with crowds either. Or people at all, really."

"I think you've been doing okay so far. You came up to me and pretty much saved my ass and you barely know me."

"You're Cooper's mom. That's all I need to know."

"That's sweet. I don't see why they call you Scary Spice."

A huff escapes me before I can hold it in. "Don't let my Prince Charming moment fool you. It probably won't ever happen again."

"Lucky me for getting to bear witness to such a rare occurrence, then," she jokes.

"You're funny. I see Cooper got that from both his parents."

My honesty must surprise her because there's a beat of awkward silence that follows my words. Beth looks around the empty field behind us and blurts out, "Has Adam told you? About me?"

"Most of it. He said there was certain stuff he thought you should have the right to tell me yourself."

"He's a good man. A great dad," she says.

"Yeah, he is."

"I was unfair to him when I told him about Cooper," she starts, her gaze falling to her shoes. "What he probably didn't tell you or want you to know at all was that I told him it was his fault. How I screamed at him in that alley and told him such awful things that weren't true, but that flew out before I could stop them. I gave him Cooper as if he were a damaged box of goods instead of a little boy, and I've never forgiven myself for that. Adam did, though. He forgave me, offered me money, welcomed me into our son's life even after I gave up my rights and told him he was his best chance at a good life. That's just who Adam is, and I want you to know that I am so happy he has found you.

"You don't need my support or acceptance, but you have it anyway. Adam and Cooper both deserve to have you in their lives. Knowing you'll be there for them makes me so, so happy."

The next time Beth looks at me, she's smiling. It's a smile fit with a thousand emotions, but I can only decipher one. Happiness.

"I don't know what to say . . ." I mumble, at a loss for words.

Out of all the things I was expecting Beth to tell me, her confessions were definitely not one of them. I don't know whether to cry or smile. I'm leaning toward smile, but my nerves have short-circuited my mind. I release an awkward, short laugh instead.

Much to my surprise, Beth starts laughing too. "That's okay. I think we'll get along quite well, don't you?"

I nod. "Yeah, I really do."

And just like that, we head toward where Ava is waiting, devouring a corn dog, suddenly more comfortable and at ease with each other.

Adam

Cooper has never been into sports. He's always chosen music and art over anything that requires physical activity, and unlike my own parents, I made sure to never fault him for realizing what makes him happy and what doesn't.

However, once a year, at this festival, he entertains me for a few minutes by putting a pair of skates on and gliding around the rink with me. He's a natural, even with a lack of experience.

"It's freezing in here!" he shouts from the opposite side of the ice.

"I told you to put a sweater on!" I shout back, laughing.

Like any twelve-year-old boy, he figured he knew better than me and insisted he would be fine. Oh, how I love proving him wrong.

I watch him speed up and head right for me, a silly grin splitting his pink cheeks. There's a joy in his eyes that has me taking off in his direction.

"Dad!" His eyes go wide when he notices I'm coming at him. "Slow down!"

"No can do!"

He shrieks when I skate up to him and grab him around his middle, lifting him off the ice and holding him sideways against my side as I keep skating.

"You're going to kill us both," he warns before I briefly loosen my grip and pretend to drop him.

He shakes against me as he breaks into a fit of laughter. The happy sound rings off the walls of the arena and settles in my chest.

"This will teach you for not listening to your old man."

"You think you're so funny." He slaps my abdomen.

I cluck my tongue to the roof of my mouth. "I don't think, buddy, I *know*."

"I'm way heavier than I was the last time you did this."

From the burn in my bicep, that much is obvious. Still, I make it my mission to hold him for at least another minute. "I would hope so. The last time I did this, you were eight. You didn't wiggle so much then either."

"I could slice your butt with my skate. Then you would let me down."

I laugh. "Try it, funny guy."

"It's not as satisfying when you agree like that," he grumbles.

The unmistakable sound of the rink door slamming shut captures our attention. I spin us around to face the entrance and find Scarlett and Beth standing by the boards.

"Don't let us interrupt all the fun," Beth says.

I barely hear her, though. I'm too focused on the woman beside her, smiling at me like I'm the answer to every single one of the questions she's ever had.

She raises her hand and wiggles her fingers. My lips tip up as I carefully set Cooper down on his own two feet. He huffs a quick *good riddance* before Scarlett's placing something by the boards and skating onto the ice.

Those yellow-laced skates are bright on her feet as she moves toward me, not stopping until the tips of them brush mine. "I was looking for you," she whispers, tilting her head to meet my stare.

Unable to help myself, I slip my hand in her hair and palm her nape. "Really? Because I was waiting for you."

"What are the odds of that?" she teases.

"Apparently pretty slim. I was beginning to think you got lost along the way."

"Me? Lost? Let's go with sidetracked."

My laugh kisses her mouth before I do the same. She grabs my waist and curls her fingers into my sweatshirt, responding eagerly.

"I missed you," I groan when we break apart, all too aware of our surroundings.

"I missed you too. Let's not do that time apart thing again, accidental or not."

"You just don't want to have to use the espresso machine again," I poke at her, loving the way her nose scrunches when I say the word *espresso.*

"Speaking of, I sort of got you something," she says nervously. "I'll be right back."

I cock a brow and watch as she quickly skates to the boards and picks up whatever she had set down when she arrived. My curiosity only grows when she comes back to me with a small gift bag in her hands.

"What did I do to deserve a gift?" I tease.

She rolls her eyes, handing me the small white bag. Feeling antsy, I take it from her and dig through the tissue paper to find a mug. A loud laugh escapes me when I pull it out and hold it up in the air, inspecting the black writing and hot pink bunny ears splayed over the white mug.

"Adam the Puck Bunny, huh? I told you it had a nice ring to it."

"It was only fair you had one too. Considering the one you slipped into the staff room for me."

I grin and reach for her, holding her warm waist. "It's perfect, baby. Thank you."

She returns my smile before leaning up and pressing her lips to mine, stealing a quick yet earth-tilting kiss.

Too quickly, a throat clears, and we reluctantly break apart. We look at Cooper at the same time, but I don't release her waist.

"Dad, I like SP, but kissing is so nasty," he tells me before looking up at Scarlett. "I like your skates. They remind me of bumblebees. Do you like bumblebees?"

She shrugs. "As much as the next person, I think. Do you?"

"Same. They're alright. Hey, do you think you could teach me how to take a slapshot?"

Her lips twitch. "Do you have a stick?"

"Yeah. Dad makes me bring it when we do this." He skates to the side of the ice and bends over the boards. When he comes back, it's with a stick in his hands. "Will this work?"

Scarlett looks at me, almost like she's asking for permission, and I don't hesitate to nod.

"Yeah, that will work. Come on," she tells Cooper before leading him to the puck bucket and getting him set up on the centre of the ice.

I feel Beth wobble up beside me as I watch them. "She's not what I expected, but maybe that's why you work so well. You're obsessed with each other."

Fuck yeah, we are. "Cooper likes her too."

"He does."

Scarlett uses his stick to demonstrate the positioning, regardless of the fact it's far too small for her. After showing him the proper movements, she hands it to him.

"Come on, buddy!" I shout.

I stifle a laugh when Cooper tries to copy Scarlett's moves, but his blade skims the puck. She's calm with him and walks him through the steps again. The next time he swings, he sends the puck a few feet in front of them and twirls in a circle with a loud whoop.

"Boo-yah!"

Scarlett claps, grinning at Cooper before we all watch him lose his balance and fly backward. He lets out a low sound of pain when his butt makes contact with the ice, but not even a second later, starts laughing.

After pushing himself to a sitting position on the ice, he looks up at Scarlett with a mischievous grin. "Help me up?" he asks her, blinking innocently.

She doesn't hesitate to offer him a hand. "You wanna try again? Maybe with a bit less twirling?"

As soon as the words escape her, Cooper's clutching her hand and pulling, bringing her down to the ice beside him. She squeals when she hits the ice before a loud laugh cuts through her surprise.

When she sits up, Cooper leans his head on her shoulder. "Sure, SP. Maybe we can do this another time too. You're actually pretty cool."

"What do you mean 'actually pretty cool'?" she asks him.

His reply is a cheeky smirk as he pushes off the ice and collects another puck, ready to try shooting again.

Scarlett's eyes meet mine then, and the spark in them makes my heart thump harder in my chest. I give her a thumbs-up and watch as she mouths the three words I can't wait to hear her say for the rest of forever.

I love you.

32

Scarlett

I ADJUST THE SLEEVES OF MY VANCOUVER WARRIORS JERSEY AND play with the neck of the sweatshirt beneath, doing anything to keep my hands busy.

I'm nervous—terrified, actually. It's game seven of the Stanley Cup finals, and both teams are tied with one goal each.

While I would love to see Leo raise that giant silver cup over his head and plant a kiss on its belly, the little girl inside of me who idolized the VW her entire life needs them to win this. I need them to win while I'm here, watching and chanting and yelling curses at the referees.

It wasn't five minutes after we arrived at Rogers Arena that it hit me. It hit me that this is the first time I've been to a game of this calibre that wasn't my own. Where I wasn't the one feeling the suffocating pressure, the exhaustion and adrenaline that pumps through you in one chaotic cocktail with each second that ticks down on the clock.

Every hockey player dreams of this moment—fantasizes about it, hoping one day it will be *their* blades cutting into this ice. *Their* stick connecting with that final game-winning puck.

When I was very young, I had dreams of being here, but things aren't the same for women in the hockey world, and that's just how it is. Instead, I got to play on an even bigger stage, with just as much on the line.

The Olympics were everything I had hoped for. The little girl inside of me sobbed when we made it to that arena in Pyeong-Chang. It was like suddenly everything was worth it. Every bill that was paid late because Mom made sure hockey came first, every pulled muscle and ache in my body that lingered for weeks, and all of the years I spent with skates on my feet and gloves on my hands.

It. Was. All. Worth. It.

The Olympics were my Stanley Cup playoffs. The gold medal that was slipped over my head and hung heavy on my neck was my Stanley Cup. And those memories will live inside of me for the rest of my life.

Hopefully, the girl sitting next to me in a matching jersey and green-painted cheeks will be there next. And maybe I'll be the one to help her get there.

"This is insane. I can't thank you enough for this," Willow says to Adam. She's staring in awe at the rush of players from our lower-level seats, three rows from the ice itself.

Tyler Bateman throws his body against the boards when he notices us on his way to the bench, and Willow's gasp is so audible I laugh into my hand. Cooper doesn't try to hide his laugh from his place beside Adam.

"It pays off to have friends in high places." Adam grins at her.

He's been holding my thigh in that large hand of his since the start of the third period, and I have a suspicion it's because he's just as nervous as I am. With his foot tapping at an unsteady beat and his hair a mess from his fingers constantly sliding through it, he looks a mess.

A ridiculously handsome mess.

"You good?" I ask in a hushed voice.

He turns his head and looks at me, a bit panicked. I blink back my surprise and place my hand over his.

"Oakley never won a Stanley Cup with this team. The VW haven't won one since long before he joined them. This is it, baby. This has to be the year. Tyler's going to get that moment."

"This is it," I echo. "And we get to witness it."

The time on the clock ticks to the final one minute before an icing is called against the Woodmen, sending them back to the left of their own net.

Adrenaline sparks beneath my skin. My pulse races.

"This could actually happen," Willow breathes, reaching for my hand, holding it for dear life. I give hers a tight squeeze and settle them on the armrest between us.

We must all look like a bunch of unstable superfans, and that's because we are. All three of us bleed hockey, but we each love it in a different way.

For Adam, it's a friendly kind of love. It's a familiar face in a crowded room. A comfort.

For Willow, it's a passionate love, a blazing fire burning inside her chest. That fire is what fuels her, and without that fire, she's cold, numb.

And for me, hockey is like my version of a high school sweetheart. It's my first love, the one who broke my heart. But it's also what helped teach me everything I needed to know about myself. It's the type of love that grew into something I'll always remember.

It's memories. It's the highest highs and the lowest lows.

I won't ever stop loving hockey. I'll use my experiences to mentor others and to just enjoy the sport that I fell in love with back when I was too young to realize what I was really getting myself into.

Some people aren't lucky enough to find a passion like mine in their entire lives, and I don't plan on ever letting that go to waste.

The last minute of the game is a blur. The crowd is deafening; the hands clutching mine are both slick with nervous sweat.

Leo clears the puck from their zone, but in a blink, Tyler's there, trapping it and quickly passing it off. A Warriors player—a rookie with the name Marshall stitched on his jersey—is the one to receive the hard pass from Tyler.

He freezes for the smallest of moments when the puck hits his blade, just long enough for anyone looking close enough to notice, before taking off toward the goalie.

I hold my breath when he crosses the blue line and avoids the Woodmen defenseman who had his stick positioned to steal the puck. My grip on Adam's hand is punishing, but I don't let go. I don't think I can.

The rookie player whips his head back and forth, suddenly seeing the players in front of him. They want to shut him down, regardless of what they have to do to accomplish it, and I'm sure he's thinking that exact thing right now.

My entire body locks up when he spots Tyler and, without a second thought, sends the puck between the Woodmen players and directly to Tyler's stick.

Tyler doesn't hesitate. He looks directly at the group of players surrounding him and pulls a maneuver worthy of the trophies and awards he's won and shoots the puck.

I jump to my feet, and a shout rips through me the second that red buzzer flares to life above the goalie net and Tyler sails across the ice with his hands and stick straight in the air.

I focus on the net through wet eyes, and there it is. The puck is nestled in the left corner.

"Oh my God!" Willow screams, launching herself in my arms as Adam hugs Cooper. "They did it!"

If I thought the crowd was deafening before, it was nothing compared to now. Hats, jerseys, and the flags that were laid over our seats when we got here—they're raining down over the stands. Plastic clappers are going crazy, and the band perched in one of the boxes is banging on drums and playing the most random music in celebration.

Willow releases me at the same time Adam scoops me in his arms and pulls me against him. He bends down and captures my mouth in a soul-shattering kiss that tastes like popcorn and the tears streaming down my face.

His hands are on my hips, my waist, my face, anywhere he can touch. We're high on adrenaline, on pure elation, and it takes everything in me to pull away before our clothes wind up everywhere but our bodies.

"Holy shit," I gasp, shaking my head in disbelief. "Is this for real?"

The Warriors are in an emotionally gripping hug on centre ice, their gloves and helmets lying around them. I lift my head to the jumbotron and see coverage of the box I know Gracie and the rest of the group was watching from.

Oakley has his sister tucked in his arms, holding her tight as she cries tears of happiness and pride. They break apart just enough for Oakley to turn Gray toward the ice as Tyler lifts his arm, pointing right at her.

She gives him a watery smile and puts her hand over her heart before shaking her head and pointing back.

The moment has me looking back at Adam, my heart in my throat. I lift my hands and grab his face, pulling him down to kiss me one more time.

But before our lips connect, I whisper, "There isn't anyone I would have rather experienced this with."

He wraps a hand in my curls and tilts my head back. "Here's to a lifetime of memories like this, Scary Spice."

EPILOGUE 1

TWO MONTHS LATER

Scarlett

COOPER PULLS BOTH ME AND ADAM BY THE HANDS UP THE pavement toward his school. His excitement is potent as he grins wildly at his friends and waits for Adam to pull open the door before yanking us inside.

"SP! Look, I painted these ones in the mural!" he shouts, pointing to the wall by the entrance made up of painted tiles that all together create a mountain range with high, snow-covered tips and bundles of trees lining the bottom.

"Coop, remember what I told you about having an indoor voice?" Adam chuckles.

Cooper essentially shrugs him off and pulls my hand tighter, bringing me closer to the mural. "You can say that mine are the best. I know they are."

Arching a brow, I lean toward the two tiles and hum under my breath. "Yeah, Cooper, they're by far the best." I gently shove his shoulder with mine.

"That's not sarcasm, is it?" He narrows his eyes quizzically at me.

"Not this time." I wink.

A large hand spans the width of my back, and I lean back into its embrace. Looking over my shoulder, I see Adam standing close behind me, watching the two of us with blazing love in his eyes.

I've seen that look more times than I can count over the past few months, and I plan on seeing it for a long time to come.

"I can paint you some tiles next time we do that in class, Scar. Maybe I could paint you a gold medal or something," Cooper offers casually.

My heart squeezes. I smile down at him. "I would love that."

"Sick. Maybe I can as soon as we're done with this stupid people unit. I hate drawing people—hold on, is Grandma A still coming?" Cooper rambles, his thoughts scrambled.

Adam bends down, and his words brush the tip of my ear. "She would burst into tears if she knew he had called her that."

"She's only been nagging at him to say it since the festival." I snort.

He kisses the side of my head, laughing. "Yeah, she'll be here, Coop."

It's been a month since we found the right caretaker for my mom, and she's been handling the change better than I was hoping. She enjoys the company of Bridgett, and they've really hit it off. They're friends, in a way. The relationship they have has helped with the onslaught of guilt and selfishness I felt after telling her I couldn't take care of her on my own anymore.

That day was hard. It was probably one of the hardest days I've ever had. But ultimately, it was the right decision.

Her memory is faltering quicker as the months go on, and with that, her personality is changing, altering. There are some days when I don't recognize her at all, but somewhere, she's the same woman who held my hair back when I puked after my first night out drinking and quit her job when I was sixteen because her boss wouldn't approve her vacation days to take me to a hockey tournament.

It's been hard, but we've survived. She adores Cooper and Adam, and when days are good, they're *so* good. We've been holding on to those days.

She's been looking forward to Cooper's fall art show for weeks now, and he's thrilled to show off to her. It'll be good for all of us.

"Yo, Cooper! Come see the pictures I took of my new RC car!"

We all turn to see a group of boys staring at us by the water fountain. The tallest one with a backward baseball cap waves like a madman.

Cooper looks at his father and me and groans. "I don't care about RC cars."

Adam ruffles his hair. "Be a good sport. We'll see you inside the gym."

"Fine, make sure you wait to look for my table. Don't do any sneaking around," he mutters before dragging his feet toward the group of boys.

I stifle a laugh, watching him paint a smile on his face and say hi to his friends. He looks over at us once and sticks his tongue out before turning back and joining the conversation.

"I'm realizing you two have more in common every day," Adam says.

"Are you trying to say that I'm not a people person?"

"Oh, baby, I know you're not a people person."

I roll my eyes at him. "You like it because it gives you a chance to turn on your charm to make up for my lack of conversation."

"Precisely." He nips at my ear and uses the hand on my back to steer me in the direction of the open gym doors.

We pass multiple sets of parents, all of whom say hi to Adam and, in turn, me. By the time we actually make it inside the gym, my cheeks are sore from all the smiling.

As we get settled against one of the walls and wait for the official start of the show, Adam turns to face me and grabs my hand, threading our fingers. "I'm proud of you, you know?"

I look at him, and as our eyes meet, butterflies erupt in my stomach. "For what?"

"Everything. Your mom, Cooper, your new job. You've come so far since the first time you came into my office."

Excitement bubbles at the mention of my new job. It's only been a couple of weeks since I took a coaching position for Willow's U15 hockey team, but it only took a few days to realize it was the perfect position for me.

After one of her previous coaches decided to drop everything and move to Quebec with her fiancé, they had an opening that needed to be filled urgently, and Willow didn't hesitate to bring my name up for the position. It was a bit of a shock to get a call from a woman offering me a job I never applied for, but Adam was the one who gave me the push I needed to go for it.

Now, I still train at WIT on days I don't have practice, but I have something else to give me purpose. Something to push me.

"Now that I think about it, I've been really missing our therapy sessions lately," I admit.

His lips pull into a smirk. "We can always have one when we're done here."

"I think that's probably a good idea. We don't want all our hard work to be for nothing." A liquid heat falls between my legs as I stare up at him, my lips parted.

His eyes flare, and as much as I know that a school gym isn't the right place to be contemplating jumping Adam's bones, I can't help it. He does something to me nobody before him has ever done.

"You're going to end up getting your ass spanked as soon as I get you home and into my bed," he rasps, squeezing my hand.

My pulse starts to race. "Haven't I told you before not to threaten me with a good time?"

I gasp when he slips his hand between my back and the wall and inconspicuously grabs my ass, kneading it in his palm. "Remember that you brought this on yourself, sweetheart."

"I don't think that will be a problem," I whisper, pushing back into his hand. He groans quietly, and I smile wickedly. "Are you sure you can contain yourself for the next couple hours? I wouldn't want you to be . . . uncomfortable." My eyes fall to the bulge in his jeans.

He bends down, and his lips caress my forehead. "Fuck, I love you."

Tilting my head, I capture his lips in a quick kiss. "I love you too."

"I love you *both*. I mean, look at you. In love and not afraid to show it," I hear my mom sigh. Adam's hand falls to his side as we both turn to greet her.

"Hey, Mom."

"You look beautiful this evening, Amelia," Adam compliments her. He always does this, and she always turns to putty. It's adorable, really.

Mom blushes a bright pink as I turn to the onyx-haired woman beside her. "Thank you for coming, Bridgett."

Bridgett smiles kindly. "Of course. Amelia couldn't stop talking about it all afternoon."

"Now, where's my little guy? I'm feeling antsy to see the little Picasso's work," Mom huffs.

Adam answers for me. "He should be out any minute. Why don't you and I go see if we can find something to drink while we wait? I think Cooper mentioned there would be lemonade."

"I would love that. You know how much I adore my lemonade."

With a lingering kiss on my cheek, Adam tells me he'll be right back before placing his hand on my mom's back and steering her past all the art tables and up toward the front of the gym.

I don't know which table is Cooper's, but I wouldn't dare disobey his orders. Not when he's been so excited to show everything off.

Speaking of, I spot the curly-haired boy heading right for me. He grins when he notices me looking at him. I wave.

"Hey, SP. Where's Dad? We're ready to start."

I nod to the drink stand, where Adam is nodding along to

something my mom is drawling on about with a full glass of lemonade in her hand. He laughs, and I swear, even from this far away, I can feel the joy in it.

"Oh well. I'll show you my table first, and then they can find us after." He grabs my hand and, for the second time tonight, drags me behind him. "I wanted to see your reaction before anyone else, anyway. Before Dad steals your attention and I lose my moment. You know?"

Nerves spark beneath my skin. "That sounds pretty ominous."

"What does that mean? I don't think I've heard that word before."

"You're talking vaguely. It's kind of scary, nerve-racking."

"Ah, okay. Yeah, I know I am."

"Can you maybe be a bit less ominous?"

"No," he says bluntly.

I choke on a laugh. "Okay then."

"It will be worth it, I promise."

"Well, if you're promising, then I'll believe you."

"That's the right move. Thanks."

We pass by two art tables and a pair of crying parents before coming to a stop in front of one with a blue covering and Cooper's name written on a white banner pinned to the front.

"Okay," Cooper starts, dropping my hand and twirling to block my view of something on the table. "I made this for you, but if you think it's bad or ugly or something, we can make it disappear."

Emotion swells in my chest at those words alone. I nod excitedly, too afraid to speak, not knowing if I'll make any sense when I do.

"Here it goes," he mumbles before stepping out of the way and shoving his hands in the pocket of his hoodie.

The painting in front of me blurs as my eyes fill with tears. I blink profusely to try and clear my vision but only make the moisture slip down my face instead.

A turquoise-coloured lake rests behind three people. Three people who look way too similar to Adam, Cooper, and me. I flick my watery gaze to Cooper and find him watching me nervously, his eyes wide.

"Oh boy, I made you cry. Should I get my dad? Yeah, I'll go get him," he rambles, looking like a dear in headlights.

"No!" I rush out. "No, it's okay. Is that us?"

He nods once. "Yeah. I told you I hated painting people, and I do, but Mrs. Johnson insisted that maybe I wouldn't hate it as much if I drew people that I loved."

I cover my mouth with the back of my hand and swallow back a sob. Between him and his father, they're going to kill me. "You can't just blurt out to people that you love them. You need to give them some warning," I croak.

Cooper smiles apologetically. "Oops."

"I didn't know you loved me."

Curiosity crosses his features. "Why wouldn't I?"

"You've only known me for a few months."

"I think that's long enough. I like having you in our family. You complete it, I think."

A watery whimper-like sound escapes me. This kid . . . this kid is something special. I rush toward him and pull him into a tight hug, mumbling, "I love you too, Cooper. I'll be here as long as you guys want me to be."

"So always," Adam says, joining us. I look at him and notice how his eyes shine as he watches me hug his son.

"Pretty much," Cooper agrees.

Adam wraps the both of us up in his embrace, and I close my eyes, content and at peace.

I kiss the top of Cooper's head. "Always sounds perfect to me."

EPILOGUE 2

THREE YEARS LATER

Adam

NAILS GENTLY SCRATCH AT THE PATCH OF HAIRS ABOVE THE waistband of my boxers, making me groan. I cover the soft hand with my own, capturing it and bringing it up to my mouth. My lips brush the palm, kissing it.

"It's early. Go back to sleep," I rasp.

The smell of cherry blossoms hits me, and I grin despite the exhaustion pulling at my eyelids. Scarlett buries her head in my shoulder, peppering the skin with kisses.

"I can't. I think I'm too excited."

Subconsciously, I twirl the cold silver band on her ring finger until I touch the diamond in the centre. "Yeah? Me too. What time are we going to visit your mom?"

"One, after she's had lunch. They say it's when she's most lucid."

I squeeze her hand and move it to my chest. She hums sleepily, but I know by now there's no hope of her falling back asleep. Scarlett is the world's testiest sleeper. It was one of the first things I noticed when I had managed to convince her to move in with me and Cooper two years ago.

Even though I had wanted her to move in pretty much as soon as she could, I knew it wasn't possible. We all needed time to adjust to the changes in our lives, and she didn't want to leave her mother until there was no other choice but to seek out assisted-living housing. Supporting her decision was easy, especially when I knew what it meant to her.

It wasn't until Amelia could no longer safely live in their home without 24/7 care that Scarlett made the decision to get her approved into assisted living. She kept the house for a couple of months, but it was empty and lonely, and as she told me the night before it went up on the market, it just wasn't a home anymore.

"What do you think she's going to say to the news?" I ask my fiancée, loving the way that sounds. It's been three weeks since I asked her to marry me, and I still haven't gotten used to how much I love using the title whenever possible.

"She loves you as much as she loves me. She'll be happy. Elated, probably."

"I don't think it's possible for her to love anyone as much as she loves you, but I'll take it."

Scarlett pushes up on her elbow and looks at me. Her hair is a mess of curls, and I can't help but reach out and push them out of her face, letting the silky strands slip between my fingers.

"When is everyone coming over? I'll need a couple hours to charge my social battery beforehand," she jokes, although there's some truth to that.

I chuckle. "Before dinner. I told them not to stay late with how tired you've been lately."

"Mm, thank you," she whispers before leaning forward and capturing my lips in a soft kiss.

When she goes to back away, I nip at her mouth and use the hand tangled in her hair to pull her closer, keeping her trapped in my orbit. Her lips part on a gasp the second I grab her waist with my other hand and pull her to straddle me.

"Where do you think you're going?" I mumble against her mouth.

She twirls her hips and grinds against the growing bulge in my underwear. "Nowhere now. I think I'm stuck right here."

"You make it sound like it's a punishment to have my cock inside you, but I never hear you complaining while you're getting fucked, baby," I whisper, sliding my mouth down her jaw to the sensitive skin beneath it and sucking, leaving a mark for everyone to see later.

A whimper escapes her before she's making quick work of freeing my cock and pushing her panties to the side. A groan gets caught in my throat when she lifts her hips and lines herself up with the tip before sinking down on it, taking every fucking inch.

"*Oh yes . . .*" she sighs.

I slide my hand under the shirt she threw over herself last night—my shirt—and move it up her side and to her front until I have her breast in my hand. "You feel like heaven. Tight and soft and made just for me." I drive my hips up into her and watch her eyes roll back as she starts to ride me harder, faster.

Reaching between her legs, I slide my fingers over her warm, wet skin and pinch her clit, twirling it over and over as her pussy pulses and beautiful noises spill from her lips.

"Oh, my—Adam, I—shower," she gasps, tossing her head back. Her thighs quiver as she reaches for me.

Knowing what that means, I slip out of bed with Scarlett shaking in my arms and my cock still buried inside of her and head into the ensuite. She hides her head in my neck and shudders, her nails digging into my back as I turn on the shower and step inside, not bothering to wait for the water to warm up.

"Holy fuck," she groans, and I'm not sure if it's from the shock of the cold water or the way I press her into the shower wall and start to fuck her like a madman.

"Are you going to come for me, baby? Are you going to come all over this cock?"

She nods frantically before tensing up and biting down on my neck. Her legs shake as her pussy clenches tight around me.

"Adam—oh my *fuck*," she whines before I feel her start to explode, soaking my cock in her cum.

Her orgasm triggers mine, and I groan low and long as I fill her, leaving myself buried balls-deep until I can trust myself to pull out without dropping her.

When I do, I keep us pressed tightly together and reach between Scarlett's legs, careful not to bump her swollen, over-sensitive clit.

"What are you doing?" she asks when I slip a finger through her swollen flesh and push the cum that's leaked from her pussy back inside.

I keep my finger buried inside for a few seconds, almost in a trance, before I catch her lust-blown stare and grin.

"We need every drop if we're going to get you pregnant, Scary Spice, not lose my swimmers in the drain."

A smile cracks through her curiosity. "You're ridiculous."

The water is way past warm by now, but after being kept pressed to the shower wall, she's shivering. I remove my hand and move her into the water, stepping behind her to start helping wash her hair.

The idea of having a baby with Scarlett isn't a new one. We've discussed it a few times over the past few months and recently talked to Cooper about what he thought of the idea. I think he was more excited about the subject than either of us was. It was a proud moment for me.

"Wanting to see you carry my baby is not ridiculous. Some would say it's hot for a guy to have a breeding kink. Oakley mentioned it to me once."

Scarlett lets out a loud laugh. "You guys talk about kinks? What, do you have meetings like a book club, but instead of books, you talk about what kinks you have?"

I squirt her shampoo in my hand and start to rub it into her hair. "Maybe we do."

"Funny, I haven't noticed you sneaking out to meet with this club at all."

"I've been meeting them in our kinky clubhouse after you pass out at eight thirty every night."

"Right, right. Totally." She moans softly as I massage the shampoo in her hair until it's foaming. Stepping under the steady stream of water, she rinses it out while I grab her fancy conditioner. "Maybe I'll have to ask the guys about it when they get here later, then."

I laugh in response, but her mention of later has me wanting to hurry up and get a move on with our day. It's been torture not telling everyone I know that I'm finally going to make Scarlett my wife, and now that I can, I don't want to waste any more time.

BY THE TIME our house has transformed into a full-blown circus, both Scarlett and I are bursting to shout our news and get the secret off our chests. I'm not sure how we made it through dinner without spilling the beans, but with how crazy our dinners get with the size of our group now, there was no way we would have been able to get a word in, even if it was to announce something as exciting as an engagement.

Now, an hour later, Cooper and the older kids are in the yard, most likely terrorizing the younger ones with water guns or Nerf bullets, while the grown-ups sit on the back patio, chatting and getting wine drunk.

Scarlett adjusts herself on my lap until her back is flush to my chest, and her head falls back to my shoulder. I wrap my arms around her middle and pull her as close as possible, loving the way she feels pressed against me. All warm and content.

"We should just blurt it out, you know. They won't stop gossiping until something more exciting comes along," I whisper, brushing my nose over the tip of her ear.

She shivers. "True. The ring is in your pocket, right?"

I answer her by reaching into said pocket and pulling it out, carefully sliding it on her finger. "Maybe just stick your hand out and see who's the first to notice."

Ava's laugh carries across the yard, and I look to see her flicking Oakley in the ear and pointing at the group of kids. Following her finger, I find Adalyn sitting on Maddox's butt as Cooper shoves his face into the grass.

"Cooper!" I yell, trying to grab his attention. "Hands off!"

"No way! This asshole just nut punched me!"

Adalyn starts to giggle and pull at Cooper's hair. "He did! He did!"

He reaches up to swat at her while keeping his other hand on Maddox's head. "Don't pull my hair, or I'll pull yours," he grunts.

She does it again anyway, pushing his boundaries like she always does.

Muffles come from the ground as Maddox tries to say something. Cooper eases off enough to let him speak.

"I nut punched you because you called me Doxxy Poxxy again. It's not funny anymore."

"So, what? Only your girlfriend is allowed to call you that? I invented that nickname."

"For the last time, Braxton is not my girlfriend!" Maddox shouts.

Cooper grins smugly. "I never said anything about Braxton."

"Cooper, you're the oldest. You know better than to shove someone's face into the dirt," I scold, albeit half-heartedly.

He and Maddox have been like this since they were kids. They fight over everything but are also closer than any two people I think have ever been. They're brothers in the strongest sense of the word. No amount of scolding will ever change their ways.

My son fully looks at me now, annoyed to the max. "You're seriously pulling the oldest card right now?"

Scarlett intertwines our fingers and squeezes. I shut my

mouth and look at her. There's mischief in her eyes, and just like that, I know exactly what she's thinking.

One second, we're staring at each other, and the next, she's turning to face the group, saying, "We're getting married."

Silence, and then a bomb goes off.

"Finally!" Ava shrieks, jumping out of her seat and hauling ass toward us. As soon as she gets close enough, she's pulling Scarlett into her arms and squeezing her tight enough that I worry I'll have to butt in before she pops her.

"What about me, O? I'm not feeling the love right now," I tease her.

With a scoff, Ava peels herself off my fiancée and gathers me in a hug just as tight. "I love the shit out of you, A. And I'm *so* proud of you."

I swallow a sudden lump of emotion and kiss the side of her head before she backs up. "Love you too, O baby."

The rest of the group makes their way over to us next, showering us with love and congratulations.

Braden tells me he can't wait to be my best man and then acts offended when I tell him I could never trust him with that much responsibility. Oakley, the only guy in the group who knew when I was planning on proposing, hugs me tight and tells me he couldn't have hand-picked anyone better for me. And Tyler, well, he hugs me for the first time in our entire friendship and tells me not to bring it up again, or he'll put *my* face in the grass.

Scarlett slides up next to me and grabs my hand, placing it on her stomach, and I stare at her with an outpouring amount of love, tempted to convince her to go with me to city hall right now.

It's not until she shakes her head and grins that I grow confused. My jaw falls open when she leans up on her tiptoes and whispers two words in my ear, blindsiding me.

"I'm pregnant."

THE END

EPILOGUE 3

TWO YEARS AFTER THAT

Cooper

I GRADUATED HIGH SCHOOL TODAY, SO I GUESS THAT KIND OF MAKES me an adult now. Or maybe not. I definitely don't feel like one, nor do I think I want to.

The beer in my hand is cold but tastes like a troll's morning piss, so I dump it down the kitchen drain and grab a blue Gatorade from the fridge instead.

The house is loud, crowded, and hot despite the air conditioning blowing on full blast. Happy Graduation banners and streamers are hung everywhere, and a half-eaten cake is on the dining room table that I'm surprised my dad hasn't put away yet.

I jump, surprised when something pulls at my leg. Look down, I find my little sister, Amelia, smiling at me with a toothy grin. Her red hair is decorated with a yellow bow and a miniature ponytail at the top of her head that resembles water shooting out of a whale.

I crouch down to her level and say, "Well, aren't you a pretty girl. Did Mama do your hair like that? There's no way Dada did."

I try not to cringe at the baby terms. We're all on strict orders from "Dada" to use baby words as much as possible to help

Ames learn how to speak. It seems a bit premature if you ask me, but oh well.

"Dada did do her hair, actually," I hear from the entryway. "And put that blue drink away. The orange ones are yours."

I look at my dad and roll my eyes. "You can keep telling me not to drink the blue ones, but I will always sneak them when you're not looking."

"You're a little shit."

"Yeah, yeah. That's me."

Scarlett's voice rings through the kitchen as she yells for Amelia. The toddler takes off, her tiny legs wobbling as she walks.

I stand and grip the drink in my hand. Dad watches me curiously for a moment before walking past me to the cupboard above the fridge and rooting around in it.

Being a little over six feet tall, I can watch everything he's doing. "You thirsty, old man?"

"No. But if you're not into beer, you should have the option of having something else. It's your graduation. Have fun instead of sitting inside drinking Gatorade. Dox is already drunk enough to have told his dad he's no longer a virgin, and he's not the one with the diploma yet."

"No shit. Actually?" I lean back against the counter, my chest shaking with a laugh.

With a full bottle of Jack in his hand, Dad turns to face me. "Yep. Ava's out back trying to coax him into drinking a bottle of water. I guess I don't have to worry about that with you, my little homebody."

I grab the bottle from his hand and twist off the cap before taking a huge gulp. It immediately burns my throat, and I spin around, coughing up a lung into the sink.

"Strong?" Dad chokes on a laugh.

I throw him a punishing glance over my shoulder. "You're a jackass."

"Who, me?" He blinks. I shove the bottle back at him, and he grins. "Usually you mix it with something, not drink it straight, hotshot."

"You know, this is why I don't drink."

"No, you don't drink because you don't want to end up like your best friend out there. You should really go save him from his parents before he ends up spilling a lot more than just losing his V card. I don't think Ava could take hearing that stuff about her baby boy."

"No, she definitely couldn't," I agree. Suddenly, Dad slaps a hand over my shoulder and pulls me into a sudden hug. I return it easily. "What's this for? Not being able to stand the taste of booze?"

"No. It's because I love you, and I'm proud of you. You're a high school graduate with an admission to university in the fall with an art scholarship. Sue me for wanting to hug the shit out of you."

The sound of footsteps in the kitchen joins us before another set of arms wrap around me from the side. The smell of cherry blossoms clues me in that it's SP.

"I know you weren't having an 'I'm proud of you' moment without me," she mumbles, tightening her grip on me.

A feeling of appreciation and love has me slipping an arm around her shoulders and bringing her further into our hug. "No way. I would have come and collected my SP moment right after this. I swear."

She hums. "Right. That's what I thought."

"Cooper the pooper!" Maddox's baritone voice hollers.

"Is he yelling from the backyard and still that loud?" Scarlett asks no one in particular.

My dad laughs and breaks up the hug. "Yes. Yes, he is." He looks at me. "Go, pooper. You're being beckoned."

"Call me pooper again and you're going to feel my wrath, Dad."

"What if I call you pooper?" Scarlett asks innocently.

I grab my blue drink from the counter and walk backward to

the door, grinning. "Nu-uh. You won't catch me giving special treatment. It's a parent rule and goes for both of you, got it?"

I FIND Maddox sitting on the grass in the backyard. He's wearing a ball cap backward like always and has his button-up under his ass, leaving him shirtless. The tattoo he just got on his sixteenth birthday is still covered in a clear wrapping, hidden from view in the dark of the backyard.

A girl with wild black curls and a hockey jacket with the name Hutton hung over her shoulders is beside him, close but not too close. She reaches toward him and pulls his ball cap off his head before pushing it over her hair. It looks like it's on the verge of popping right off.

"Braxton Heights, when the hell did you show up?" I ask, walking in front of them and flopping down on the grass.

Ice-blue eyes meet mine when she looks at me, smiling gently. Her dimples have popped out, like they always do. That girl smiles like she's paid to do it. Unlike Maddox. If looks could kill, I'd be meeting Death right about now as he glares at me for simply talking to her. As if we haven't all been best friends since elementary school.

"A few minutes ago. I'm sorry I missed your ceremony. I was stuck babysitting my sister because my dad's out in Vegas dealing with one of his clients. You know how it is with free-agent signings," she says.

Her father, Roy Heights, is an agent for several pro hockey players. One of the guys known to latch onto big money opportunities like a low-level leech. He's not respected in the industry, but neither Dox nor I have ever told her that.

Dox grunts, and I swear I see him move his arm behind her. "You say that like he's not always gone. Busy season or not."

She sighs. "Don't start. Not tonight. It's Cooper's big day!"

"I graduated high school, Brax. I didn't get married or unveil one of my paintings in the Louvre."

"Not yet. But that's beside the point. It's still a big milestone, Cooperoni," she says.

"God, I hate that nickname," I groan and lie back on the grass.

"Too bad I'm never going to stop saying it," she sings.

The stars are out tonight, decorating the dark sky like white paint flicked on an empty black canvas. Cassiopeia winks at me before I turn my head and look at my friends.

Neither of them has any interest in stars, or anything that doesn't involve sports in Maddox's case, or animals in Braxton's. They're both a bit narrow-minded, but somehow, we all get along as if they were into everything I am.

Maybe how different we are is why we work so well together. The Three Musketeers, as my aunt Ava calls us. We've always meshed, clicked on a molecular level despite the small age difference between me and them. We've fought and made up more times than I can count, but no matter what happens, we are never apart for too long.

I can't help but wonder if that will change when Maddox makes his move on her—which I know he will. He's been in love with her since before his balls dropped. Brax, on the other hand, she's harder to read. And that's what scares me.

I like our dynamic now. Yeah, I'm older and soon will be off to university while they're still living in the hell that is high school, but I have faith that won't be the cause of our inevitable change.

And as I watch Dox look at our best friend with a deep-rooted desire that I've seen countless times when Dad looks at SP, I know my fears might become a reality sooner than I'd like.

BONUS CHAPTER

Scarlett

PRESSURE BUILDS ON MY BLADDER, AND I BEND OVER AT THE WAIST with a loud groan. My massive protruding belly pushes against my thighs before I straighten my back out and drop my head back. I cup the underside of my belly in two hands and lift, sighing out at the relief that follows.

"Let me do that," Adam rushes out, coming around me and replacing my hands with his.

I rest my forehead on his shoulder and breathe him in as my skin sparks beneath his fingertips. "God, that feels good."

"Good, sweetheart. You're a goddamn superhero for carrying our big girl."

I smile sleepily into his T-shirt. "Can we go home now?"

He hums into my hair. "Of course, we can. Just let me get someone to ring up all this stuff and then we can get out of here."

"I'm hungry."

"What do you want?"

"I don't know."

"What a surprise." He laughs, his chest shaking against my forehead. "You decide while I go pay for this stuff. Can I drop your belly?"

"Slowly," I mumble.

He lowers my belly and crouches to give the area above my belly button a kiss before leaving one on the tip of my nose and leading the cart of baby stuff over to the till. My eyes fall to his ass as he walks, and I'm sure I have hearts in my eyes. He has the perfect butt. And in those jeans? Shiiit.

I used to have a nice butt, too, back before I got pregnant and started eating everything in my path. Now instead of a ripe peach of an ass, it's more of a squishy, rotting tomato.

My scowl is deep as I waddle to the automatic doors and step outside. The cool breeze is exactly what I need as a goddamn fire

burns beneath my skin. I'm officially five days over my due date and this baby isn't making any move to leave my womb. We have an induction date set for next week, but at this point, I don't know if I'll make it that long.

Everyone talks about how amazing it is growing a child inside of you, but why doesn't anybody tell you how equally agonizing it is? At least in my case, it has been anything but glamourous. Between heart burn, morning sickness that kept me bed ridden for almost the entirety of my second trimester, and the swollen extremities, I've never been more ready to push out this baby. We should normalize not loving being pregnant but still loving our babies more than words.

It's about time for our little girl to make her official debut. She has so many loved ones waiting patiently to meet and love on her. I smile at my swollen feet—the ones I forced inside a pair of flip-flops in this mid-November cold because they're the only shoes that fit at this point.

I sense him behind me seconds before a strong-arm wraps around my waist and I'm pulled into a hard side. "I should have given you the keys. Sorry, baby."

Leaning into him, I let him lead us through the parking lot while pushing the cart in front of us. "I needed the cold air, anyway."

"You do look a bit flushed."

"I feel like I'm on fire."

Suddenly, A cramp builds in my abdomen, stronger than the ones I've been getting for the past couple of days.

"Sweetheart? What's wrong? Are you okay?" His tone fills with concern.

I hiss out an exhale. "Yes."

"Are you sure?"

"Adam."

"Maybe we should take you to the hospital for a quick pop in," he says, unlocking the car and turning to press the back of his hand to my forehead. "You're burning up."

"I'm burning up because I'm filling with rage and my body hurts. Let me get in the car and take me home before I punch you. You're too handsome to be all bruised up."

The cramp slowly fades away, and I shoulder my way past him, all but falling into the passenger seat. He goes to buckle me in, but as soon as he notices my glare, he backs up and rushes around to the truck to load up all the stuff we bought. There is not a single thing in any of those bags that we actually needed, not with the glamourous baby shower Ava threw us last week, but this baby has turned me into an impulse shopper, apparently.

Nobody in their right mind can walk past a pair of baby booties and *not* buy them. No pregnant person, at least.

I turn down the heat blasting from the vents and spread my legs as far as they'll go to try and get comfortable. It doesn't work, and I just get more annoyed instead as another cramps builds. By the time Adam gets into the car, I'm about ready to explode.

"You're freaking me out, baby," he says, looking me over.

"They're just braxton hicks. I've been having them since last night. The girls told me about them. They mimic contractions to prepare your body for birth."

"Okay. What do you need from me? Tell me what to do to help."

"Drive us home, please."

I blow out a breath and rub my belly, adjusting myself in the seat to try and find a better position, knowing there isn't one. Biting my tongue, I covers my eyes with my hand and try to relax. I've never been this uncomfortable in my entire life.

"You're living up to your name right now, Scary Spice." He says, choking out a laugh.

I slowly turn my head and blink at him. "I should have asked Cooper to come with me instead. He would have already gotten me McDonald's by now."

His laugh is loud and unrestrained this time as he pulls the car out of the parking spot and lays a hand on my thigh.

"You're right. But then you would be even more stressed out because he's an awful driver."

"He's not *that* bad."

My lie is obvious. By some miracle, Cooper passed his driver's test a couple of weeks ago right after his sixteenth birthday, but neither Adam or me have tried to put ourselves into situations where we need him to drive us anywhere since.

He isn't bad in the expected sense. Instead of being a reckless teenage driver, he drives like a grandpa. A grandpa who left the house without his glasses on.

"Right." Adam snorts.

"God," I mutter, leaning forward as much as I can. "I'm going to punch the window."

He squeezes my thigh. "Please don't. We'll be home in a few minutes."

The next cramp comes even stronger than the last one and steals my breath. My eyes water as I hold in a whimper.

"I'm taking you to the hospital," Adam mutters, and when he takes a sudden turn, I slam my hands to the dash and stare wide-eyed out the windshield.

"Adam," I squeak.

"I'm sorry, sweetheart. That was a lot sharper than I thought it would be."

The puddle between my legs has my cheeks flaming red. "No. My water just broke."

Jerking the car, he stiffens up, eyes flicking between me and the road. Panic flashes across his face, and I would find it adorable had my inner liquids not been dripping down his expensive leather seats.

"What do I do?" he asks, voice cracking.

"Now is the time to take us to the hospital. Give me your phone so I can start calling everyone. My bag is at home."

He nods frantically, tossing me his phone. "I feel like I should be the one making the calls."

"Maybe if you weren't driving. I can handle it." At least I can between contractions. "Can you time the contractions? I'll tell you when the next one comes."

"Yes. Of course, I can."

I start to make all of the calls as he rushes us to the hospital, and by the time we get there, my contractions are exactly three minutes apart.

An hour later, a tiny, squirming baby girl wrapped in a pink blanket is placed on my chest for the second time. A sob tears free as I hold our daughter, her eyes so wide and blue as she cries softly and curls into me.

"You did it, Scarlett. Look at this angel. Fuck, that's our girl right here," Adam whispers, cheeks wet with tears. He brushes my hair off my forehead while running a gentle hand over Amelia's soft brown curls.

An overwhelming feeling of joy fills me, and I grin despite the pain I'm in. I kiss the top of Amelia's head over and over, trying to convince myself that she's really here, in my arms.

Adam's presence helps ground me, and I lean into it, greedy for his love right now. He's my pillar of stability in any situation. God, he's the love of my life.

"Dad? SP? Oh my god," I hear from the doorway. Cooper is standing there, eyes trained on the baby in my arms.

"Come here, Bud," Adam says, voice thick with emotion. "Come meet your little sister."

Tears blur my vision when he comes walking over and stops beside his dad, arms tight at his sides. Adam drops an arm over his shoulders and pulls him close.

"Want to hold her?" he asks.

Cooper blinks quickly and then looks at me expectantly.

"You can hold her, Coop," I confirm.

"Okay…yeah, I want to hold her."

I smile gratefully at Adam when he takes Amelia from my arms and slowly shifts her toward Cooper, explaining to him how to properly hold her.

The moment she's in Cooper's arms, I fall apart, tears streaming freely over my sweat-stained cheeks. He stares down at her with soft eyes and offers her his finger, mouth parting in awe when she grips it in her small fist.

"She's holding my finger," he whispers.

Adam hums. "She does."

"I think I love her already. Is that weird?"

This time it's Adam that loses it. A strangled noise slips from his lips as he nods, quickly wiping at his eyes.

"It's not weird. She loves you, too. We all do."

And my husband is completely right. We all love this sweet baby girl just as much as we love our gentle, soft-spoken son. It hits me then that this is my family. This is really my life.

How did I get so lucky?

After another barely contained sob, I ask my boys to come close and as they move in, I finally let my eyes fall closed, feeling completely at peace.

Feeling happier than I ever have.

Thank you for reading Vital Blindside! If you enjoyed it, please leave a review on Amazon and Goodreads.

This is officially the end of the Swift Hat-Trick series, but there is much more to come in this world. The second-generation series is coming in 2023.

Her Greatest Mistake, a fake dating romance– Maddox and Braxton (Out now)

Her Greatest Adventure, a forbidden romance – Adalyn and Cooper (May)

His Greatest Muse, a *dark* themed romance– Noah and Tinsley (September)

Book 4 – Oliver Bateman and ? (TBA)

Book 5 – Jamieson Bateman and ? (TBA)

To be kept up to date on all my releases, check out my website!
www.hannahcowanauthor.com

If you have not read the previous books in the series, now is the time to do so!

Lucky Hit — Oakley and Ava
Between Periods (Novella and BH prequel)
Blissful Hook — Tyler and Gracie

Keep reading for a sneak peek of Her Greatest Mistake.

PROLOGUE

Maddox

AGE SEVENTEEN

Soft, tight black curls tickle my throat, and the hard wooden planks beneath me have made my ass numb. Slivers from the unsanded, worn-to-shit wood bite into my exposed thighs, but Braxton's fruity perfume blows in the wind, helping mask the discomfort with something *so* damn good. Something that has my heart thumping hard inside my chest.

My best friend is curled into my side, sitting beside me against one of the walls of the tree house my dad and uncles built for my siblings and me when we were just kids. We've spent the past two hours pretending our curfews don't exist and praying for the rainstorm predicted on the weather radar to hit Vancouver and trap us in here.

I keep waiting for my mom to come running outside, yelling at me to drive Braxton back home before our parents ream both our asses, but it's been silent. I'm the only one in our friend group to have my license yet, and I've been known to use that to my advantage—conveniently "forgetting" to bring Brax back home on time just to wrangle a few more minutes with her.

Braxton never pushes me to bring her back, so I keep my mouth shut. Happily, at that.

"I can almost hear you thinking," she says, turning her face into my shoulder and heaving a sigh. I hold back a shiver.

"If you focus, I'm sure you could slip right inside my head."

She hums. "You would think so, but you're guarded up tight tonight. What are you thinking about?"

"You."

I don't know whether to laugh or cry when she doesn't seem surprised by my blunt reply. If anything, she seems comforted by it because her body shifts closer to mine. She grips my shirt in her fist, right over my heart.

With a swallow, I adjust my hold and slip my arm around her back, brushing the curve of her hip with my fingertips before resting my hand safely on her bent knee. My hockey jacket is splayed out beneath her, keeping her bare legs protected from the wood. We used to have blankets in here, back when our other best friend, Cooper, would hang out with us up here, but he graduated high school two years before us, and Mom has since cleaned up the tree house, thinking we would have gotten too old to hang out in here.

In a sense, she's right. We haven't played in this tree house since we were thirteen, but I'll continue to take Braxton up here every damn day for the rest of my life if it means we can be like this. It's easy to forget the rest of the world when we're within these walls, protected from the outside world.

"What about me are you thinking about?" she asks softly.

I drag my thumb over her knee. Back and forth, back and forth. What I want to say is too much, even if I think she already knows. Everyone does.

"Have you chosen a school yet?"

"No. There are too many."

"It's because you're brilliant. Every school wants you."

Her lips brush over where my neck and shoulder meet, and I

grind my teeth together to keep from groaning. Does she know she's doing these things? Or is it all subconscious?

"Thank you. I haven't chosen where I want to go yet."

"I always pictured you at some prestigious school in Ontario or Quebec, but you hate big cities, and your French sucks."

She pinches my chest. I laugh. "My French is better than yours."

"Tais-toi."

"Funny. How long did you practice that one?"

I shrug. "Long enough to know I wasn't cut out to speak another language."

Her fingers release my shirt as she opens her hand and presses it against my sternum. *"Je ne veux pas te quitter,"* she mutters.

My brows drip. "I don't know what that means."

"The draft is coming up. Soon, you'll be gone regardless of where I choose to go to school." She changes the subject. My French is crap, but even I know that isn't what she said.

"So come with me. Find a school close to wherever I end up."

She shakes her head. "I can't chase you."

I shove a hand through my hair before removing my arm from around her and twisting my body so we're facing each other. My legs are long, and my muscles are too tight from my workout this morning, so I have to stretch them out along her sides, forcing her to sit with me wrapped all around her. Placing my hands on her bent knees, I lean close.

"Then let me chase you." I press my thumb to her bottom lip, feeling how soft and warm it is. How kissable her mouth must be . . . "I'll follow you anywhere. No matter what, I'll make it happen."

Her electric-blue eyes hold my stare with expertise, trapping me in her bubble. "I don't doubt that for a minute."

"Promise me something," I whisper, dropping my forehead to hers. Our noses brush ever so slightly. God, I'm breathless.

"Anything," she replies instantly.

I press my mouth to the corner of her soft lips and exhale. "Be my best friend forever. No matter what. Even when we fight or the distance between us grows. Promise you'll fight for us as hard as I will."

"I promise," she lies.

CRAVING THE PLAYER

Braden has never been the type to dream about settling down. Just the smell of commitment is enough to chill him to the bone.

And after finally being free of a toxic four-year relationship, Sierra plans on staying single for as long as she can. With her sights set on getting her much-deserved promotion at her dream job, it seems like a straightforward plan.

But after one spontaneous night spent tangled up in Braden's sheets, will it be as easy as both of them expected to continue on with their normal lives? It is just sex, after all.

One risky agreement later and their lives are intertwined.

Is it really possible to keep the lines between lust and love from blurring? Or are they just postponing the inevitable?

Keep reading for a sneak peek!

CHAPTER 1

BRADEN

Sharp nails tear their way down my back, ripping through the sensitive skin and drawing blood. The blonde beneath me moans in my ear, begging me to pick up the pace.

We've been going at this for what feels like hours now. She's come more times than I can count, quite the opposite of myself. I've been unwantedly edging myself.

"Just like that!"

My frustration is obvious as I pull out of her in one swift movement and lean back on my legs, dick starting to sag.

"What are you doing?" she whines, lips jutting out in a juicy pout.

"Sorry. I just remembered that I have to go pick up my grandpa's friend's dog from the vet." My tone is dry and careless. I move off of the silk red sheets left in a disarray on her bed and toss the unused condom into the nearby trash can.

"You could say my name, you know." Her breathless voice only frustrates me more. In all honesty, I don't remember her name.

I try to block her out and focus on finding my clothes. I can just about plant a thank you kiss on the lamp in the corner of her room when I spot my button-up hanging from it. "And you expect me to believe that you have to pick up this dog in the middle of the night?"

She doesn't spare me an unconvincing frown as she wraps the blanket around her otherwise naked body—a wise decision on her part. It was her hot body that enticed me enough to come here in the first place, and as much fun as it is to stare at her smooth, olive skin, I already have a terrible case of blue balls. The thought makes me reach down and anxiously rub at my limp cock with a deep, aggravated sigh.

"Sorry, what?" I slide my arms through my shirt. My back burns when the material rubs across the new cuts in my skin.

"What is your deal?" she snaps.

I run a hand through my messy hair and pull my phone from the pocket of my jeans. As soon as I switch it on, I'm met with several texts asking about my whereabouts and disappearance.

"You're unbelievable!" she scoffs, pulling the blanket tighter around her. In a flurry, she rushes into the ensuite bathroom, slamming the door behind her.

Well, that makes things easier.

I pull my keys out of my pocket and the cold metal bites into my palm. The nauseating smell of her fruity perfume wafts throughout the house, making me rush to the front door even faster. I slide my sneakers on and fight back the urge to kick myself in the ass for letting my dick get me in trouble again.

I'm out the door and in the driver's seat of my car before my stomach has a chance to start swirling with disappointment.

"If you keep dropping your arms like that, I'll gladly bruise up that pretty face, Clay."

Clayton takes another risky swing at my chest and I roll my

eyes at his poorly placed move. "C'mon, buddy. You gotta do better than that." I grab and twist his arm behind his back. I turn the six-foot ginger around and shove his face into the boxing bag in front of us.

Poor guy didn't stand a chance in hell with that sloppy throw.

"Your mouth twitches before every swing. That needs to stop. Anyone who studies you even in the slightest will know your tells. You'll never win like that. *Ever*." I move back a step and lift my arms into position before nodding for him to try again.

His eyes narrow as he bounces on his feet, observing me. Trying to learn *my* tells. As if I would put them on display for him. Less than a second later, his top lip lifts just the slightest bit, causing mine to lift in a grin

In an instant I'm tucking myself under his right hook and swinging my left arm. I make contact with his abdomen, and the air is pushed from his lungs in a raspy wheeze. He clutches his stomach and curls over.

"Fuck you," he coughs.

"Damn, I guess I should have put my gloves on. My bad." I shrug.

"Remind me again why I can't have another trainer?" He asks me the question like he doesn't already know the answer while pushing himself upright again. After a few seconds, his grimace slowly evens back out into a scowl.

"Because nobody else wants your whiny ass," I snicker, walking toward my gym bag and pulling out my gloves. The gold stripes wrapping around the slick black material never fail to make my chest swell with pride. I worked day and night to afford these babies, and damn are they *ever* worth it.

"We both know that you just don't want to get rid of me."

"Yeah." I snort. "That's it."

Sliding my hands in my gloves, I clench my fingers and

tighten the Velcro strap. Patting both gloves together, I raise my brow and nod for him to try again.

The balls of my feet tap against the concrete floor as I bounce, keeping my eyes locked on my best friend. He's finally got his arms in the correct position, at least, but the tension in his shoulders worries me.

"Drop your shoulders!" I bark. "You're going to hurt yourself."

"I'm trying," he snaps but drops his shoulder slightly, most likely to humour me more than anything.

Without a second thought I send my fist toward him, but stop mid-throw when he drops his arms just enough to expose his face to me.

I warned him. Pushing my arm forward again, I hear a loud *smack*.

"What the fuck!" he shouts with eyes full of fire as he grabs his now bleeding nose. I bite back my laugh.

"It's not broken. Relax." I grin to myself and give my head a quick shake. "I told you that if you dropped your arms again, I would mess with your pretty face."

I turn away from him and reach into my gym bag, pulling out two towels. After I toss him the darker coloured one for his gushing nose, I keep the lighter one for myself. The sweat covering my bare torso is wiped away quickly before I discard the towel.

"What if you would have broken it?" he groans.

"Then you wouldn't have dropped your arms next time. Take the pain as a learning experience."

"You were coming for my stomach!"

"It looked like I was aiming for your stomach. You would have no idea if that were a trick or not. That's why you don't drop your arms," I say with unwavering confidence. I've trained to be a boxer nearly my entire life, learned almost everything there is to know about the sport. He needs to gain a bit of confidence in me. If my ego weren't the size of Texas I would have been offended. "Anyways, pizza for dinner?"

"Sure," he replies, voice nasally from the pressure he's applying to his nose. His ability to go with the flow is one of the reasons we get along so well.

"Come on, if you get blood on the floor Dad will kill me." I lead the way to the showers.

"Maybe I'll leave a trail then."

I scowl.

Working for your dad has its benefits, but dealing with his rage when you break one of his rules is not one of them. No bloodshed is the most crucial rule in this gym. It has been since before I can remember. We Lowry men don't follow many rules, but the ones we do, we live by. As if by breaking a single one would throw the entire universe off kilter.

"If you want to go that far, I might as well get a couple more hits in. Soak the floor in your misery," I half-heartedly threaten.

He just scoffs, shaking his head. "I'd like to see you try."

"Yeah? Want to bet on how long you'd last in the ring with me?" I tilt my head and straighten my back so all six-foot-three of me tower over him.

Clay gulps but keeps his lips pressed together. "Whatever. Arrogant bastard."

I laugh. "Always full of compliments, Clay. So, stuffed or regular crust?"

"Grab me a beer, would you?" I shout as I drop back on the couch. My words are muffled as a slice of pepperoni stuffed-crust pizza is clenched between my teeth.

"Do I look like your damn mother?" Clayton calls back.

I shove my hand between the couch cushions and grab hold

of the TV remote. My greasy fingers fiddle with the remote before finding the power button and the familiar sound of my favourite, hot as hell sports announcer fills the room.

"Pretty please can you bring me a beer?" I try again, snickering to myself when I hear the fridge door slam shut.

"Here."

I catch the cold can midair when he throws it toward me like a softball. I turn to face him and crack it open nice and slow. I take a long swig and rest my head back against the couch. "Thanks."

"Don't mention it," he grumbles and sits down beside me, holding out a paper plate. He wears a look that dares me not to use it, so I take it with a huff and set it down on my lap.

My attention drops to my phone when it vibrates, shaking the glass coffee table it's lying on. Reaching for it, I notice the several names spread across the screen.

I lean back and unlock the phone, grinning. A picture of a naked body fills the screen, and my eyes narrow. The girl's athletic, toned figure lies outstretched on what looks to be a bed, with a sheer, white, silky robe sagging off of her narrow shoulders. Her knees are bent, legs are spread wide open, the soft pink skin of her bare pussy glistening between them.

"What are you smirking at?" Clay asks. When I don't answer, he leans over my shoulder to look for himself. "Holy shit. Who is that?"

Locking my phone, I roll my eyes. "Fuck off and go find your own."

"I have my own." He sounds less than mildly confident in that statement.

"Then what are you waiting for?" I raise a brow, testing him before he flips me off and pushes off the couch. "Maybe if you got laid, you wouldn't be so damn uptight. You're acting like a twenty-seven-year-old virgin."

"Not everyone wants to be a 'fuck it and chuck it' kind of guy until the day they die. We're not all that young anymore, dude."

Registering his words, I nearly blow chunks all over the living room. "I stopped ageing when I turned twenty-four, remember?"

"Right." He snorts.

The reminder of how old we are was unnecessary. It's not like I don't know how close I am to reaching my thirties. With Clay getting his shit together with most things, I'm reminded nearly every damn day of the week. The thought of becoming someone that needs to start meeting society's standards makes a knot form in my stomach the size of Texas and my blood run ice cold.

I feel proud of Clay for realizing what he wants in life goes farther than a good fuck and a cold beer afterward. But his path will never be mine. The whole idea of going to a job I hate five days a week before coming home to a wife and three identical kids waiting on the porch of a two-story suburban home makes me want to kneel and pray to be shipped off to another planet.

Nah, I'm happy with staying twenty-six forever. Society can kiss my pearly white ass for demanding a change

I've just wrapped a towel around my waist when Clayton pushes open the bathroom door, eyes droopy and dull as he shoves past me, stopping in front of the sink.

He follows the same routine as every night: wets his toothbrush with cold water, smears a thick line of spearmint toothpaste onto the rough bristles before shoving it into his mouth and brushing his teeth for precisely two minutes. I'm no shrink, but I would confidently diagnose Clay with a case of obsessive-compulsive disorder any day of the week.

We've been living together for two years now, and I'm still trying to come to grasps with his overly cleanly, organized ways.

After exactly two minutes of scrubbing every square inch of his mouth, Clay spits into the sink and wipes a fresh towel across his lips. He doesn't tear his concentration from the small container of dental floss pinched between his fingers as he mumbles, "I forgot to tell you that there's some sort of concert tomorrow night at SP, and you need to be there."

I raise my brow. "There's a concert? At Sinners? Since when do they do that shit there?"

"Don't know. Ethan got tickets or something from one of the bouncers last week. There's one for both of us."

"Could be fun." I shrug and rub at the sting in my eyes, exhaustion stepping on me with its dirty shoe. I don't give the invitation much thought. Ethan is an eighteen-year-old boy stuck in the body of a twenty-six-year-old man. This isn't the first time that we've been *told* to go to out with him, and it won't be the last. I just nod my head and follow along. Night clubs aren't my venue of choice anymore, but a beer is a beer regardless of where you drink it.

Clayton gives me a nod but doesn't look away from the mirror.

"I'm going to bed. Don't forget that I need you ready to go to the gym at eight," I remind him before leaving the bathroom. I don't get anything more than a brief grunt in response, and I chuckle.

Our two-bedroom apartment—if you could call a full bedroom and a small den without a window two bedrooms—is so damn tiny that it only takes me a whole two seconds to walk down the hallway and reach my room.

I was lucky enough to earn my right to the actual bedroom by sucking back two more shots of tequila than Clay at a pub on Halloween the night before we moved into this place. I'm damn grateful for my stomach of steel, too, since there's no door or a lick of privacy leading to the den Clayton calls the Boom Room. But boom, it does not.

Where I might seem picky about the women I bed, Clayton damn near refuses anyone that doesn't meet his iron-set criteria to the absolute T. It's safe to say the Boom Room is filled with more tepid echo than anything else.

I don't bother turning on the light as I quickly swap out the towel for a pair of briefs that I find in a rare, clean basket of laundry and crawl into bed. When I get under the covers, I close my eyes and pray to God himself that I'll pass the fuck out soon.

Acknowledgements

Writing "the end" on this book was surreal. This is my sixth book but the one I'm most proud of. These characters have been with me since I first put words to paper, and I feel at peace now that this one is finished.

Adam was a special character to me as I spent the first few years of my life being raised by a single mother. Even though I was young, I remember how hard it was for her having to be both a mother and a father to me. But I also remember what an amazing job she did. Thank you, Mom. I love you dearly.

This series is everything to me, and although I'm closing this chapter, I am so happy that I get to continue on with the second-generation characters in the future. For that, I have to thank all of my readers. You gave me my dream job. You'll never know how much I appreciate your support and love.

When it comes to thank yous, I feel so blessed that I have so many to do. My team has grown exponentially since I wrote Lucky Hit, and some days I can't believe it.

Booksnmoods, thank you for creating all of the covers for these books. You truly brought these characters to life, and I am so grateful that I found you.

To my editor, Sandra, oh boy am I happy I found you. I'm going to continue to thank you in every single acknowledgments page until you get bored of seeing the same old thank you each time. You're SO appreciated.

A massive thank you to my ARC and Beta teams. The fact you love my work and characters enough to keep coming back and reading and loving all of these books does a number on my heart. I appreciate the fuck out of you all.

To my fiancé, Mitch, thank you for taking the chance on my crazy, far-fetched career choice and supporting me through it all. You let me quit my job after only writing and publishing a single book and carried the weight of that for two years while you waited for me to catch up. You stuck up for me when people thought I was making a mistake and wouldn't make it anywhere in the writing world, and that means more than I can ever tell you.
Without your support, I wouldn't be here doing this. I love you.

Mikayla, my littlest sister, your red hair is beautiful, and so are you. I know kids can be mean, but they're just jealous. Remember, you have hair thousands of people will pay hundreds of dollars to get.

Monica, thank you for loving Adam the way he deserved from the very beginning. I hope this was everything you wanted for him and then some.

Thank you to my sensitivity readers who helped me write Beth's character. You're amazing.

To everyone struggling with family and loved ones diagnosed with dementia, know you are not alone. You are strong, amazing, and loved. You're allowed to cry and hurt. You're doing everything you can.

About The Author

Hannah is a twenty-something-year-old indie author from Canada. Obsessed with swoon-worthy romance, she decided to take a leap and try her hand at creating stories that will have you fanning your face and giggling in the most embarrassing way possible. Hopefully, that's exactly what her stories have done!

Hannah loves to hear from her readers, and can be reached on any of her social media accounts.

Instagram : @hannahcowanauthor
Facebook : @hannahdcowan
Facebook Reader Group : Hannah's Hotties
Website : www.hannahcowanauthor.com

Printed in Great Britain
by Amazon

23113008R00170